James Hadley Chase) was
born in London in 1 luring
which time he was ʼriters
and went on to writ ːories,
also set in the United States. He first found success with
No Orchids for Miss Blandish which was published in 1939
and was one of the most successful books of the thirties,
selling several million copies. George Orwell described it as
'a brilliant piece of writing with hardly a wasted word or a
jarring note anywhere'. It was subsequently dramatised and
performed on London's West End and also made into a film.
Chase went on to gain popularity for his numerous other
gangster stories, and by the end of the war he was one of
Britain's most successful thriller writers. During his career
he produced some ninety books, also writing under the
names of James L Dochery, Ambrose Grant and Raymond
Marshall. He travelled widely, though only visited the USA
late in life. He died in 1985 whilst in Switzerland

BY THE SAME AUTHOR
ALL PUBLISHED BY HOUSE OF STRATUS

JAMES HADLEY
CHASE

THE GUILTY ARE AFRAID

This edition published in 2001 by The House of Stratus, an imprint of House of Stratus Ltd, Thirsk Industrial Park, York Road, Thirsk, North Yorkshire, YO7 3BX, UK.
Also at: House of Stratus Inc., 2 Neptune Road, Poughkeepsie, NY 12601, USA.

www.houseofstratus.com

Typeset, printed and bound by The House of Stratus.

A catalogue record for this book is available from the British Library and the Library of Congress.

ISBN 1-84232-104-8

Cover design: Marc Burville-Riley
Cover image: Photonica

1

The first thing that attracted my attention as I came out of St Raphael City station was a blonde doll in a bikini swimsuit, a straw hat as big as a cartwheel and doughnut sized sun goggles. Her skin – and you could see a lot of it – was a golden satin, and she had a shape on her that Mr Varga himself would have been proud to have designed.

She was getting into a hard-top Cadillac, taking her time while the unattached males feasted their eyes on her.

I feasted my eyes too.

She settled herself behind the driving-wheel and surveyed her male kingdom with lifted eyebrows. As she drove off she sneered in my direction.

The red cap with my baggage nudged me.

"If that makes your eyes pop, brother," he said, "you're in for a rare time when you get to the beach. Do you want a cab?"

"Are there more like her?" I asked, slightly dazed. "If a girl showed that much of herself where I come from, she'd land in jail."

"The place is lousy with them," the red cap told me. "This is St Raphael City. Anything goes here. But don't kid yourself. The more these chippies show, the less they give away. The only thing that talks with them is money. Do you want a cab?"

I said I wanted a cab, took out my handkerchief and mopped my face.

It was eleven-thirty a.m. and the sun blazed down. People streamed out of the station to waiting cars, cabs and horse-drawn carriages. This was vacation city, and I earnestly hoped Jack had thought to reserve a room for me.

A cab drew up and the red cap piled in my baggage. I tipped him and he went away.

"The Adelphi Hotel," I said to the driver, got into the cab and started mopping my face again.

The cab fought its way through the traffic, and after two or three minutes, turned into the main road to the sea: an imposing, broad boulevard with smart-looking shops, palm trees and cops in tropical uniforms. The town had a rich look to it. Big Cadillac and Clipper convertibles lined the street on either side: every one of them the size of a bus.

As we crawled with the traffic, I sat forward, staring out of the window at the women. Most of them were in beachwear: some in lounging pyjamas, some in halters and shorts, some in French swimsuits: the fat ones invariably favoured the shorts. Every now and then I spotted a pippin, but most of them were the middle-aged and the fat.

The driver caught my tense expression in his wing mirror and he leaned out of the cab to spit.

"Looks like the meat market on a Saturday night, doesn't it?" he said.

"I was wondering what it reminded me of," I said, and sat back. "Quite a little town you have here."

"Think so? I wouldn't give you a dime for it. You've got to be a millionaire or you might just as well cut your throat as live here. There are more millionaires here to the square mile than any other country in the world. Did you know that?"

I said I didn't know and wondered uneasily if I had brought enough money with me. I knew it would be hopeless to try to borrow anything from Jack.

We climbed a hill, going away from the sea, and after a while, we came to a quiet road lined on either side with orange trees. The cab pulled up outside the hotel.

I looked at the hotel as I got out of the cab. There was nothing de luxe about it. The kind of hotel I would expect Jack to have chosen: probably the food was good. He had a talent for finding hotels that served good food.

A boy in buttons came out and collected my bags. I gave the driver a dollar and went up the steps into the hotel lounge.

It was fairly large, furnished with basket chairs and a few decaying palms in brass tubs: if it wasn't gaudy, at least it was clean.

The reception clerk, a balding fatty with a silk cravat to support his second chin, showed me his teeth and offered me a pen.

"You have a reservation, sir?"

"I hope so. The name is Lew Brandon. Did Mr Sheppey tell you I was coming?"

"Certainly, Mr Brandon. I've put you in the room next to his." He placed his finger on the bell push and the bell hop materialized. "Take Mr Brandon to room 245." He showed me his teeth again. "Mr Sheppey is in room 247. I hope you will enjoy your stay with us, Mr Brandon. Anything we can do ... any little thing ..."

"Thanks. Mr Sheppey in?"

"No. He went out about an hour ago." He gave me a coy little smile. "With a young lady. I imagine they were going to the beach."

That didn't surprise me. Jack was no great worker and women were his weakness.

"When he comes in, tell him I've arrived. I'll be in my room," I said.

"I'll do that, Mr Brandon."

I and the bell hop and my baggage squashed ourselves into the ancient elevator and were dragged up two floors.

Room 245 was no larger than a large rabbit hutch and as hot as a blast furnace. The bed didn't look big enough to take a midget at full stretch, the shower leaked and there was no view from the window. I only hoped it would be cheap. It had no other recommendation.

After the boy had gone through the routine of lowering and raising the blind and turning the electric switches on and off and seemingly surprised to find anything worked, I got rid of him.

I called room service and asked for some ice and a bottle of Vat 69 at the double. Then I stripped off my clothes and got under the shower. As long as I remained under the shower I felt fine, but when I returned to the bedroom I broke out into a sweat again.

I gave myself a slug of Scotch, then just as I was about to get under the shower again, someone hammered on my door.

I wrapped a towel around my middle, unlocked the door and opened it.

A big man with a red weathered face and freckles across his nose that looked as if it had been stamped on at one time, and who had cop written all over him, rode me back into the room and closed the door.

"Your name Brandon?" he asked in a voice as gritty as gravel.

"That's right. What do you want?"

He took out his wallet and showed me his buzzer.

"Sergeant Candy, Homicide," he said. "You know Jack Sheppey?"

I felt a prickle of apprehension crawl up my spine.

This wouldn't be the first time Sheppey had been in trouble with the police. Six months ago he had punched a detective in the eye and had drawn a ten-day stretch. Three months before that he had taken a poke at a patrolman and had been fined twenty-five bucks. Jack was a great cop hater.

"Yes, I know him. Is he in trouble?"

"You could call it that!" Candy said. He produced a pack of chewing-gum, tore off the wrapping and fed gum into his face. "Can you identify him?"

That really jarred me.

"He hasn't met with an accident?"

"He's dead," Candy said. "Hustle some clothes on, will you? I've a car outside. The Lieutenant wants you down there."

"Dead?" I stared at the big, red face. "What happened?"

Candy lifted his heavy shoulders.

"The Lieutenant will tell you. Let's get moving. He hates being kept waiting."

I put on my shirt and trousers, ran a comb through my hair, slid into my coat and sat on the bed to put on my socks and shoes.

My hands were shaking a little.

Jack and I got along fine together. He had always had a fierce enjoyment of life: living every second of it and getting much more out of it than ever I did. It seemed impossible he was dead.

When I had fixed my shoes, I poured myself another slug of whisky. I felt I needed it.

"Join me?" I said to Candy.

He hesitated, licked his thick lips, fought with his conscience and lost.

"Well, I'm not exactly on duty ..."

I gave him a slug big enough to knock over a horse and cart, and he poured it down his throat as if it were water.

"Let's go," he said, putting down the glass. He blew out his cheeks and thumped himself on the chest. "The Lieutenant doesn't like being kept waiting."

We travelled down in the elevator. As we crossed the lobby I saw the reception clerk was staring at me, bug-eyed. The bell hop was also staring. They probably thought I was under arrest.

A couple of old gentlemen in white flannels and Harvard blazers were sitting in basket chairs by the door. They too stared, and as Candy and I passed, one of them said, "I'll be damned if that fellow isn't a policeman."

We went down the steps where a car waited. Candy got under the wheel and I sat beside him. We drove fast, using the back streets, and avoiding the traffic on the main roads.

"Where was he found?" I asked suddenly.

"At Bay Beach," Candy told me, his heavy jaw working as he chewed. "There's a row of cabins there for hire. The attendant found him."

I put the question that had been bothering me ever since I had been told he was dead.

"Was it a heart attack or something?"

Candy touched his siren button as a Cadillac tried to edge in front of him. The Cadillac swerved and slowed down at the sound of the siren and Candy went past, glaring at the driver.

"He was murdered," he said.

I sat still, my hands squeezed between my knees, while I absorbed the shock.

I hadn't anything to say after that. I just sat staring ahead and listening to Candy hum under his breath some tuneless song. In under five minutes we reached the beach. Candy drove fast along a wide road that ran parallel with the sea. Finally, we came to a row of red-and-white-painted beach cabins and a small parking lot.

The cabins were shaded by palm trees, and there were the usual gaudy beach umbrellas. Four police cars were parked on the road. I could see a crowd of about two hundred people, mostly in swimsuits standing near the cabins. I spotted the Buick convertible Jack and I had bought second hand, and for which we were still paying, in the parking lot.

We pushed through the crowd who stared curiously at me. As we neared the cabins Candy said, "The little fella's Lieutenant Rankin."

Rankin saw us and came forward.

He was a head shorter than Candy. He wore a lightweight grey suit with a slouch hat placed carefully and at a jaunty angle over his right eye: a man nudging forty-five with a smooth, hard face, ice grey eyes and a small slit that served him for a mouth. His hair, white at the temples, had been recently cut. He was dapper, neat and as hard as forged steel.

"This is Lew Brandon, Lieutenant," Candy said.

Rankin looked at me. His eyes were as intense as searchlights. He took from his pocket a flimsy slip of paper and thrust it at me.

"Did you send this?" he asked.

I looked at the paper. I was the telegram I had sent Jack telling him when I would be arriving.

"Yes."

"He was a friend of yours?"

"We were in business together. He was my partner."

Rankin continued to stare at me. For a long moment he just stared, rubbing his jaw, then he said, "You'd better take a look at him, then we can talk."

Bracing myself, I followed him across the hot sand and into the cabin.

II

A couple of beefy-looking men were dusting powder on the window-ledges for fingerprints. A thin, elderly man sat at a small table, a black bag at his feet, filling out a buff-coloured form.

I scarcely noticed them. My eyes went immediately to where Jack was lying on the floor by a kind of divan bed. He was hunched up, close to the bed, as if he had been trying to get away from someone when he was dying.

Except for a pair of swimming-trunks, he was naked. In the hollow of his neck and right shoulder was a blue-red hole. The skin around the hole was badly bruised. There was a scared expression on his sun-tanned, dead face.

"That him?" Rankin asked quietly, his ice grey eyes watching me.

"Yes."

"Okay." He looked at the thin man. "Nearly finished, Doc?"

"All but. It's a straightforward job. There's a professional touch about it. I'd say a rat-tail ice pick. Whoever did it knew where to strike. Got him just by the occipital bulge. Driven in with considerable force. Death would be instantaneous. I'd say he was killed within the hour."

Rankin grunted.

"You can take him away when you're ready." He turned to me. "Let's get out of here." He went out into the hot sunshine, blinking a little in the fierce light. He waved to Candy, who came over. "I'm going back to Brandon's hotel," he said. "See what you can find here. Doc says it's an ice-pick job. Hughson will be down with some more men. Get them looking for the pick. There's a chance the killer threw it away, but I doubt it." He looked at his gold strap watch he wore on the inside of his thin wrist. "See you in my office at fourteen-thirty hours."

He crooked his finger at me, then set off across the sand, walking through the crowd as if it didn't exist. The crowd gave way hurriedly, staring at me as I followed him.

As we passed the parking lot, I said, "The convertible Buick belongs to Sheppey and me, Lieutenant. He had the use of it down here."

Rankin paused, looked over at the Buick, then waved to one of his men.

"Tell Sergeant Candy the convertible over there is the car Sheppey came in. Get it checked for prints and give it a going over. When you're through with it have someone take it to the Adelphi Hotel and leave it there." He looked at me. "Okay?"

"Thanks."

We went to a police car and got in the back.

Rankin said to the driver, "Adelphi Hotel. Take the long way round and drive slow. I've got some talking to do."

The driver touched his cap, engaged gear and moved the car into the traffic.

Rankin settled himself in the corner, took a cigar from his pocket, shook it out of its metal container, pierced it and put it between his small white teeth. He lit it, drew down a lungful of smoke, held it, then let it drift slowly down his pinched nostrils.

"Well, let's have it," he said. "Who are you and who is Sheppey and what is all this about? Don't rush it. Take it slow, but give me the complete picture."

I lit a cigarette, thought for a moment, then began to talk.

I told him Sheppey and I had been running a successful inquiry agency in San Francisco for the past five years.

"I've been on a job in New York for three weeks while Sheppey has been looking after the office. While I was in New York I got a wire from him telling me to get to St Raphael City as fast as I could. He said he had a big job on and there was money in it. I had more or less tied up my job, so I flew to Los Angeles and took the train here, arriving this morning at eleven-thirty. I went to the hotel, found Sheppey had reserved a room for me and was told he had gone out. I was taking a shower when Sergeant Candy picked me up. That's all I can tell you."

"He didn't say what the job was?" Rankin asked.

I shook my head.

"Jack isn't much of a letter writer. I guess he decided it would be quicker and easier to tell me than to write."

Rankin brooded for a moment, then said, "Have you got your licence on you?"

I gave him my billfold. He examined the contents quickly and expertly, then handed it back.

"You've no idea who employed him here or what the case was about?" he asked.

"No idea at all."

He gave me a hard stare.

"You'd tell me if you did?"

"Possibly, but as I don't know, the point doesn't arise."

He scratched the side of his face, screwing up his eyes.

"Do you think he kept notes on the case? Progress reports?"

"I doubt it. He wasn't keen on any paper work. Usually we worked together and I did the reports."

He rolled his cigar between his lips.

"How is it you go to New York when you've an office in Frisco?"

10

"This happened to be a client I had had dealings with before. He had moved to New York and particularly wanted me to handle the job."

"Sheppey was off his beat, too, wasn't he? Think he was working for an old client?"

"Could be, but I don't know any of them who has moved out here."

"Do you think he was killed because of something he turned up on this case?"

I hesitated, remembering the reception clerk at the hotel had said Jack had gone out with a woman.

"I don't know. The clerk at the hotel told me a woman picked him up and they went out together. He chased women: it was his big fault. He'd leave a job flat if he saw a woman who interested him. This may be one of those times and her husband objected. I'm guessing, but he's been in an awful lot of messes through women in the past."

Rankin grimaced.

"Did he run around with married women?"

"He didn't care what they were so long as they had looks. Don't think I'm knocking him. He was my best friend, but he certainly made me sore sometimes the way he lay down on the job because of some floozy."

"It doesn't often happen a husband shows his disapproval with an ice pick: that was a professional job."

"Maybe he was a professional husband. Have you got anyone on your records who uses an ice pick?"

Rankin shook his head.

"I don't know of anyone, but this is a very rich town. There are plenty of boys here on the make, and some of them are dangerous. No one's ever been skewered by an ice pick, but there's always got to be a first time." He tapped ash off his cigar. "Can you get a line on this case he's working on? That's our first move. I've got to be sure his death isn't hooked up to it."

"Unless he's left a record in his room, there's nothing I can do about it," I said untruthfully.

I was going to satisfy myself first that Jack's client was in the clear before I let Rankin know I might be able to get his name. It was a long shot, but it was just possible Ella, our typist, who looked after the office back in Frisco might have a line on him.

Rankin leaned forward and said to the driver, "Okay, step on it now."

In less than five minutes we pulled up outside the Adelphi Hotel.

We crossed the lobby together to where the reception clerk was waiting, his fat chins wobbling and his eyes bulging with suppressed excitement.

The two old gentlemen in white flannels had been reinforced by their wives, who looked as if they had stepped out of the pages of a Victorian novel. They sat motionless, staring at us, their ears growing out of the sides of their heads.

"Let's talk where these old crows can't listen," Rankin said, pitching his voice so they could hear him.

"Why certainly, Lieutenant," the reception clerk said, his voice flustered. He took us behind the desk into a small office. "Is there anything wrong?"

"Not here, there isn't," Rankin said. "What's your name?"

The reception clerk looked even more flustered.

"Edwin Brewer."

"What time did Sheppey leave here?"

"It would be about half past ten."

"There was a woman with him?"

"Yes. She came to the desk and asked for him. While she was speaking to me, Mr Sheppey came from the elevator and joined her."

"Did she give her name?"

"No. Mr Sheppey appeared before I could ask for her name."

"Did they seem friendly?"

Brewer licked his lips nervously.

"Well, yes. Mr Sheppey was pretty familiar with her."

"In what way?"

"Well, he walked up to her and said, 'Hello, baby-doll,' put his hand behind her and pinched her."

"How did she react?"

"She laughed it off, but I could see she didn't like it. She wasn't the type I'd care to take liberties with myself."

"What type was she then?"

"She had a sort of dignity. It's hard to explain. She just wasn't the type to take liberties with."

"And yet he did?"

"That doesn't mean anything," I said. "Jack had no respect for anyone. He'd pinch a bishop's wife if he felt in the mood."

Rankin frowned.

"Can you describe this woman?"

Brewer rubbed his hands together nervously.

"She was very attractive: dark with a good figure. She wore big sunglasses and a big hat. I couldn't see much of her face. She had on navy slacks and a white shirt."

"Age?"

"In the twenties, but I wouldn't be sure: twenty-five perhaps."

"Could you identify her if you saw her again?"

"Oh, yes, I'm sure I could."

Rankin stubbed out his cigar in the ashtray on Brewer's desk.

"If she wasn't wearing the big hat and sunglasses, but happened to be wearing no hat and a white dress, do you think you could still identify her?"

Brewer thought for a moment, then looked sheepish.

"Well, perhaps not."

"You can identify the clothes, but not the woman?"

"Well, yes."

"That's not a lot of help, is it?" Rankin said. "Okay, never mind. After Sheppey had said hello, what happened?"

"He said he had to be back in a couple of hours and they had better get going. They went out together and I saw them drive away in his car."

"Did she leave her car here?"

"I didn't see one. I think she must have walked."

"Let me have the key to his room."

"Shall I call Greaves? He's our house detective."

Rankin shook his head.

"No. I don't want your house dick tramping around lousing up any clues."

Brewer went out of the office and over to the key rack. We followed him out. The four old people were staring.

Brewer said, "He must have taken his key with him. I'll give you a spare."

He found a key and gave it to Rankin.

As Rankin took the key, Brewer asked, "Has anything happened to Mr Sheppey?"

The old people leaned forward. This was something they were panting to know.

"He's given birth to a baby," Rankin said. "I believe it is the first time in history but I'm not absolutely sure, so don't quote me."

14

He walked with me to the elevator.

The old people stared after us, amazed expressions on their faces.

As Rankin pressed the button to take us to the second floor, he said, "I hate old people who live in hotels."

"You'll get old yourself," I said. "They don't live in hotels for fun."

"A sentimental shamus," he said, his mouth turning down at the corners. "I thought I had seen everything."

"Did you get a line on the girl from the cabin attendant?" I asked as we crawled past the first floor.

"Yeah. The same description. There're two changing-rooms in the cabin. She used one and he the other. We found her slacks, shirt, hat and sunglasses there. His clothes were in the other room."

"The girl left her clothes in the cabin?" I said sharply.

"That's what I'm telling you. It could mean either of two things: she wanted to fade out of the picture and decided she could do it by leaving in her swimsuit. Everyone in this lousy town wears a swimsuit or else she took a swim and someone knocked her off after knocking Sheppey off. My boys are searching the beach now. I think she faded out of the picture myself."

"No one saw her leave the cabin?" I asked as the elevator stopped at the second floor.

"No, but we're still asking around."

We walked down the corridor to room 247.

"That was a pretty good disguise she was wearing," Rankin went on as he sank the key into the lock. "People in this town don't look at faces, they look at shapes." He turned the key and pushed the door open.

We stood looking around the room. It was a little larger than mine, but not much and it was just as hot and airless.

"Sweet suffering Pete!" Rankin said under his breath. The room looked as if it had been hit by a cyclone. All the drawers of the chest hung open. Jack's belongings lay scattered on the floor. His briefcase had been ripped open and papers lay everywhere. The bed had been stripped and the mattress cut open, the stuffing dragged out. The pillows had also been ripped and feathers were heaped on the floor.

"Pretty quick work," Rankin said. "If there was anything to find, we won't find it now. I'll get the boys up here. Maybe there're some prints although I'm ready to bet there won't be."

He closed the door and locked it.

2

I lay on my bed and listened to the heavy tramping feet plodding around in the room next door, and to the murmur of the voices as Rankin's men hunted for clues.

I felt depressed and lonely. Although Jack had had his faults, he had been a good man to work with. We had met five years ago when I had been working as special investigator to the District Attorney's office. Jack had been the crime reporter on the *San Francisco Tribune.* We had got friendly, and one night, over a bottle of Scotch, we both had decided we were tired of taking orders and being pushed around by two fat slags who sat behind desks and who seemed to take pleasure in running us ragged.

Even though we were a little drunk, we were both uneasy about leaving the security of a regular salary for the risk of setting up on our own. We hadn't much capital: I had five hundred more than Jack, but we had a lot of experience and we thought we could make a go of it.

There were a number of inquiry agencies in town. We knew most of them and they were no great shakes. After we had worked through half the bottle of Scotch we had decided to burn our boats and go into the business.

We clicked lucky right from the start. After a year we were making a reasonable living, and we hadn't looked back since.

I wondered what it was going to be like working without a partner. I wondered if I should look around for someone to team up with. There was enough money now in the bank to buy out Jack's wife. She was a dumb redhead who had driven Jack nuts at times and I was pretty sure she would jump at the chance of getting the money back she had lent Jack to put in the business.

Switching my mind from that problem, I considered Jack's end. I didn't think his death was hooked up to the case he had been working on. It was more likely he had made some racketeer's girl, and the racketeer had killed him. A rat-tail ice pick, as Rankin had said, was a professional weapon, and it had been used professionally. But I would have to find out who Jack's client had been. Jack had said the job was larded with money. It must have been, otherwise Jack wouldn't have come all this way from his home ground. That meant the client was a man of substance. Not that that helped me. Most men, so far as I could see, who lived in St Raphael, had to be of considerable substance.

I had to be certain that the client was in no way connected with the murder before I gave his name to Rankin. Nothing can damage the reputation of an inquiry agent more than to land the law in the lap of his client: that's a brick that gets talked about quicker than anything.

As soon as Rankin's men had gone, I would put a call through to Ella, but not through the hotel switchboard. I didn't know how smart Rankin was, but if he was as smart as I suspected he was, he would have a man standing by the switchboard waiting for me to put through just such a call.

I looked at my watch. The time was now twelve forty-five. I was feeling hungry. I hadn't had any solid food since the previous night. I thought it would save time if I ate now while the boys next door were busy enough not to bother about what I was doing. I swung my legs off the bed and stood up.

The door opened as I was fastening my collar-button and Rankin looked in.

"Phew! Like an oven in here."

"Yeah. I was just on my way to eat. Do you want me?"

He leaned against the doorpost, rolling a dead cigar between his teeth.

"Nothing in there." He jerked his thumb to the other room. "Hundreds of prints that probably don't mean a thing. They don't clean these rooms with any enthusiasm. I'd say we have prints of at least thirty old customers. Couldn't find a progress report: didn't expect to. Nothing to tell us who Sheppey was working for."

"I bet the guy who searched the room didn't find anything either. Jack didn't make reports."

"You still don't know who the client is?" Rankin said, his stare searching.

"No idea."

"This crap about protecting a client's name, Brandon, doesn't mean a thing when it comes to a murder case. You'd better hustle up the name: don't kid me you can't find it."

"I wouldn't kid you, Lieutenant. If Jack hasn't left a report, then I'm foxed."

"Let's have your office address. You've got a secretary or someone there, haven't you?"

I gave him the address.

"We have a typist. She's just turned seventeen and she's as dumb a moron as ever drew a salary. We don't tell her anything."

Rankin didn't look as if he believed me.

"When you find out who the client is, come and see me. If I don't hear from you within twenty-four hours, I'll come and see you."

He went away, closing the door behind him, leaving the threat hanging in the air like a cloud of poison gas.

I decided to skip the meal. I had an idea Rankin was going to call police headquarters in San Francisco and get a man to talk to Ella before I could contact her.

I took the elevator to the lobby, walked a block before I found a drug store, shut myself in a pay booth and called my office number.

I had been telling Rankin only half the truth about Ella. She was only just seventeen but she was no moron. She was as smart as they come and as sharp as a razor.

It was good to hear her young crisp voice say, "This is the Star Agency. Good afternoon."

"This is Lew," I said, speaking fast. "I'm calling from St Raphael City. Jack came down here on a job and wired me to join him. I have bad news, Ella. He's dead. Someone knifed him."

I heard her draw in a quick, sharp breath. She had liked Jack. From force of habit he had given her the treatment when she had first come to the office, but I had persuaded him that at her age she should be left alone. He had seen reason and had transferred his personality to maturer pastures. All the same he had made an impact on her, and I knew she was more than half in love with him.

"Jack – dead?" she said, and there was a shake in her voice.

"Yes. Now listen, Ella, this is important. The police want to know what the job was and who the client was. Jack didn't tell me. Did he tell you?"

"No. He just said something had come in and he was going to St Raphael City. He said he would wire you to join him, but he didn't say what the job was."

I could hear her fighting her tears. I felt sorry for the kid, but this was no time for sentiment.

"How did he get the job: a letter or a telephone call?"

"A man called on the telephone."

"Did he give his name?"

"No. I asked him, but he wouldn't give it. He said he wanted to talk to one of the principals."

I pushed my hat to the back of my head and blew out my cheeks. The atmosphere in the booth was thick enough to lean against.

This looked as if I was at a dead end. Then I had a sudden idea. I remembered Jack's habit of doodling whenever he talked to anyone on the telephone. Give him a pencil and a telephone and he had to doodle. He either drew nudes – and he had talent in this direction – or he wrote down snatches of the conversation that was taking place. It was second nature to him to scribble while he used the telephone.

"Go into his office, Ella, and take a look at his blotter. There's a chance he wrote down the client's name. You know how he doodled."

"Yes. I'll look."

I waited, feeling sweat running down my spine. It was so hot in the booth that I had to open the door to let in a little fresh air. That was when I saw the flatfoot. He was leaning against the soda bar. He had cop written all over him, and by the exaggerated way he was staring at a cup of coffee I knew he was anxious not to let his glance stray in my direction.

I cursed myself for not thinking that Rankin would slap a tail on me. This guy must guess I was calling my office.

Ella's voice jerked my attention back to the telephone. "There's a lot of stuff on the blotter," she said. "I have it right here. But there's only one name. It's Lee Creedy, written in block letters."

"Okay, Ella. It might be something or it might not. Get rid of the blotter right now, will you? I'll hold on. Tear it up and flush it down the toilet. You could have a call from the cops any moment and they mustn't find it."

I waited for three minutes, then she came on the line again.

"I've got rid of it."

"Good girl. Now listen, I've told the police here you're a dim-wit and we don't tell you anything. Play it that way. Tell them Jack had a telephone call and he told you he was going to St Raphael City, but you don't know why or who called him. Okay?"

"Yes."

"Don't let them faze you. They'll probably get tough and talk about accessories after the fact, but don't worry. Stick to your story. They can't prove anything and they'll soon get tired of trying."

"All right, Lew."

"One more thing. I don't like asking you to do it, Ella, but I can't do it from here. Will you break the news to Jack's wife? Tell her I'm writing. I'll get a letter off tonight. I'll fix the funeral. When she's got over the shock, I'll call her."

"Aren't you coming back yet?"

"No. I'm going to find out why Jack was killed and who killed him. Will you go around and see her, Ella?"

"Yes, of course." Then she said in a lower tone, "Two men have just come in. I think they are detectives ..." and the line went dead.

I took out my handkerchief and wiped my face, then I left the booth and crossed over to the counter and stood close to the waiting detective. He gave me a stony stare, then turned his back on me.

I ordered a sandwich and a coffee.

He finished his coffee, lit a cigarette, then, with exaggerated nonchalance, he went out of the drug store, got into a black Lincoln and drove away.

II

I got back to the hotel soon after one-thirty and went straight up to my room. I had to pass Jack's room and, seeing the door was open, I looked in.

A heavily built man in a baggy suit was standing by the window, his hands on his broad hips, looking around. He turned and stared at me, his eyes hard and hostile.

He looked like an ex-cop. I guessed he would be the house dick.

"Have they folded their tent and stolen away?" I asked, coming into the room.

"What do you want in here?" he demanded in a rasping, bass voice.

"I'm Brandon. My room's next door. You Greaves?"

He relaxed a little and nodded.

The room had been tidied up to some extent. At least the feathers had been swept up, although a few still remained.

The drawers in the chest were shut, the stuffing had been put back into the mattress cover and the papers had been collected.

Jack's belongings were piled in a corner of the room: two shabby suitcases, a raincoat, a hat and a tennis racket in a frame. They looked a pathetic little heap: not much to show in place of a guy with his looks, strength and fun.

"They finished with that lot?" I said.

Greaves nodded.

"I'll have to send them back to his wife. Will someone do it for me?"

"Joe will, the bell hop, if you ask him."

"If you have nothing better to do, come into my room. I have a bottle of Vat 69 that needs a work-out."

His fat face brightened. It wouldn't have surprised me to learn he hadn't many friends.

"I guess I can spare a few minutes."

We went into my room and I shut the door. Greaves sat on the upright chair while I sat on the bed. The ice had long since melted. I didn't bother to phone for more. I gave him three fingers of whisky and myself one.

I studied him as he sniffed at his glass. His round, fat face was devoid of guile. His moustache had a few white hairs. His eyes were hard, suspicious and a little weary. It couldn't be much fun to be a house dick to a hotel of this standing.

"Do they know who killed him?" he asked after he had taken a healthy gulp at his drink.

"If they do, they haven't told me," I said, then went on, "Did you see the girl he went out with?"

Greaves nodded.

"I saw her." He produced a crumpled pack of Luckies, offered me one and lit up. "The cops in this town only co-operate with the dicks of the big hotels. Little guys like me they ignore. Okay, that's no skin off my nose. If that city slicker Rankin had talked to me, I could have told him something, but no, he has to talk to Brewer. Know why? Because Brewer can just afford to buy himself a silk cravat. That's why."

"What could you have told him?" I asked, sitting forward.

"He asked Brewer for a description of the girl," Greaves said. "That shows you the kind of cop he is. All Brewer saw of her were her clothes. I was watching her. I could see she was wearing that outfit because she didn't mean to be recognized again. The first thing I spotted about her was she was a blonde. She was either wearing a wig or she had dyed her hair. I don't know which, but I know she was a blonde."

"Why are you so sure?"

Greaves smiled sourly.

"By using my eyes. She had short sleeves and the hairs on her arms were blonde. She had a blonde's skin and complexion."

I wasn't particularly impressed by this reasoning. The hair on her arms could have been bleached by the sun. I didn't say so because I didn't want to discourage him.

"I've been trained to look for the little give-away habits people have and she had one," Greaves went on. "She was in the lobby for five minutes. All the time she was playing the piano on her thigh." He stood up to demonstrate. "With her right hand, see? Moving her fingers against her thigh like this." He went through the motions of playing a scale. "All the time, and that was a well-developed habit. It wasn't a stunt: she didn't know she was doing it."

I took a drink while I considered this information.

"The police would have quite a job looking for a girl who had that trick, wouldn't they?" I said.

Greaves sneered.

"You'd have to get close to her first. But it would clinch it if they thought they had found her and weren't sure."

I nodded.

"Yeah, I guess that's right. From what you saw of her, what line do you think she was in?"

He lifted his heavy shoulders.

"Hard to tell. She could have been in show business. I don't know: a model, a singer or an actress. She wore her clothes well and she had plenty of style."

"Are you telling Rankin all this?"

Greaves killed his cigarette then shook his head.

"He wouldn't listen even if I could be bothered to take a trip down to headquarters. He has no time for small guys like me. The hell with him."

"Any idea how the guy who searched Sheppey's room got in?"

"He used Sheppey's key. Sheppey took it along with him: forgot to hand it in. It's my guess the guy who killed him found the key, hot-footed back here, walked up the stairs, let himself in and took the room to pieces. It needed nerve, but he was safe enough. We're under-staffed, and at that hour of the morning there wouldn't be anyone up here."

I decided it was time to let him know I was more or less in the same line of business as he was. I took out my card and handed it to him.

"I'm not asking questions for the fun of it," I said.

He read the card, frowned, rubbed his fat nose and handed the card back to me.

"Was he your partner?"

"Yes."

"I've always wanted to get into your racket. There's a lot more money in it than mine. How are you doing?"

"I can't grumble until this happened. Now I'll have to shut down until I find the killer."

He stared at me.

"That's police work. What do you think you can do?"

"It'd look good, wouldn't it, if I went back to Frisco and carried on as if nothing had happened? What sort of advertisement would it be if I didn't do something towards tracing the killer? Besides, Jack was my best friend. I couldn't sit still and let the police handle it."

Greaves pulled a face.

"Then watch out. Rankin isn't so bad: he's a reasonable cop, but Captain Katchen is in a class all by himself. If there's one thing he hates more than a hotel dick, it's a shamus. If he gets the idea you are poking around on his territory, you're in for trouble, and I mean trouble."

I finished my drink, then wiped my wrists with my handkerchief. The room temperature was up in the eighties.

"What kind of trouble?"

"There was a private eye who came here from Los Angeles to check on a suicide case. The widow was convinced it was murder so she hired this guy to poke around. Katchen warned him off, but he still kept trying. One day when he was out driving, a prowl car slammed into him, wrecked his car, put him in hospital with a broken collar-bone and when he came out he got six weeks for drunken driving. He swore the cops had poured half a pint of whisky over him before taking him to hospital, but no one believed him."

"He sounds a nice type. Thanks for the tip. I'll keep clear of him."

Greaves finished his drink regretfully and put down the glass.

"You'd better. Well, I guess I'll be hauling my butt. I'm supposed to be in the lobby around this time to make sure none of the old gentlemen smuggle in a floozy. They never have done it, but the manager is sure they'll try some time. Thanks for the drink. Any time you want help, I'll do what I can."

I said I'd remember that.

As he was leaving the room, I said casually, "Does the name Lee Creedy mean anything to you?"

He paused to stare, then pushed the door to and leaned against it.

"He's the biggest man we have in this town."

I managed not to show my excitement.

27

"How big?"

"He's worth a hundred million bucks for a start. He owns the Green Star shipping line. They have a fleet of tankers plying between Frisco and Panama. He owns the Air Lift Corporation that runs air taxis from here to Miami. He owns three newspapers and a factory that employs ten thousand men and women who turn out electrical components for cars. He owns a piece of the Casino, a piece of our light-weight champion, a piece of the Ritz-Plaza Hotel and a piece of the Musketeer Club, the only really exclusive night club in this lousy town, and when I say exclusive, I don't mean expensive although it's expensive enough. You have to have a five-figure income and maybe a blood test before you get in. That's how big he is. Maybe he owns other things as well, but that will give you the general idea."

"He lives here?"

"He's got a place out at Thor Bay: about five miles along the coast: a fifteen-acre estate with a little shack of about twenty-five bedrooms, a swimming pool you could float an aircraft carrier on, six tennis courts, a zoo with lions and tigers, a staff of forty, all falling over their flat feet to give him service, and a little harbour just big enough to take his four-thousand-ton yacht."

"Married?"

"Oh, sure." Greaves wrinkled his nose. "Remember Bridgette Bland, the movie star? That's her."

I had a vague recollection of once seeing her in some movie. If she was the girl I was thinking of, she had caused a minor sensation four years ago at the Cannes film festival. She had received a lot of publicity by riding a horse into the lobby of the Majestic Hotel and tossing the reins to the reception clerk before strolling to the elevator to be whisked up to her five-room suite. She had lasted about two years in pictures and then she had faded out. If I wasn't confusing her with someone else, I remembered she had the reputation for being wild and tiresome.

Greaves was regarding me with question marks in his eyes.

"What gives with Creedy?" he asked.

"Nothing," I said. "His name came up. Some guy mentioned him. I wondered who he was."

Greaves stared thoughtfully at me, then nodding, he opened the door and went away.

I lit a cigarette and stretched out on the bed.

Jack had said the job was larded with money. If his client had been Lee Creedy then there would be money to be had. But why should a man in Creedy's position hire an obscure inquiry agent three hundred miles from his home town? With his set-up and bank balance he could have got Pinkerton or any other of the de luxe agencies.

I ran my fingers through my damp hair.

A man like Creedy would be surrounded by secretaries, bouncers, flunkies and yes-men whose job it would be to keep people like me away from him. It wouldn't be easy to get near him; it wouldn't be easy to ask him if he had hired Jack and why.

I drank a little whisky to get me in the right mood, then I lifted the telephone receiver.

"Give me Greaves," I said to the switchboard girl.

There was a delay, then Greaves came on the line.

"I have a call to make," I said. "How clear is your switchboard?"

He didn't need a blue-print to understand what I meant.

"You've nothing to worry about. There was a cop hanging around for a while, but he's gone now."

I thanked him, then flashed the operator and asked for directory inquiries. When the girl answered I said I wanted to be connected with Lee Creedy.

She told me to hold on and after a while a man's voice said, "This is Mr Creedy's residence."

He sounded as if he either had a plum in his mouth or should have had his adenoids snipped in the past.

"Put me through to Mr Creedy," I said briskly.

"If you will give me your name, sir," the voice said distantly, "I will put you through to Mr Creedy's secretary."

"My name is Lew Brandon. I don't want Mr Creedy's secretary, I want Mr Creedy in person."

I didn't think it would work and it didn't.

"If you will hold on, sir, I will connect you with Mr Creedy's secretary."

The boredom in his voice was as insulting as a slap in the face.

There were a few clicks, then a curt voice, sharp enough to slice bread on, snapped, "Hammerschult here. Who is talking?"

"This is Lew Brandon. I want Mr Creedy."

"Hold it, please."

By listening carefully I could hear his heavy breathing and could hear him turning the pages of what could have been an address book. This was a careful guy. He wasn't going to get rude until he knew who he was talking to.

"Mr Brandon?" he demanded, much more aggressive now. "What is your business?"

"Mr Creedy will tell you if he wants you to know. Just put me through and stop wasting my time."

I put some menace in my voice, making it sound tough. It didn't work, but it slowed him down a little.

"It isn't possible for you to speak to Mr Creedy," he said, his tone quieter. "If you could give me some idea what you want, I will speak to him and he may call you back."

I knew this was the dead-end. If I became too tough, he would guess I was trying to trample over him, so I played my last and none-too-strong card.

"Tell him I am the senior partner of the Star Agency of San Francisco. He's waiting for me to report to him."

"Is he?" The voice sounded surprised and less confident. "All right, Mr Brandon, I'll speak to him and we'll call you. What is your number?"

I gave him the hotel number and he hung up.

I stubbed out my cigarette, finished my whisky and closed my eyes.

I would have, I thought, an hour's wait, possibly longer. I might not hear at all. There seemed no point at the moment in doing anything. I relaxed, and after a while, I dozed off.

The sharp and violent ringing of the telephone bell brought me awake with a start that nearly threw me off the bed.

I grabbed up the receiver, looking at my wristwatch. I had been asleep for fifteen minutes.

"Mr Brandon?"

I recognized Hammerschult's voice.

"Yes."

"Mr Creedy will see you at three o'clock this afternoon."

I couldn't believe my ears.

"Three o'clock?"

"Yes. Will you please be punctual? Mr Creedy has several appointments for this afternoon, and he will only be able to spare you a few minutes."

"That'll be long enough," I said, and hung up.

For a long moment I lay staring up at the ceiling, then I swung my legs to the floor.

Creedy had to be Jack's client. That could be the only reason why a man of his position would bother to see me.

I looked at my watch again.

I had just under the hour to get out to his place.

I went over to my suitcase to unpack my best suit.

3

Lee Creedy's estate was built on the far end of a mile-long, narrow peninsula that projected into the exact centre of Thor Bay.

You could get a good view of it from Bay Boulevard. Before I turned off on to the private road that ran the length of the peninsula to the estate, I slowed down and took a look at it.

The house was massive: three stories high with vast windows, terraces, a blue-tiled roof and white walls covered with flowering climbers. The rear of the house appeared to hang over the cliff face. It had a magnificent view of the two arms of the bay.

I was driving the office Buick. The police had left it outside the hotel. There was a bad scratch on one of the door panels and a hub-cap was dented. I didn't know if the police were responsible or if Jack had bumped something on his drive down from Frisco. It was possible that Jack had done the damage. He had never been much of a driver, cutting in too close and taking too many chances. But I was glad to have the car. It would save me the cost of taking taxis, and from what I had been told, the cost of living in St Raphael City was so high I would need every cent I had.

I turned off Bay Boulevard on to the road to the peninsula. A hundred yards or so further on I came to a big sign that told me that this was a private road and only visitors to the Thor Estate could go beyond this point.

A quarter of a mile further on I came on one of those red-and-white poles you see on the continent blocking the road. Near by was a small white guardhouse.

Two men in white shirts, white cord breeches, black shiny knee-high boots and peak caps watched me come. Both of them looked like ex-cops: both of them were wearing .45 Colts at their hips.

"I've an appointment with Mr Creedy," I said, looking out of the car window.

One of them moved over to me. His cop eyes ran over me, and by his curt nod I knew he didn't approve of the Buick nor, come to think of it, of me.

"Name?"

I told him.

He checked a list he had in his hand, then he waved to the other guard, who lifted the barrier.

"Straight ahead, turn left at the intersection and park your car in Bay 6."

I nodded and drove on, aware they were both staring at me as if to make sure they would know me again.

A half a mile further on I came to massive gates of oak, fifteen feet high and studded with iron nails, that stood open. I then hit the sanded carriageway and I drove through woodland, and then past the ornate, magnificent gardens with their acres of close-mown lawns, their beds of flowers, their sunken rose gardens and their fountains.

Chinese gardeners were at work on one of the big beds, planting out begonias: taking their time as the Chinese do, but making a good job of it. Each plant was exactly equidistant from the other: each plant planted at the same level: an exactitude that no other gardener in the world can do as well as the Chinese.

At the intersection I turned left as directed. I came to a vast stretch of tarmac divided by white lines into fifty parking places. Some of the places had signs made of oak with glittering gilt letters.

I left the Buick in Bay 6, got out and took a quick look at some of the signs. No. 1 sign said: Mr Creedy. No. 7, Mrs Creedy. No. 23, Mr Hammerschult. There were a lot more names that meant nothing to me.

"Hot stuff, huh?" a voice said behind me. "Important people: big-shotting themselves to death."

I looked around.

A short, thickset man in a white guard's uniform, his peaked cap at the back of his head, gave me a friendly grin. His face was red and sweaty, and as he came closer, I smelt whisky on his breath.

"It takes all kinds to make up the world."

"Damn right. All this crap though is so much waste of good money." He waved his hand at the signs. "As if they should care who parks where." His small, alert eyes travelled over me. "You looking for anyone in particular, buster?"

"Old man Creedy," I told him.

"That a fact?" He blew out his cheeks. "Rather you than me. I've had all I can stomach. This is my last day here and am I rejoicing?" He leaned forward and tapped me lightly on the chest. "Why is it money always goes to the punks? This guy Creedy: nothing ever pleases him. His shoes aren't shined enough, his car isn't clean enough, the roses aren't big enough, his food either isn't hot enough or cold enough. He's never happy, never satisfied; always moaning, yelling or cursing and driving a guy nuts. If I had the tenth of his money I'd be as happy as a king, but not him."

I sneaked a look at my watch. The time was four minutes to three.

"That's the way it is," I said. "Just one of those things. I'd like to continue this theme, but I'm due to meet him at three and I'm told he takes it badly if he's kept waiting."

"He certainly does, but don't kid yourself that being punctual will mean you'll see him when he's fixed for you to see him. I've known guys wait three or four hours before they get to him. Well, you're welcome. I'd rather have a meeting with a dose of cholera." He pointed. "Up those steps and to the left."

I started off, then I had a sudden idea and I turned back. "Would you have anything to do around six o'clock tonight?"

He grinned.

"I'll have plenty to do around six o'clock tonight. I'm celebrating. I've been with this old punk for twenty months. I've got a lot of drinking to get in to soothe the pain out of that stretch. Why?"

"I've some celebrating to do myself," I said. "If you're not tied up with anyone, maybe we could do it together."

He stared at me.

"Are you a drinking man?"

"On special occasions: this could be one."

"Well, why not? My girl doesn't approve of me drinking. I was planning to have a lone bender, but I'd as soon have a guy with me. Okay. Where and when?"

"Say seven. You know a good place?"

"Sam's Cabin. Anyone will tell you where it is. The name's Fulton. First name, Tim. What's yours?"

"Lew Brandon. Be seeing you."

"Sure thing."

I left him, took the steps three at a time, turned left, walked the length of an ornate terrace to the front entrance.

I had a minute in hand as I tugged at the chain bell.

The door opened immediately. An old man, four inches over six foot, thin and upright, wearing the traditional clothes of a Hollywood butler, stood aside with a slight bow and let me walk into a hall big enough to garage six Eldorado Seville Cadillacs.

"Mr Brandon?"

I said he was right.

"Will you come this way, please?"

I was led across the hall, out into the sunshine that blazed down on a patio, through French doors and along a passage to a room containing fifteen lounging chairs, a carpet so thick and soft it made me think I was walking in snow, and a couple of Picasso paintings on the wall.

Six weary-looking businessmen, clutching despatch cases, sat in some of the chairs. They stared at me with that numbed indifference that told me they had been waiting so long they had not only lost their sense of time, but also their sense of feeling.

"Mr Creedy will see you before long," the butler said, and went away as quietly and as smoothly as if he had been riding on wheels.

I sat down, balanced my hat on my knees and stared up at the ceiling.

After the others had gaped at me long enough to satisfy their curiosity, they went back into a coma again.

At three minutes past three, the door jerked open and a youngish man, tall, thin, with one of those high-executive chins and a crew cut, wearing a black coat, grey whipcord trousers and a black tie came as far as the doorway.

The six businessmen all straightened up, clutching at their despatch cases and pointed the way a setter points when he sights game.

His cold, unfriendly eyes ran over them and stopped at me.

"Mr Brandon?"

"That's right."

"Mr Creedy will see you now."

As I got to my feet, one of the men said, "You'll pardon me, Mr Hammerschult, but I have been waiting since twelve o'clock. You said I would be the next to see Mr Creedy."

Hammerschult gave him a bleak stare.

"Did I? Mr Creedy thinks otherwise," he said. "Mr Creedy won't be free now until four o'clock. This way," he went on to me, and, leading the way down the passage, he took me into a smallish lobby, through two doors, both lined with green baize, to another massive door of solid polished mahogany.

He rapped, opened the door, looked in, said, "Brandon's here, sir."

Then he stood aside and waved me in.

II

The room reminded me of the pictures I had seen of Mussolini's famous office.

It was sixty feet long if it was an inch. Placed at the far end between two vast windows, with a fine view of the sea and the right arm of Thor Bay, was a desk big enough to play billiards on.

The rest of the room was pretty bare apart from a few lounging chairs, a couple of suits of armour and two heavy, dark oil paintings that could or could not be original Rembrandts.

Behind the desk sat a small, frail-looking man, his horn glasses pushed up and resting on his forehead. Apart from a fringe of grey hair, he was bald and his skull looked bony and hard.

He had a pinched, tight face: small features and a very small, tight mouth. It wasn't until I encountered the full force that dwelt in his eyes that I realized I was in the presence of a big man.

He gave me the full treatment, and I felt as if I were under X-rays and that he could count the vertebra of my spine.

He let me walk the length of the room and he kept the searchlight of his gaze on me. I found I was sweating slightly by the time I reached his desk.

He leaned back in his chair and eyed me over the way you would eye a bluebottle fly that has fallen in your soup.

There was a long pause, then he said in a curiously soft, effeminate voice, "What do you want?"

By then, and by his reasoning, I should have been completely softened up and ready to fall on my hands and knees and rap my forehead on the floor. Okay, I admit I was slightly softened, but not as soft as he would want.

"My name's Brandon," I said, "of the Star Inquiry Agency of San Francisco: You hired my partner four days ago."

The thin, small face was as deadpan as the back of a bus.

"What makes you imagine I would do that?" he asked.

From that I knew he wasn't sure of his ground, and he was going to probe first before he took the hoods off his big artillery.

"We keep a record of all our clients, Mr Creedy," I said untruthfully. "Sheppey, before he left our office, recorded that you hired him."

"Who would Sheppey be?"

"My partner and the man you hired, Mr Creedy."

He placed his elbows on his desk and his fingertips together. He rested his pointed, bony chin on the arch thus formed.

39

"I must hire twenty or thirty people a week to do various unimportant jobs for me," he said. "I don't recall any man named Sheppey. Where do you come in on this? What do you want?"

"Sheppey was murdered this morning," I said, meeting his hard, penetrating gaze. "I thought you might want me to finish the job he was working on."

He tapped his chin with his fingertips.

"And what job would that be?"

Here it was: the dead-end. I knew sooner or later it might come to that, but I had hoped I might flush him out of his cover by bluff: it hadn't worked.

"You'd know more about that than I do."

He sat back in his chair, drummed on the desk for about four seconds, his face still deadpan, but I knew his mind was busy. Then he reached out a bony finger and pressed a button.

A door to the right of the desk opened immediately and Hammerschult appeared. He appeared so quickly he had to be waiting just outside the door for the summons.

"Hertz," Creedy said without looking at him.

"At once, sir," Hammerschult said and went away.

Creedy continued to drum on his desk. He kept his eyes lowered.

We waited in silence for perhaps forty-five seconds, then a rap sounded on the door. It opened, and a short, thickset man came in. His right ear was bent and crushed into his head. At some time in his career someone must have hit him either with a brick or possibly a sledgehammer: no fist could have caused that amount of damage. His nose was boneless and spread over his face. His eyes were small, and had that wild light in them you might see in the eyes of an angry and vicious orang-outang. Black hairs sprouted over the top of his collar. He wore a pair of fawn flannel trousers, a white sports coat and one of those razzle-dazzle, hand-painted ties.

He moved up to the desk silently and swiftly. He was as light on his feet as any ballet dancer.

Creedy pointed his chin at me.

"Look at this man, Hertz," he said. "I want you to remember him. It may be I will want you to take care of him. It's unlikely, but he may be a bigger fool than he looks. Just make certain you will know him again."

Hertz turned and stared at me. His cruel little eyes moved over my face, his own smashed-up, ruined face was expressionless.

"I'll know him again, boss," he said, his voice husky and soft.

Creedy waved him away and he went out, closing the door silently behind him.

There was a pause, then I said, "What is he supposed to do to me – turn me into butter?"

Creedy took off his glasses, pulled out a white silk handkerchief and began to polish the lenses, staring at me.

"I don't like inquiry agents," he said. "They seem to me to be shabby little men who have tendencies to become blackmailers. I haven't hired your Mr Sheppey nor would it cross my mind to do so. I would advise you to get out of this city immediately. A man in my position is often annoyed by people like you. It saves time and irritation to bring Hertz on to the scene. He is an extraordinary character. He is under the impression that he is in my debt. I can say to him this man is annoying me and he makes it his business to persuade the man to stop annoying me. I have never inquired how he does it, but I have never known him to fail. That is the position, Mr Brandon. I don't know your Mr Sheppey. I didn't hire him. I don't wish to have anything to do with you. You may go now unless you wish to say something that might be of value."

I smiled at him. I had got over his searchlight gaze, the big room and the awe-inspiring atmosphere. I was more angry now than I had ever been before in my life, and that is saying a lot.

"Yes, I have something to say," I said, resting my hands on his desk and staring him in the face. "First, Mr Creedy, I thought you would be smarter than you are. I didn't know for certain that you had hired Sheppey, now I do. It so happened Sheppey wrote your name down on his blotter: that was the only clue I had to work on. I thought it was possible someone had mentioned your name to him and while he was talking to this someone he had doodled your name in the rather senseless way he had. Now I know different. When I called this afternoon, I was pretty sure you wouldn't see me. A man with your money doesn't grant an interview to a small-time inquiry agent unless he either wants to employ him or else he has something on his mind that is keeping him awake at nights. By giving me priority over six important-looking businessmen, one who has been waiting three hours, told me the thing on your mind was not only keeping you awake nights, but was giving you inward jitters in no mean way. You obviously couldn't wait three minutes to hear just how much I knew. When you found out how little I knew, you called in your tame gorilla and waved him in my face. You hoped I'd be so scared that I would rush back to my hotel, pack my bag and get the hell out of here. Not very smart, Mr Creedy. You should know by now that some men don't scare easily. I happen to be one of them."

He leaned back in his chair, his expressionless face telling me nothing, his bony fingers still busy with his handkerchief and glasses.

"Is that all?" he asked.

"Not quite. I am now sure that you hired Sheppey. While he was working for you, he turned up something that someone didn't like so he got killed. For all I know you hold the clue that could lead the police to his killer, but not unnaturally you don't wish to be involved in a murder case. You know if you did become involved you would have to come out with the reason why you hired Sheppey. From my experience, when a millionaire takes the trouble to hire an agent who lives three hundred miles from the millionaire's home ground, the millionaire is asking him to dig into something pretty smelly that he wouldn't want the local agents to know about. Sheppey is dead. He was a good friend of mine. If the police can't find his killer, then maybe I can. Anyway, Mr Hertz or no Mr Hertz, Mr Creedy or no Mr Creedy, I'm going to have a damn good try." I straightened, pushing myself away from his desk. "That's all. Don't bother to call your flunkey, I can find my own way out."

I turned and started down the long room towards the door.

Creedy said in his soft, effeminate voice, "Don't say I didn't warn you, Mr Brandon."

I kept on, reached the door, opened it and tramped into the lobby where the butler was waiting.

As he conducted me to the exit, Creedy's last words banged around inside my skull like demented ping-pong balls.

III

It took me forty minutes to get back to my hotel. For one thing I was in no hurry, and for another the afternoon traffic was heavy.

I was satisfied now that Creedy had hired Sheppey, but I still didn't know if Sheppey had been murdered because of something he had turned up while working for Creedy or because he had been fooling around with some cut-throat's girl. I mentally cursed his weakness for women. It made the job of finding his killer that more difficult.

I was glad now I had made a drinking date with Tim Fulton. Very often a dissatisfied employee could give away some useful information, and that was something I needed badly.

As I pulled up outside the hotel, I saw a prowl car parked a few yards ahead of me.

I got out of the Buick.

The door of the prowl car swung open and Candy appeared. He came towards me, moving heavily, his jaw working as he chewed.

"Captain Katchen wants to talk to you," he said, when he was within a yard of me. "Let's go."

"Suppose I don't want to talk to him?" I asked, smiling at him.

"Let's go," he repeated. "I can take you in smooth or rough – please yourself."

"Did he say what he wanted?" I asked, moving with him to the prowl car.

"If I needed proof that you were a stranger in this town, that dopey remark would have clinched it," Candy said, sliding his bulk into the back seat.

There was a uniformed cop at the wheel. He turned to look me over.

I got in beside Candy and the car took off as if it were answering a four-alarm fire call.

"You mean the Captain doesn't tell his subordinates why he wants anything, only that he wants it?"

"Now you're being bright," Candy said. "If you don't want to come out of headquarters a permanent cripple, you'll watch your step, speak only when you're spoken to, answer all the questions quickly and truthfully, and generally behave as if you were in church."

"Which would suggest that the Captain has a hasty temper."

Candy smiled sourly.

"I think that's a fair statement. I'd say Captain Katchen is a little quick tempered, wouldn't you, Joe?"

Joe, the driver, spat out of the window.

"No more than a bear with a boil on its ass," he said.

Candy laughed.

"Joe talks like that all the time, except when the Captain's around, then he never says a word, do you, Joe?"

Joe spat out of the window again.

"I like my food. I've only eight good teeth in my mouth as it is."

"See? A comedian." Candy took out a cigarette and lit it. "So watch out. Don't go sounding off."

"Have you found the killer yet?" I asked.

"Not yet, but we will. In the past ten years we have had five homicides in this town, and we haven't found one killer yet. We must break that record sometime and this could be the time. What do you think, Joe?"

"It depends," Joe said cautiously. "It's not as if we haven't the men because we have: good, bright, clever detectives who know a clue when they see it, but there's a bottleneck of bad luck somewhere. I wouldn't bet my salary we'll find the killer, but we might."

"There you are," Candy said, smiling at me. The smile didn't reach his eyes. "Like Joe says, he wouldn't bet his salary, but we could crack it."

"Captain Katchen think so?"

"No one ever asks what Captain Katchen thinks. He's a mite touchy about sharing his thoughts with anyone. I wouldn't ask him if I were you."

We rode on for a fast half-mile before I said, "Did you find the ice pick?"

Candy shook his head.

"No. The Lieutenant thinks the killer took it with him. He's probably right, but I wouldn't bet Joe's salary on it. It could have got buried somewhere. There's a whale of a lot of sand on that beach."

"You didn't find the girl's body?"

Again Candy shook his head.

"No, and I didn't expect to. We looked because there was a slight chance she got knocked off too, but the Lieutenant thinks she slid out of the picture just before your pal got stuck."

"Maybe she killed him."

Candy blew out his cheeks.

"The pick was driven home with a lot of force. I doubt if a woman could have done it."

"Women aren't all that frail. If the pick was sharp enough and she was angry enough it wouldn't be so tough."

Candy flicked his cigarette out of the window.

"Don't bet your salary on it."

The car swerved to the kerb and pulled up outside the police headquarters. We got out, walked up the steps, through double swing doors and along a stone passage that gave off the usual smell that all police headquarters have.

"Watch your step," Candy said. "I'm telling you for my good rather than yours. The Captain gets into a rage easily, and it's bad for us all when he does."

He paused outside a door, rapped and waited. A voice as musical as a foghorn bawled, "Wadja want?"

Candy gave me a weak smile and lifted his shoulders. He turned the doorknob, opened the door and walked into a small, drab office full of cigar smoke.

"Lew Brandon, sir."

A mountain of a man sat behind a battered desk. He was getting on in years, but he was still in hard physical shape, and there wasn't much fat on him. His thinning grey hair was slicked down in a cow's lick over his low forehead. His face was massive, leathery and brutal. He rested two enormous hairy hands on his desk and glared at me while Candy closed the door as if it were made of eggshells and moved silently behind me and leaned against the wall.

"Brandon?" Katchen said, reached out and viciously stubbed out his cigar. "Huh: the shamus. Yeah, the shamus." He rubbed his face while he continued to glare at me. "To think we gotta have beetles like you crawling around our streets." He leaned forward, screwing up his small eyes. "When are you getting out of town, shamus?"

"I don't know," I said mildly. "Within a week I'd say."

"Would you? And what the hell are you going to do in this town for a week, shamus?"

"See the sights, swim, take a girl out and relax generally."

He wasn't expecting this and he hunched his shoulders. "Yeah? You weren't planning to stick your snout into this murder case, were you?"

"I'll watch Lieutenant Rankin's progress with interest," I said. "I'm sure he can get along fine without my help."

Katchen leaned back in his chair, making the back creak. "That's pretty white of you, shamus." He glared at me for maybe twenty seconds, then went on, "I don't like a beetle around the place. If I catch up with him I put my foot on him."

"I can imagine that, Captain."

"Yeah? Don't kid yourself, shamus, you can pull a fast one on me. You start interfering in this case and you'll wonder what's hit you." He lifted his voice into a bellow and yelled at me: "Understand?"

"Yes, Captain."

He showed his teeth in a big, sneering grin.

"Not a gutty beetle, are you, shamus? Okay, don't say you haven't been warned. Keep your nose clean, keep away from me and you might possibly survive. If you ever come into this office again, you won't forget the experience. Remember that. You put one foot wrong and you'll be brought in. We have ways of softening beetles, shamus."

His little eyes glittered.

"Okay, now you've been told and remember you ain't going to be told again. One step wrong, and in you come, and, shamus, if you do come in, the boys will certainly give you a work out before they kick you into a cell." He looked at Candy. "Take this yellow-gutted beetle out of here and lose him," he snarled. "He makes me sick to my stomach even to look at him."

Candy pushed himself away from the wall and opened the office door.

Katchen lifted a huge finger and pointed at me.

"Keep your snout out of this case or else ..."

I took a step to the door, paused and said, "Could I ask a question, Captain?"

He ran the tip of his tongue over his thick, rubbery lips.

"What question?"

"Did Lee Creedy call you up and ask you to talk to me?"

His eyes narrowed and his great hands turned into fists.

"What does that mean?"

"Mr Creedy hired Sheppey to do a job for him. While doing it Sheppey got killed. Mr Creedy is anxious to keep that bit of information quiet. He reckons he would be called as a witness and he would have to tell the court just why he hired Sheppey. So he had a little talk to me himself. He produced a thug called Hertz and tried to scare me with him. I was curious to know if Mr Creedy was losing confidence in his thug and had asked you to strengthen the threat to make sure it would stick."

I heard Candy draw in a quick breath.

Katchen's face turned the colour of a damson plum. Very slowly he got to his feet. Standing, he looked larger than life: a kind of Boris Karloff nightmare.

He moved away from his desk and advanced slowly towards me.

I waited, not moving, my eyes on his.

"So there is a little life in you shamus," he said, and the words seemed to come through clenched teeth. "Well, here's something to go on with."

His open hand came up and exploded against the side of my face. I saw it coming and rolled with the slap, taking some of the weight out of it, but it was hard enough to make my head ring and send me staggering.

He waited for me to straighten up, then he thrust his dark, blood-congested face into mine.

"Go on, shamus," he said in a low, vicious whisper, "hit me!"

I was tempted to hang one on his jaw. Very often a guy of his build can't take a punch on the jaw, but I knew he wanted me to hit him. I knew if I even threatened to hit him I'd be in a cell in seconds flat with three or four of his biggest men to keep me company.

I didn't move. The side of my face where he had hit me burned hotly.

We stared at each other for a long moment, then he stepped back and yelled at Candy, "Get this punk out of here before I kill him!"

Candy grabbed my arm and swung me out of the room and pulled the door shut. He let go of me and stepped back, his red, weathered face angry and scared.

"I told you, didn't I, you damned fool?" he said. "Now you've really started something. Get the hell out of here!"

I touched my face.

"I'd like to meet that ape up a dark alley. So long, Sergeant. At least I don't have to work for him."

I walked down the passage, through the double swing doors and on to the street.

It was nice to see the sun was still shining and the men and women coming back from the beach were still looking like human beings and still acting like them too.

4

Sam's Cabin, at the unfashionable end of St Raphael's promenade, was a big wooden shack of a place, built out over the sea on steel piers.

There was a parking lot and though it was only five minutes to six o'clock, there were some thirty cars already parked, and not a Cadillac nor a Clipper among them.

The parking attendant was a fat, elderly man, who smiled cheerfully as he told me that the parking was free.

I walked the length of the narrow jetty and into the bar room. The bar ran the width and one side of the room. There was also a snack bar equipped with twelve electric spits which at this moment were busily roasting twelve fat chickens.

About eight or nine men were propping themselves up against the bar, drinking beer and dipping into the dill pickle bowl.

Beyond open double doors at the far end of the room I could see a railed verandah, shaded from the evening sun by a green awning. There were tables out there, and that's where the crowd was. As I was hoping to do some serious talking with Fulton, I decided I'd stay inside and away from the crowd. I went over to the doors and looked the crowd over to make sure he hadn't already arrived, then, not seeing him, I picked a corner table in the bar room by a big open window and sat down.

A waiter came over, wiped the table and nodded at me. I told him to bring me a bottle of Black Label, some ice and two glasses.

A few minutes after six o'clock Tim Fulton came in. He was wearing a pair of baggy grey flannel trousers and an open-neck, blue shirt. He carried his jacket over his shoulder. He looked around, saw me and grinned. Then he came over, his eyes on the bottle of Black Label.

"Hey, there, buster," he said. "So you've got the flag waving already? Couldn't you wait for me?"

"The bottle's not open yet," I said. "Sit down. How's it feel to be a free man?"

He blew out his cheeks.

"You don't know anything until you've been through what I've been through. I should have my head examined for staying so long with him." He flicked the bottle with his fingernail. "You reckoning to uncork this or do we just sit and admire it?"

I poured him a drink, dropped a chunk of ice into his glass, then made myself one.

We touched glasses as boxers will touch gloves and nodded to each other. We drank.

After my interview with Creedy and then with Katchen, the ice-cold whisky certainly hit a spot.

We lit cigarettes, sank further down in the basket chairs and grinned at each other.

"Pretty nice, huh?" Fulton said. "If there's one thing I like better than anything else it's to sit where I can listen to the sea and drink good whisky. I don't reckon a man could wish for anything nicer. Okay, there are times when a woman can take the place of pretty well anything, but when a guy wants to relax he doesn't want a woman. I'll tell you why: women talk, whisky doesn't. This is a bright idea of yours, buster."

I said I was full of bright ideas.

"I've another bright idea," I went on. "After we've had a few drinks, it might be an idea to try some of that chicken cooking there."

"Yeah. Those birds are the best on this stretch of coast," Fulton said. "Make no mistake about that. Okay, you can go to Alfredo's, the Carlton, the Blue Room, or if you can get in, even the Musketeer Club. They serve chicken too. They give it to you with five waiters, silver forks and orchids. The bill will knock your right eye out. Here, they just throw it at you, but, brother, is it good! And it's cheap." He finished his drink, put down his glass and sighed. "I come here twice a week. Sometimes I bring my girl; sometimes I come alone. It makes me laugh to think of all the rich suckers going to the shake-down joints and paying five times what I pay and getting something not so good. The joke is none of them would dare be seen here because their rich pals would imagine they were economizing, and in this town, to economize is a deadly sin."

I made him another drink and freshened mine to give him the illusion that I was drinking level with him.

"But, and there's always a but," he said, shaking his head, "this place is beginning to slip. A year ago we got guys and dolls in here who were friendly, nice and homely. Now the tough boys have discovered it. They are as fond of stuffing their bellies as I am, so they come. We've got this gambling ship anchored out in the bay: that attracts them the way rotten meat attracts flies. Sam's worried. I was talking to him only the other week. He tells me the people who made his business are fading away and these tough boys are taking their place. There's nothing he can do about it. Last month there was a fight here and a knife was flashed. Sam got it under control quick, but that's the kind of thing that'll scare people away. He reckons if there's another knife fight in here, he'll be owning just another racketeer's restaurant."

I said it was bad and looked over at the group of men standing at the bar. They were big and flashily dressed, with the hard watchful eyes of men who don't care how they make their money so long as they make it.

"Bookies," Fulton said, following my gaze. "They're okay so long as they stay sober. The boys who cause the trouble don't show until it's dark." He lit another cigarette and pushed the pack over to me. "Well, how did you get on with the old man: lovely character, isn't he?"

"Yeah. That long room of his and his searchlight eyes. I'd hate to have to work for him."

"You said it, brother! I've got me a nice little job now driving an old lady to the shops, holding her shopping bag and generally helping to make life easier for her. She's a nice old thing, and, after Creedy, I reckon she's going to do my ulcer a lot of good."

"Talking about nice old ladies," I said, "who is this character Hertz?"

Fulton grimaced.

"What are you trying to do – spoil my evening? Have you run into him?"

"He was with Creedy when I blew in. He struck me as a pretty tough egg. Who is he? What's Creedy doing mixing with a type like that?"

"He takes care of people," Fulton said. "Creedy employs him now and then as a bodyguard."

"What's Creedy want with a bodyguard?"

Fulton shrugged.

54

"These rich punks get inflated ideas. They think people are going to shoot or stab them. Have a bodyguard and people imagine you're important: window dressing, like the signs in his parking lot. Big-shotting himself to death. But you don't want to get the wrong idea about Creedy. He's tough. Maybe he doesn't look like it, but he's as tough and as dangerous as any of the gun-and-knife punks who come in here. He practically runs this town. It was his idea to have a gambling ship in the bay. He reckoned it would encourage the tourists and it certainly did. He couldn't care less if it also brought the tough boys as well. He owns half the ship anyway, and takes half the profits."

"And Hertz is as tough as he looks?"

Fulton nodded.

"He certainly is. Creedy has no use for a phoney. When he hires a tough guy that guy has to be tough. Hertz is that and more. He scares me. I reckon he has a bat in his attic."

If what he was saying was true, there didn't seem much to choose from between Katchen and Hertz.

"Did you read about the guy who was killed out at Bay Beach this morning?" I asked.

"I did see something in the evening paper," Fulton said. "Why bring that up?"

"He was my partner. I have an idea he called on Creedy during the past few days and I'm wondering if you saw him."

Fulton showed interest.

"Come to see the old man? Well, maybe I did. I was on the gate most of this week. What was he like?"

I described Sheppey carefully. He had flaming red hair, and I was pretty sure if Fulton had seen him he wouldn't have forgotten him, and I was right.

"Sure," he said. "I remember him: big guy with red hair. That's right. Logan passed him through. I was on the barrier and I didn't get his name."

"Would you swear to seeing him? This is important. You might have to, and in a court of law."

Fulton finished his drink, then said, "Of course I'd swear to it. He came last Tuesday: a big, red-headed guy with a crew cut, wearing a grey flannel suit and driving a Buick convertible."

That was good enough. The car was a clincher. So I had been right. Jack had been to see Creedy. Now I had to find out why, and that wouldn't be easy.

"You say he was murdered?" Fulton said, looking curiously at me.

"Yes. The police think he was fooling around with some thug's girl and the thug fixed him. Could be: he was over fond of women."

"Well, what do you know? You had to go to the cops about it?"

"I went. That Captain Katchen is quite something, isn't he? Belsen missed a great boss in him."

"You're right. Every so often he comes out to see Creedy: about four times a year. It's my guess he comes for his rake-off. You'd be surprised at the number of night clubs and high-toned brothels that stay open because Katchen looks the other way."

"What are night clubs and brothels to do with Creedy?"

"I tell you he owns most of this town. Maybe he doesn't collect the gravy direct from the rats who run these places, but indirectly he gets the rents, and Katchen gets his cut."

"He's married, isn't he?"

"Who – Creedy? As far as I know he's been married four times, but it could be more. His present wife is Bridgette Bland, the ex-movie star. Ever seen her?"

"Once, I think. If I remember rightly she was quite a looker."

"She still is, but she can't hold a candle to her stepdaughter. Now there's a beaut, about the loveliest dish I've seen, and I've seen quite a few in my day."

"Does she live at home?"

Fulton shook his head.

"Not now: she used to, but the other one couldn't take it. Whenever the old man threw a party, Margot, that's the daughter, took all the limelight, and the other one was left out in the cold. She didn't like it. They were always quarrelling, so Margot packed and cleared out. She has an apartment on Franklyn Boulevard. From what I hear the old man misses her. I miss her too. She was the one bright light in that lousy place. Bridgette gave me a pain: just like Creedy: never happy, always moaning, stays up all night and sleeps all day."

I was learning things. We had the evening before us and there was no point in rushing at it. I turned the conversation to the coming world championship fight and let Fulton sound off on why the Champ couldn't lose. From that we went on to ball games and finally to the old, old standby: women.

It was around nine o'clock by the time we had finished the bottle of Scotch. The sun had gone down, making a great red splash across the sky, and it was now dark.

I waved to the waiter, and after a while he came over.

"Let's have two chicken dinners with all the trimmings," I said.

He nodded and went away.

Both Fulton and I were a little high by now, but pleasantly high, as, after the first quick rush, we had been taking the Scotch slowly, which is the way good Scotch should be taken.

I looked through the open window at the lights of St Raphael City. It looked a pretty nice place from where I was sitting.

"Does Mrs Creedy get along all right with Creedy?" I asked.

Fulton shrugged.

"No one could get along with him," he said. "Anyway, he's too busy making money to bother with women. She gets her fun elsewhere."

"Anyone in particular?"

"Well, the current favourite is a husky, curly-haired hunk of meat who calls himself Jacques Thrisby. He's a French Canadian."

I became aware that a man had moved up to our table. For a moment I thought it was the waiter bringing our food. I was looking out of the window, listening to Fulton talk, so my reflexes were a little slow; besides, the Scotch had made me just that woolly in the brain.

Then I heard Fulton catch his breath sharply, the way only a very frightened man will gasp, and I looked quickly around.

Hertz was standing right up at the table looking at me. Behind him in a semi-circle, blocking the way of escape, were four men, tall, beefy, dark and tough, and the expression in Hertz's wild little eyes sent a chill crawling up my spine.

II

The noise in the big room was suddenly hushed: heads turned, and eyes looked in my direction.

I was in a bad position. My chair was only a foot or so from the wall. The table was between me and Hertz, and it wasn't a big table. Fulton was better placed. He was on my right, with no wall behind him.

Obviously there was no doubt in the minds of the crowd that there was going to be trouble. Already some of them were heading with restrained panic towards the exit.

Hertz said in his husky voice, "Remember me? I don't like peepers, and I don't like a punk."

Out of the corner of my eye I saw a big Negro, wearing a white apron and in shirtsleeves, come fast from behind the bar. He was built on the lines of Joe Louis, and there was a vague, apologetic smile on his big, battered face. He crossed the room, weaved around the four men and arrived at Hertz's side quicker than I can tell it.

I caught hold of the edge of the table and braced myself.

The Negro said pleasantly to Hertz, "Don't want trouble here, boss. If you and your friends have business to talk over, you talk about it outside."

Hertz turned his head to look at the Negro. There were tiny red sparks in his eyes making him look a little insane.

I saw his shoulder drop slightly, then his fist flashed up and landed in the Negro's face. The blow sounded like a thump on a tympani. The Negro went staggering back, then fell on his hands and knees.

All this happened fast. I put my weight against the table and rammed it hard into Hertz, who was slightly off balance from the punch he had thrown.

The edge of the table caught him against his thigh and he reeled backwards, cannoning into two of the men with him.

I now had a little space in which to move and I jumped to my feet and grabbed hold of my chair. I swung it shoulder high, using it like a scythe, and cleared some more space in which I could manoeuvre.

Fulton was also on his feet, his chair above his head. He slammed it down on the head of the nearest thug, knocking him to the floor.

Two bouncers, big men, one of them a Negro, clubs in hand, came rushing through a doorway near by. The three thugs with Hertz scattered, then converged on the bouncers. That left Fulton and me facing Hertz.

I smashed my chair down on Hertz's head and the chair back broke, leaving me with a strip of brittle wood that had the staying power of a toothpick as far as an animal like Hertz was concerned.

Hertz staggered, then snarling, he came at me, his right hand flashing up. If I had stepped back, he would have caught me, but I jumped forward and planted my fist in the middle of his face. It was a good, jabbing punch and it rocked his head back. I moved away from him and cannoned into one of the bouncers, who slugged me with a backhand blow that sent me staggering into Hertz as he came at me again. I managed to grab his wrist with both hands. I half-turned, got his arm over my shoulder, pulled down and heaved. He went over my head with the speed of a jet-propelled rocket and landed on the floor with a crash that shook the building.

I spun around, looking for Fulton. He was leaning against the wall, holding a handkerchief to his face, his knees sagging. I went to him, grabbed him by his arm and bawled, "Come on – out!"

One of Hertz's thugs reached me. I ducked under the blackjack that swished towards my head, sent me right into his ribs, then knocked his legs from under him. I didn't wait to see him go down. I grabbed hold of Fulton and dragged him across the room to the door.

There wasn't much comfort outside. Facing us was the narrow, long jetty, brilliantly lit, with the sea either side, and at the far end, the big car park, also brilliantly lit.

Fulton was hurt badly and seemed on the point of collapse. Any second now Hertz and his thugs would be out and after us.

"Beat it," Fulton gasped. "I can't go any further. Get away before they catch you."

I grabbed his arm, swung it around my shoulder, then half-supporting him, I dragged him in a rushing run down the jetty towards the parking lot.

The quick patter of feet behind me told me I wasn't going to get far.

I let go of Fulton and turned.

Hertz was coming down the jetty.

"Run!" I said to Fulton. "I'll handle this ape."

I gave him a quick shove and he went staggering off as Hertz came at me. He moved with the speed and the shuffle of a professional boxer. I backed away fast, circling him so the light from the overhead standard would be in his eyes. I watched his fists. He looked insane with rage. That was in my favour. A man in a rage isn't anything like as dangerous as a man who keeps his head in a fight. He came at me like an enraged bull and I slammed my fist into his face, jerking his head back. I swayed away from a right that would have decapitated me had it landed, then thumped my own right into the side of his neck. He caught me with a left, and it felt as if I had been hit with a sledgehammer. I backed away fast as he came in again, jabbed him off, slid away from a crushing punch that started from his ankles, jumped back and took a quick look down the jetty. Fulton had disappeared. I decided it was time I took off.

But I shouldn't have taken my eyes off Hertz. Although he telegraphed his punches, he had the speed of a flyweight. He caught me with a hook to the jaw. I saw it coming just a shade too late, but I had started to roll with the punch and that took a little of the steam out of it. It was hard enough to bring me to my knees, but not hard enough to fog my brain. As he rushed, I fell forward and grabbed him around his thick thighs, raised myself and heaved. He went over my head and slid along the planks of the jetty on his face.

I was up and running before he came to rest. As I bolted into the car park, I heard a voice call, "Hey, Brandon! Right here!"

I changed my direction as I saw Fulton waving at me from the front seat of my car. I heard Hertz lumbering down the jetty after me. The engine of the car was running and I scrambled in under the steering wheel, slammed in the gear and trod down on the accelerator.

Hertz was within twenty yards of the car now, his battered face a snarling mask of fury as the car shot away. I went through the parking lot gates with an inch to spare and stormed out on to the boulevard. Still at high speed, I swung the car into a side turning, drove flat out to the top of the road, stood on the brake pedal and flung the car into another road, then slowed down.

"Are you badly hurt?" I asked, looking at Fulton.

"I'll survive," he said.

"Where's the nearest hospital? I'll take you."

"Third left at the top of this road, then straight on for half a mile."

I increased speed. In five minutes I pulled up outside the emergency entrance to the hospital.

"I can manage now." He got out of the car. "I was a mug to have opened my big mouth. I should have kept clear of you."

"I'm sorry. I didn't mean to land you in for that kind of party. You could bring a charge against Hertz. There were plenty of witnesses."

"Much good that'd do. It'd never stick, and I'd be in more trouble. I'm packing and getting out of this town. I've had about enough of it."

He went away, moving unsteadily.

I watched him disappear through the doorway, then I U-turned and headed back fast to my hotel.

III

It wasn't until I was in the quiet of my bedroom, and after I had bathed my bruises, that I remembered I had missed my dinner, and found I was hungry. I called down for some hot turkey sandwiches on rye bread and a pint of iced beer. While I waited for the sandwiches to be brought up, I stretched out on my bed and considered the activities of the day.

I knew I was sticking my head into a hornets' nest, and I wondered how long I would survive if I continued to do so.

Sooner or later I would run into Hertz again, and the next time I might not get off with only a bruised neck and a slight swelling under my right eye. I thought of Tim Fulton and grimaced.

Even if I managed to side-step Hertz, there was Katchen. If he got the slightest suspicion I was continuing my inquiries, he would fix me on some charge and have me in. I didn't kid myself that that would be any kind of picnic.

It seemed, if I were going to make any safe progress, I would have to get some sort of protection, but how I was to do it defeated me. Was there anyone in town more

63

powerful than Creedy and who could warn Katchen to lay off? It didn't seem likely, but if there was, and I could get him on my side, that would be the solution to my problem.

Leaving that, I considered what I had discovered. I knew now that Creedy had hired Jack. Creedy's money was behind some of the rackets of the town. He was married, and his wife was playing around with a man called Jacques Thrisby. He also had a daughter, Margot, whom he was fond of and she had an apartment on Franklyn Boulevard. I reached for the telephone book, looked her up and found her apartment was in a block called the Franklyn Arms. As I put the book down, there came a knock on the door and a waiter brought me the sandwiches and the beer. He stared curiously at my swollen eye, but didn't comment on it, which was as well for him. I was in no mood to be sociable with a waiter right at this minute.

When he had gone, I got off the bed and, sitting in the lone armchair, I ate the sandwiches and drank the beer.

Someone had taken Jack's things out of the room next door and put them in a neat pile in the corner of my room. I was reminded by the sight of them that I had to write to his wife. After I had finished my meal and had lit a cigarette, I took a sheet of the hotel notepaper and wrote to her. It took me until half past ten to complete the letter to my satisfaction. I offered her a reasonable sum as compensation for losing her husband. I purposely made the sum a little low because I knew she would bargain long and bitterly to get more out of me. She had never liked me, and I knew she would never be satisfied no matter what I gave her.

I stuck the envelope down and left it on the dressing table to post the following morning.

I then sat down and unlocked Jack's suitcase. I went through his stuff to make sure there was nothing in the case that might upset his wife when I returned it. It was as well that I did, for I found photographs and letters that proved he had been cheating her for the past year or so. I tore them up and dumped them in the trash basket.

I went through the rest of the suitcase and I found, hidden in the lining of the case, a match folder: one of those things restaurants and nightclubs give away as an advertisement. This was something special. It was covered with dark red water-silk and across the outside in gold letters was the legend: *The Musketeer Club* and a telephone number.

I turned the folder over between my fingers, remembering that Greaves, the hotel detective, had said that the Musketeer Club was the most exclusive, apart from being the most expensive club in town. How had Jack got hold of the folder? Had he gone to the club? Knowing him, I was sure he wouldn't go to a de luxe nightspot like that unless it was for business reasons. He was far too careful with his money to take any girl to a place that expensive.

Still holding the folder, I got to my feet, thought for a moment, then, leaving my room, I took the elevator down to the lobby.

I asked the reception clerk if Greaves was around.

"He'll be in his office right now," the clerk said, staring at my swollen eye. "Downstairs and to the right. Did you have an accident, Mr Brandon?"

"This eye? Why, no. I ordered some sandwiches to be sent up and the waiter threw them at me. Think nothing of it. I go for that kind of service."

I left him with his mouth hanging open and his second chin quivering and went down the stairs to Greaves' office.

It was more of a cupboard than a room. I found him sitting at a small table, laying out a hand of patience. He looked up as I came to rest in the open doorway.

"Someone take a dislike to your face?" he asked, without much show of interest.

"Yeah," I said and, leaning forward, I dropped the match folder on the table.

He looked at it, frowned, looked up at me and raised his eyebrows.

"How come?"

"I found it in Sheppey's suitcase."

"I'm willing to bet a buck he never went there. He hadn't the class, the money nor the influence to get past the bouncers."

"No chance?"

"Not a chance in ten million."

"Maybe someone took him in. That possible?"

Greaves nodded.

"Maybe. A member can take in who he likes, but if the other snobs don't like who he brings in, he could lose his membership. That's how it works."

"He could have picked it up somewhere."

Greaves shrugged.

"First one I've seen. The guys and dolls who go to the Musketeer Club wouldn't soil their lily-white fingers touching a thing like that. They'd be afraid it'd give them a germ. I'd say someone took him in and he brought this away with him to prove he had been there. It's something to brag about if you're the bragging kind."

"Know where I can get hold of a members' list?"

He smiled sourly, got up, edged around his table and went to a cupboard. After rummaging around for a few moments, he offered me a small book, bound in faded red water-silk with the same gold lettering on it as the match folder.

"I found it in one of the rooms at the Ritz-Plaza and thought it might come in useful one day. It's two years out of date."

"I'll let you have it back," I said, retrieving the match folder from the table and putting it and the members' book in my pocket. "Thanks."

"Who gave you the shiner?"

"Nobody you'd want to know," I said, and went out and up to the lounge. I found an armchair away from the old ladies and gentlemen and read through the names in the book. There were about five hundred names to wade through. Four hundred and ninety-seven of them meant nothing to me: the other three did: Mrs Bridgette Creedy, Mr Jacques Thrisby and Miss Margot Creedy.

I closed the book and slapped it gently against my hand.

I sat for some minutes thinking. Then out of the blue came an idea. I considered it, decided after a moment or so that it wasn't perhaps a brilliant idea, but at least it wasn't a bad one, and I got to my feet.

I went over to the hall porter and asked him where Franklyn Avenue was.

He told me to take the second on the right, then the first on the left by the traffic lights.

I thanked him and went down the steps to where I had left the Buick.

5

The Franklyn Arms turned out to be one of those snooty, high-toned apartment blocks reserved only for those in the upper social register, and who have more than a six-figure income.

There were, at a guess, not more than thirty apartments in the block. The building was three stories high and sat with the dignity of a dowager duchess in an elaborately cultivated acre of land with lawns, a fountain in which stood a reproduction of Donatelli's Boy with a Dolphin, flood-lit to underline the architect's good taste, and set beds with silver centaurea and sky blue petunias.

I steered the Buick into a vacant space between a Silver Wraith and a Silver Dawn Rolls-Royce, got out and walked past a Continental Bentley, a sixty-two coupé Cadillac, and a Packard Clipper. There was enough money rolled up in all that hardware to keep me happy for ten years.

I pushed my way through the revolving doors into an oak-panelled lobby decorated with carnations growing in chromium-plated boxes set against the walls, and a small fountain with half a dozen well-fed, contented-looking goldfish swimming in the lighted water.

Over in the far corner was the reception desk behind which stood a tall blond man in an immaculate tuxedo, who wore a bored, disdainful expression on his handsome, effeminate face.

I went over to him and gave him one of my friendly smiles. This was probably a mistake, for he reared back as if I had hung a decayed fish under his aristocratic nose.

"Miss Creedy please," I said.

He fingered his immaculate tie while his brown eyes travelled over me. He would know to the exact cent what my suit, tie, shirt and hat cost. The valuation didn't seem to impress him.

"Is Miss Creedy expecting you?"

"No. Will you call her and tell her I have just been talking to her father and would now appreciate a word with her. The name is Lew Brandon."

He tapped his beautifully manicured fingernails on the top of the polished counter while he thought. From the strained expression in his eyes, I could tell this was a process that would never come naturally to him.

"Perhaps you had better write first," he said at length. He lifted his arm and consulted a solid gold Omega. "It is a little late for a call."

"Look, buster," I said, making my voice suddenly tough, "you may be a thing of beauty, but don't kid yourself you're a joy forever. Just call Miss Creedy and let her make her own decisions."

He stared at me for a brief moment, surprise and alarm in his eyes, then he went into a room behind the counter and shut the door.

I took a cigarette from my pack and pasted it on my lower lip. I wondered if he were going to call the law. I'd look pretty sick if some ambitious cop rushed me down to headquarters on a charge of annoying the elite of St Raphael City. But a couple of minutes later, he came out looking as if he had swallowed a bee. He indicated an automatic elevator across the way and said curtly, "Second floor. Apartment seven." Then, tossing his blond curls, he turned his back on me.

I found apartment seven after walking down a long oak-panelled corridor. As I paused outside the front door, I could hear a radio playing something from Mozart. I pushed the bell button, and after a moment or so the door was opened by an elderly, pleasant-looking woman in a black silk dress and a frilled white apron.

"Mr Brandon?"

"Yes."

I surrendered my hat as I walked into a small hall which was furnished with an oval-shaped table on which stood a silver bowl of orchids.

The maid opened a door, said, "Mr Brandon," and stood aside for me to enter.

I walked into a big lounge, decorated in white and apricot. The walls and drapes and the leather lounging chairs were in apricot; the carpet and Miss Creedy were in white.

She stood by a big radiogram, looking towards me, slim and quite tall, with ash-blonde hair, the quality of spun silk. She was sensationally beautiful in the classic tradition, and her eyes were the colour and seemed to have the same texture as those giant mauve-black pansies you see from time to time at the better flower shows.

She was high-breasted, long-legged, with hips that had curve and just the right weight. She was wearing a white evening gown with a plunging neckline, and around her throat was a string of diamonds that had probably been given to her on her twenty-first anniversary and must have set old man Creedy's bank balance back quite a long way. She wore elbow-length gloves, and around one wrist was a diamond-and-platinum watch, and on her little finger, worn over the glove, was a long flat ruby set in a thin gold hoop.

She looked what she was: every inch a multi-millionaire's daughter. All in all I could understand why Mrs Creedy had found her hard to compete with. She must have flung her bonnet over the roof when this young woman had packed her bags and left home.

"I would be glad if you would excuse me for making such a late call, Miss Creedy," I said. "I wouldn't be troubling you only my business is urgent."

She gave me a small smile. It was neither friendly nor hostile: a hostess welcoming a stranger in her home, a show of good manners; no more, no less.

"Has it something to do with my father?"

"Well, no: remotely perhaps, but to be honest I didn't think you would see me unless I mentioned your father's name." I gave her a boyish smile, but it made no impression. She was now looking straight at me and her dark eyes had a disconcerting directness. "I am head of the Star Inquiry Agency," I went on. "I'm hoping you might be willing to help me."

She stiffened a little and frowned. Although she looked severe, she still managed to look beautiful.

"You mean you are a private detective?"

"That is right. I am working on a case and you could help me, Miss Creedy."

I could see she was beginning to freeze.

"Help you? I really don't know what you mean. Why should I help you?" The freeze was now in her voice.

"No reason at all except some people don't mind helping others now and then." I tried the boyish smile again, but still with no results. "This business might interest you if you will let me tell you about it."

She hesitated, then she waved at a chair.

71

"Well, all right," she said. " Perhaps you had better sit down."

I waited until she had sat down on the settee opposite before I dropped into the chair she had indicated.

"Five days ago, Miss Creedy,' I said, "my partner Jack Sheppey came here from our office in San Francisco on an assignment he received over the telephone. The caller didn't give his name to the girl who handles our switchboard. I was away at the time. Sheppey left without saying who the caller was, but he did write your father's name on his blotter."

While I talked, I watched her and I could see I was holding her attention. She was thawing out.

"Sheppey sent me a cable asking me to come down here. I arrived this morning. I went to the hotel where he was staying but he had gone out. A little later, the police came for me to identify him: he had been murdered in a bathing cabin out at Bay Beach."

Her eyes widened.

"Why, of course. I saw it in the evening paper. I didn't realize ... was he your partner?"

"Yes."

"You say he wrote my father's name down on his blotter?" she said, frowning at me. "Why should he have done that?"

"I don't know unless it was your father who called him."

She looked away then and began to turn the ruby ring around on her finger. I had an idea she was suddenly uneasy.

"Daddy wouldn't do that. If he wanted an inquiry agent, he would get his secretary to do it."

"Unless it happened to concern a matter of an extremely confidential nature," I said.

She continued to look away.

"I really can't see what all this has to do with me," she said. "I am going out in a few minutes …"

"I saw your father this afternoon," I said, and saw her stiffen. "I asked him if he had hired Sheppey and he said he hadn't. He was very emphatic about it. He produced what looked like an ex-fighter named Hertz and told him to take a look at me. He implied if I didn't mind my own business, Hertz would discourage me."

A slight flush mounted to her face.

"I still can't see what this has to do with me. So if you will please excuse me …"

She got to her feet.

"I am trying to trace Sheppey's movements, Miss Creedy," I said, standing up. "Apparently he went to the Musketeer Club and I want to find out who he went with. You are a member of the club. I was wondering if you would sponsor me at the club so I could make a few inquiries."

She stared at me as if I had suggested she should take a trip to the moon.

"That's quite impossible," she said, and she sounded as if she meant it. "Even if I did take you into the club, and I have no intention of doing such a thing, they wouldn't tolerate you asking anyone questions."

"I'm with you there, Miss Creedy," I said. "From what I hear of the place it seems pretty high-toned, but if you were to ask the questions, I'm sure you'd get the answers."

She stared at me, biting her under-lip.

"That is impossible. I'm sorry, Mr Brandon, I must ask you to go now."

"This isn't a frivolous request," I said. "A man has been murdered. I have reason to believe the police won't make much effort to find his murderer. I realize that's a pretty sweeping thing to say, but I've talked to Captain Katchen of the Homicide Department, and he more or less told me if I didn't keep clear of this business he would make me sorry. I'm not kidding myself that he wouldn't do it. A little less than an hour ago I got involved in a fight because I was asking questions. Someone in this town is anxious to have Sheppey's death hushed up. Sheppey was my friend. I don't intend to let anyone hush up his death. I'm asking you to help me. All I want you to do ..."

She reached out and touched a bell push on the wall near her.

"This has nothing to do with me," she said. "I'm sorry, but I'm unable to help you."

The door opened and the maid came in.

"Oh, Tessa, Mr Brandon is leaving now."

I smiled at her.

"Well, at least you haven't threatened me as Captain Katchen did, nor have you as yet sent a thug after me as your father did," I said. "Thank you for giving me your time, Miss Creedy."

I went out into the hall, picked up my hat and, opening the door, I set off down the corridor.

It had been a long shot, and it hadn't come off, but at least I hadn't wasted I my time. I had an idea that Margot Creedy knew just why her father had hired Sheppey. If she knew, it meant that Sheppey was hired on a matter concerning the family. I decided to take a look at Bridgette Creedy's new boyfriend, Jacques Thrisby. Maybe Sheppey had been hired to find out just how friendly these two were. That could make sense. Creedy would naturally clam up and turn tough if he thought he might have to tell a court that he had hired a private eye to watch his wife: that was something no man would want to broadcast.

The time now was ten minutes past eleven: a little early for me to return to the hotel.

I got back into the Buick and sat for a long moment, thinking, then I trod on the starter and headed down to Bay Beach.

II

As I drove along the promenade, I could see people still bathing in the sea. In the light of the big white moon the water was the colour of old silver.

I reached Bay Beach after a ten-minute drive. This part of the beach was away from the fashionable end, and I found the bathing station was closed, and the row of cabins, under the shadows of the palms, in darkness.

I left the Buick in a side street just beyond the bathing station, then I walked down to the beach. Apart from a few cars, drifting along the beach road with nowhere to go and all the time in the world in which to get there, this section of the promenade was as quiet and as deserted as a railroad waiting-room on a Christmas morning.

The gate down to the beach was closed and locked. I looked to right and left, satisfied myself there was no one watching me, then put my hand on the top rail and vaulted over. I landed in soft sand with no noise.

Moving fast, I reached the sheltering shadows of the palms and then paused.

I had no concrete idea why I should have come down here except that I hadn't anything better to do, and I wanted to see again the place where Sheppey had died.

Keeping in the shadows, I looked over at the row of cabins.

There was a chance that Rankin had left a cop on duty, and the last thing I wanted at this moment was to run into the law. But there was no sound nor movement on this strip of lonely beach except from the murmur of the sea and the occasional car that drove along the promenade above me and out of my sight.

Satisfied I had the place to myself, I moved down the row of cabins until I reached the second one from the end. In that one, Sheppey had died.

I pushed against the door, but found it locked. Taking a flashlight and a gadget of thin steel from my hip pocket, I examined the lock. Then I inserted the gadget between the lock and the doorpost and levered hard and pushed. The door swung open.

I paused in the doorway, feeling the pent-up heat of the little room coming out at me like the blast from a fierce oven. I stepped just inside, turned the beam of my flashlight on and swung it slowly around the room.

There were two stools, a table and a divan bed. In the corner where Sheppey had died, there was a big dark stain on the floor that gave me a cold, creepy feeling.

Opposite me were two doors, leading into the changing-rooms. One of them Sheppey had used: the other, the girl who had been with him.

I wondered about her. Had she been a decoy to get Sheppey down here? He had been mug enough about women to have fallen into that kind of trap. Had his death nothing to do with Creedy? Had he been fooling around with the girl belonging to some thug who had caught up with them?

If the boyfriend had suddenly walked in on them it would explain why the girl had left her clothes in the cabin. While he was killing Sheppey she had probably run out and away. But why hadn't she got help? Wouldn't she have tried to get someone to stop this thug killing Sheppey? Or had it happened so fast that Sheppey was dead before she could get out and, seeing he was dead, she had just run?

I pushed my hat to the back of my head and wiped my forehead with my hand.

Or had she killed him?

I moved into the hut and closed the door. I didn't want any swimmer or someone in a boat to spot my light through the open door.

I went over to the first door leading into the dressing-room, opened it and glanced inside. It was a cupboard of a room with a bench and four hooks for clothes and a small mirror. I swung my beam around as I wondered if this was the room Sheppey had used. I didn't expect to find anything. The police had already been over it, and it was too small for them to miss anything: I didn't find anything.

I stepped out, thinking I was wasting time. There was nothing here for me: not even atmosphere. Maybe I wouldn't have bothered to have looked in the other little room, but suddenly I had a feeling I was no longer alone in the dark cabin. I stood motionless, listening, hearing my heart thumping. My finger eased on the button of the flashlight and thick darkness engulfed me.

For a long moment I heard nothing, then just as I was thinking my imagination was playing me tricks, I heard a sound that seemed close: the sound of a faint sigh: the sound someone makes when letting his breath out slowly through his open mouth.

It was a sound so slight that if I hadn't been listening intently, and if there hadn't been any other sound during that brief moment, I wouldn't have heard it.

I felt the hair on the nape of my neck move. I wished now I had brought a gun. Stepping back two steps brought me against the door of the changing-room. I lifted the flashlight and pressed the button.

The white beam of the light made a meaningless circle on the floorboards. I swung it around, saw nothing, and listened again.

On the road a car went by with a roar and a whoosh of someone in a hurry.

I turned the beam to the door of the second changing-room, reached forward, turned the handle and gently pushed open the door.

I lifted the flashlight.

She was sitting on the floor, facing me, in a pale blue French swimsuit, her golden skin shiny with sweat. Her eyes were fixed in a vacant stare. Down her left shoulder was a long stream of dried blood.

She was a dark, good-looking girl with black silky hair; around twenty-four or five with the figure of a model. She was much too young to be dying.

She stared sightlessly into the beam of the flashlight. I stood transfixed, sweating ice, my heart hammering, my mouth dry.

Then, very slowly, she began to topple sideways.

I was unable to move. I just stood there, staring.

It wasn't until she slid with a horrible ghost-like silence to the floor that I moved forward to clutch at her.

But by then I was just that much too late.

III

She lay on her side, her dark hair covering her face. Looking down at her, I saw on the floor an ice pick with a white plastic handle. It was a reminder that this girl had died the same way as Sheppey had died, although this time the killer's hand had lost some of its cunning, for Sheppey had died instantaneously.

I bent over her, sweat running down my face and dripping off my chin. The spasm, completely unmistakable, that I had seen run through her as she had spread out on the floor told me the exact moment when she died. I didn't have to feel for an artery nor lift her eyelid to know she was beyond any help I could give her.

I kept the beam of light on her. There was nothing to tell me who she was. All she had on was this swimsuit. The fact that she was well groomed, that her hair had been recently shampooed and set, that her nails were manicured and stained dark red and the costume itself was a good one told me nothing. She could have been rich or she could have been poor. She could have been a model; she could have been just one of the thousands of workers in St Raphael City: she could have been anything.

There was one thing I was certain of: she was the girl who had called for Jack Sheppey at the hotel: the one Greaves had been so certain had been a blonde. Remembering he had thought she had either been wearing a wig or had dyed her hair, I held the torch closer to satisfy myself that he had been wrong, and I did satisfy myself. She was neither wearing a wig nor had she dyed her hair. There was no doubt about that and that proved just how wrong a trained house dick could be.

I turned the beam of light on to her arms. In the bright light, the soft down looked fair. It wouldn't have been natural if it had been otherwise. She had been worshipping the sun for months to judge by her tan: the down on her arms would naturally be bleached.

I straightened up. Taking my handkerchief from my pocket, I wiped my face.

The heat in the tiny room was awful. I found I had sweated right through my clothes and I moved back into the larger room.

It was then that I noticed another door that obviously communicated with the next-door cabin. There was a bolt on the door, but it wasn't pushed into its socket.

That gave me a jolt.

I realized it must have been through this door that the killer had come and gone. For all I knew he was still in the cabin next door, waiting for me to go away, and wished even more that I had brought a gun with me.

Moving softly I crossed the room, snapped off my flashlight, and put my ear to the panel of the door. I listened for a long moment, but heard nothing. I groped for the door handle, found it and, gripping it tightly, I slowly turned it. When it was as far back as it would go I put a little pressure on the door, but it didn't move.

Someone had gone into the next cabin through this doorway but had bolted the door after him.

Was he still in there?

I stepped back, aware that my mouth was dry. He probably hadn't a spare ice pick with him, but it was possible he had a gun.

Then a sound came to me that made me stiffen and set my nerves crawling.

In the distance came the wail of a police siren: a sound that grew in volume and told me a police car was coming along the promenade at high speed.

I wasn't kidding myself that those prowl boys were sounding off for the fun of it. They were on business and the most obvious place for them to be coming to was right here.

I turned on my flashlight, took out my handkerchief and wiped the door handles in the little cabin. Although I worked fast, I didn't skimp the job: I knew how important it was not to leave a print that would bring Katchen after me. Finished, I jumped for the door, opened it and looked quickly to right and left.

The beach was still deserted, but apart from the shadows made by the group of palms, it was as bare of a hiding place as the back of my hand.

The note of the siren was much louder now and still coming fast. If I returned the way I had come I was certain to run right into them. There was no hope of hiding among the palms. They would be sure to spot me as they came down towards the cabins. That left me with the wide-open beach.

When I have to I can run. There was a time when I had won a couple of impressive-looking cups for the half-mile: not Olympic stuff, but moving in that direction.

I didn't hesitate.

I started off across the sand at not perhaps my best speed, but close to it.

I heard the siren blasting its way along the promenade. I didn't look back. I had to put about a thousand yards or so between me and those boys or else they would start shooting at me. I didn't kid myself they wouldn't see me. Against the white sand and with the moonlight, I would be in sight for miles.

I had covered about five hundred yards when I heard the siren come to a wailing stop. This was the time for a spurt, but running through the soft yielding sand was tougher than I had imagined. I was beginning to pant and my legs were aching. I made my spurt, but it was nothing to get excited about.

It was then that I saw the beach sloped sharply to the sea, making a razorback in the form of a long sand dune.

In a few seconds the cops would have left their car and be down on the beach, and then the fun would start. If I could get on the lower level of the beach before they spotted me I would be out of their sight.

I turned and legged it for the top of the dune, running as I had never run before. Reaching the top, I dived head first down the slope, arriving nearly to the edge of the sea in a cloud of dry sand.

There had been no shout to tell me if I had been seen. For a moment I lay still, gasping air into my lungs. Then I got to my feet and, bending low, I climbed back until I could just see over the top of the dune.

I looked towards the cabins.

Standing in the moonlight was a patrolman, his back turned to me. The door leading into the cabin where the dead girl was stood open, and as I watched another cop came out. He joined his companion, and they talked for a few moments, then the one who had been waiting outside started to run back to the promenade.

It would only be a matter of a few minutes before the whole beach would be crawling with the law. I didn't have to be told what would happen to me if they found me.

Captain Katchen would know what to do with a gift like me. He had already told me what to expect. Even if he didn't ride me into the gas chamber, I'd be in his hands for weeks, and that was something I was going to avoid if I could.

Keeping below the top of the ridge, I started to run again.

By the time I had put a mile between me and the row of cabins, I was pretty near bushed, but I was now far enough away to strike back inland, knowing I wasn't likely to be seen.

I walked across the sand, trying to control my laboured breathing. A flight of steps took me up on to the promenade.

A few courting couples were dotted along the front, sitting under the palm trees: too busy with their own affairs to notice me. I crossed the road and then began to walk back to where I had left my car.

It took me close on ten minutes to draw level with the entrance to the bathing station. By that time there was a big crowd, blocking the road, gaping as crowds will gape. I saw three police cars parked along the kerb.

This was only the beginning. Two murders in one day at the same place was a sensation that would really pack the crowd in once the news got around.

As I stood there watching, four more police cars came tearing up. I saw Lieutenant Rankin get out of one of them and hurry across the promenade towards the row of cabins.

I felt I could leave him in charge, and I legged it to my car and then drove along the back street at a steady clip until I reached the Adelphi Hotel.

I left the car in the hotel parking lot, got a duster from the glove compartment and wiped away all traces of sand I had picked up on the beach. Then I entered the hotel.

The time was now just after midnight.

The night clerk, an elderly man with the springly air of a jovial priest, smiled at me as he handed me my key.

He said it was a fine night, and had I noticed the effect of the moon on the sea? He was just trying to be friendly, but I wasn't in the mood. I grunted at him, took the key and headed for the elevator.

As I waited for the cage to come down, I heard the telephone bell on the desk ring. The night clerk answered it, then as the cage appeared and as I was about to get in, he called out, "Mr Brandon, a call for you. Will you take it in your room or in the booth across the way?"

I said I'd take it in the booth.

Wondering who could be calling me, I went into the booth, shut the door and took the receiver off the cradle.

"Hello – yes?"

"Is that Mr Brandon?"

A woman's voice, clear, but low-pitched and familiar.

"Yes."

"This is Margot Creedy."

I pushed my hat to the back of my head and blew out my cheeks. How had she found out where I was staying was the first thought that jumped into my mind.

"Glad to have you call me, Miss Creedy."

"I am speaking from the Musketeer Club," she said. "I looked in the visitors' book. Mr Sheppey's name doesn't appear in it."

I was surprised, but not too surprised to say, "He could have used another name, of course."

"I thought of that. The man on the door tells me no one with red hair has been to the club for months. He is very good at that sort of thing. If Mr Sheppey had been to the club, he would have remembered him."

I tried to recall if the newspaper account of the murder had mentioned that Jack had red hair. I decided it had been mentioned.

"So it looks as if he didn't go there."

"Why did you think he had?"

"I found a folder of matches from the club in his suitcase."

"Someone, of course, could have given it to him."

"Yes. Well, thank you for helping me, Miss Creedy. I really am very ..."

The soft click over the line told me she had hung up. I stood for a long moment staring through the glass panel of the booth while I wondered why she had changed her mind about helping me, then I replaced the receiver, pushed open the booth door and walked over to the elevator.

So Jack hadn't gone to the Musketeer Club. I saw no reason why I should doubt her word. Greaves had said it wasn't likely. I had been through Sheppey's things, and I knew he hadn't brought a tuxedo down with him. He wouldn't have got beyond the doorman without wearing a tuxedo if I was to believe what Greaves had said about the exclusiveness of the club.

Then where had the match folder come from? Why had Jack kept it? He hadn't a magpie mentality. He didn't keep anything unless it was of some use.

I left the elevator, walked down the corridor, unlocked my bedroom door and entered the room. I shut and locked the door, chucked my hat on the bed and went over to Jack's suitcase. I got the match folder from the suitcase and then sat down in the armchair and took a closer look at the folder. It contained twenty-five tear-off matches: each matchstick carried the name of the Musketeer Club. The inside back of the folder carried an advertisement for one of those arty pottery shops that spring up like mushrooms wherever there are tourists.

The advertisement ran:

> *You should not miss visiting*
> *Marcus Hahn's School of Ceramics*
> *The Treasure House of Original Design.*
> *The Château*
> *Arrow Point*
> *St Raphael City.*

I wondered why an advertisement so obviously aimed at the tourist trade should be displayed in a match folder of an exclusive club that would not tolerate a tourist in any shape or form within its high-tone portals. I wondered if I were on to something or whether it was just one of those things.

I tore off one of the matches. On examining it I found printed on the back a row of ciphers: C451136. I bent back the other matches and saw they too were numbered and the numbers were consecutive up to C451160.

I wedged the loose match back into the folder, sat for several minutes wondering why the matches were thus numbered, then coming to no conclusion I put the match folder into my wallet.

The time was now twenty minutes to one o'clock. It had been quite a day. There didn't seem anything else for me to do now but to wait for the morning. With any luck the newspapers would tell me who the girl in the swimsuit was. Until then, it seemed a good idea to go to bed.

As I got to my feet, there came a knock on the door. It was delivered by a set of knuckles that would have no trouble in ramming your teeth down your throat: knuckles that didn't belong to any member of any hotel staff: knuckles you'd expect to find on the hands of the law.

I stood still, my brain racing. Had I been spotted leaving the beach? Had I left any fingerprints in the cabin?

Knuckles banged on the door again and a voice growled, "Come on! Open up! We know you're in there."

I took my wallet from my pocket, took the match folder out and slid it under the edge of the fitted carpet, then I put my wallet back, stepped to the door, turned the key, and opened the door.

Candy stood there, chewing, his dark eyes hostile. Behind him were two big plain-clothes men: their faces stony and their eyes alert.

"Come on," Candy said in a flat, bored voice. "Captain Katchen wants you."

"What for?" I said, not moving.

"He'll tell you. Are you coming rough or smooth?"

I hesitated, then, seeing the odds were against me, I picked my hat off the bed and said I'd come smooth.

6

The night clerk's eyes bulged out of his head like organ stops when he saw me come out of the elevator, surrounded by Candy and his two hunks of beef. This was the second time I had been taken away from the hotel by the law, and I had an idea that if I survived this trip, the management would probably ask me to leave.

But I wasn't any too sure that I would survive the trip. I remembered what Katchen had said at our last meeting, and I had a depressing idea he wasn't bluffing.

We went across the lobby, down the steps to the waiting police car. The two plain-clothes men got in the front, and Candy and I got in the back.

The car went off with the usual frantic rush and with the usual wailing siren, leaving the kerb so fast the jerk nearly dislocated my neck.

Candy sat beside me like a rock that has been baked in the sun. I could feel the heat of his body, and although I couldn't see much of his face in the darkness of the car I could hear the steady movement of his jaws as he chewed.

"Okay if I smoke?" I said, more or less for something to say.

"Better not," Candy said, his voice flat and cold. "I was told to bring you in rough."

"What's biting the Captain?"

"If you don't know, how should I?" Candy said, and there the conversation ceased.

I stared out of the window. I wasn't happy. There was a chance that someone had seen me on the beach and had phoned in my description. I had visions of being grilled. If Katchen conducted the grilling, I knew I was in for a bad time.

No one said anything until we pulled up outside the police headquarters, then Candy groped in his hip pocket and produced a pair of handcuffs.

"Got to put the nippers on," he said, and I thought I detected an apologetic note in his voice. "The Captain likes everything ship-shape."

"Are you arresting me?" I asked, offering my wrists. The cold bite of the steel bracelets added to my depression.

"I'm not doing anything," Candy said, getting out of the car. "The Captain wants to talk to you – that's all there's to it."

He and I walked across the sidewalk and up the steps into the charge room, leaving the two plain-clothes men in the car.

The desk sergeant, a big, fat-faced man, looked at me and then at Candy, who shook his head and kept on, through a doorway, up some stairs and along a passage to a door at the far end. I walked at his heels.

He paused outside the door, rapped once, then turned the handle and shoved the door wide open. He put his hand on my arm and moved me into a big room that contained a desk, six upright chairs, a couple of filing cabinets, Captain Katchen, Lieutenant Rankin and a tall, thin man around forty with straw-coloured hair, rimless glasses and a face of an eager ferret.

Candy said, "Brandon here, Captain," then stepped back, giving me the stage.

I took a couple of steps forward and stopped.

Katchen was standing by the window, his massive face dark with congested blood. He looked at me the way a caged tiger might look at a fat lamb that is being marched past its cage.

Rankin sat on one of the upright chairs, his hat tipped over his eyes, a cigarette burning between his fingers. He didn't turn his head to look at me.

The straw-haired man eyed me with the interest and the professional detachment of a bacteriologist confronted with an obscure germ that might or might not be a potential killer.

"Why is this man handcuffed, Captain?" he asked in a soft, Ivy League voice.

Katchen suddenly appeared to have difficulty in breathing.

"If you don't like the way I make my arrests, you'd better talk to the Commissioner," he said in a voice that could have stripped rust off any lump of old iron.

"Is this man under arrest then?" the straw-haired man asked, his voice a polite inquiry.

Even if he had the face of a ferret and an Ivy League accent, he was rapidly becoming my favourite member of this oddly assorted trio.

Katchen bent his glaring stare on Candy.

"Take those goddam bracelets off," he said, his voice muffled with rage.

Candy came over to me, slid a key into the lock, twisted and the cuffs dropped into his hand. With his back turned to Katchen he allowed himself a slow, deliberate wink at me. He moved away while I went through an elaborate pantomime of rubbing my wrists and looking injured.

"Sit down, Mr Brandon," the straw-haired man said. "I'm Curme Holding of the District Attorney's office. I heard Captain Katchen wanted to see you so I thought I would see you too."

I began to feel less depressed.

"Glad to know you, Mr Holding. I feel in need of protection. The Captain has already talked to me once today. So I'm more than pleased to see you."

Holding took off his glasses, inspected them and put them back on again.

"Captain Katchen wouldn't do anything out of the line of duty," he said, but he didn't sound as if he meant it.

I smiled.

"Maybe the Captain has a sense of humour. I took his talk seriously, but maybe you could be right. You have only to look at the deep-seated kindness in his face to realize he could be a great little kidder."

Katchen made a growling sound deep in his throat and moved from the window towards me. He looked like a gorilla disturbed at feeding time.

"Will you ask the questions, Captain, or shall I?" Holding said, sudden steel in his voice.

Katchen paused. His little red-flecked eyes moved from me to Holding, who stared at him with the bored expression of a man watching a very tough gangster movie and finding it phoney.

"Now you've got your oar in, you can handle it yourself," Katchen snarled, biting off each word. "I'm going to talk to the Commissioner. There's too much goddam interference from your office. It's time someone did something about it."

He went past me, out through the doorway and slammed the door behind him. The room rocked a little under the percussion.

Sergeant Candy said, "You won't need me, Mr Holding?"

"That's okay, Sergeant."

I heard the door open, but I didn't look around to see Candy leave. The door closed behind him gently in sharp contrast to the exit made by Katchen.

"Well, now, Mr Brandon, would you take a seat?" Holding said, and waved to a chair opposite the desk. He got up and took the desk chair.

As I sat down I met Rankin's blank stare. I got no information from it: it was neither friendly nor hostile.

Holding moved a pencil from the blotter to the pen tray, and gave me a hard look from behind the screen of his glittering glasses.

"Captain Katchen is retiring at the end of the month," he said. "Lieutenant Rankin is taking his place."

"Congratulations," I said.

Rankin moved restlessly, fingering his tie. He didn't say anything.

"Lieutenant Rankin is in complete charge of this investigation," Holding went on. "I am, of course, referring to these two murders at Bay Beach."

I could see the trap in that.

If I were going to deny being in the cabin when the girl had died, now was the time to show surprise and ask what other murder had been committed? But I got one jump ahead of that thought fast. For all I knew they had found a fingerprint of mine in the cabin or someone had seen me and had offered to identify me, or they had spotted the Buick parked on the scene. I decided to take a chance and come clean.

"Now I know the Lieutenant is handling the case," I said, "I'm ready to make a statement. I would have done so an hour ago, but Captain Katchen's threats put me off. He warned me to keep out of this business and I didn't keep out of it. When I found the girl I saw Katchen could pin the killing on me."

Holding appeared to relax a little.

"So you were the man who was seen entering the cabin?"

"I don't know about that, but I did enter the cabin and I found her dying."

"Did she say anything?"

"No. She died within seconds of my finding her."

Rankin said, "Suppose we go over it from the start?" He reached forward and took a notebook off the desk and opened it. "Why did you go down there?"

"I had no particular reason except I had nothing to do and I wanted to look the place over," I said. "I know it sounds corny, but my partner was killed there, and your men were all over the place when I went there this morning. I just wanted to have a second look at it."

He didn't seem wildly enthusiastic about this explanation, but he let it go. He asked, "What time did you get there?"

I told him, and then went on to give him an exact description of what had happened. I told him how I had heard the police siren and how I had realized that if I were caught there, Katchen's conclusion would be that I had killed her. I went on to describe how I had got away and what time I returned to the hotel.

Rankin looked over at Holding, then suddenly his hard, tight face crinkled into a smile and he looked quite human.

"Can't say I blame you," he said. "I guess I would have done the same thing. But it's not the kind of thing I'd recommend you to try again."

I said I wouldn't try it again.

"You realize how lucky you have been?" he said. "You could have got yourself nailed for murder. But the doc says she was stabbed at least two hours before you entered the cabin. She took that time to die. He could tell by the blood on her and on the floor."

"How did your men know she was there?"

"Some guy spotted you going into the cabin. He was taking a look at the scene of the crime, so he says; he spotted you and called headquarters."

"What wouldn't we do without the great American public?" I said. "No sign of the killer, of course?"

Rankin shook his head.

Then I asked the sixty-four-dollar question.

"Any idea who she is?"

Rankin stubbed out his cigarette, then sat back while he and Holding exchanged glances.

Holding shrugged.

"It's pretty obvious she's the woman who called for Sheppey at his hotel this morning. What she has been doing from eleven o'clock this morning up to the time of her death defeats me. She was still wearing the swimsuit she had on when she left Sheppey."

"Have you been able to identify her yet?"

"A girl named Thelma Cousins has been reported missing by her landlady. The landlady said she hadn't been back since she left for work this morning. We got her to look at the body. She says the girl is Thelma Cousins. We're getting a second check on her. The man she works for is on his way down now."

"Who is he?"

Rankin supplied the information which had me suddenly pointing like a gun dog.

"His name is Marcus Hahn," he said. "He's a phoney who runs a pottery racket he calls the School of Ceramics out at Arrow point. The girl worked in his showroom."

II

I had to decide whether to tell them about the folder of matches I had found in Sheppey's luggage and the odd tie-up between the folder and this School of Ceramics or whether to say nothing.

I told myself that maybe this wasn't the time for a complete exchange of confidences. I had to make sure first that Rankin was going to find Sheppey's killer. Although he was in charge of the investigation that didn't mean he had a free hand. He could still be blocked by Katchen on Creedy's orders. I wasn't going to hand him anything on a plate until I was sure he meant business.

Rankin said, "We want to find out what Sheppey and this girl were up to. It's my bet she had a boyfriend and he fixed them both."

I looked over at Holding. His face had gone blank and he had begun to fidget with the pen tray.

"It shouldn't be difficult to find out if she had a boyfriend," I said.

"Hahn may know something." Rankin looked at his watch. "I guess I'd better go over to the morgue. He should be down any moment now." He looked at Holding. "Okay?"

"Oh, sure," Holding said.

I made a move to get up, but Holding lifted his hand. "I'd like to run over your statement just once more, Mr Brandon. You get off, Lieutenant."

Rankin got to his feet, nodded to me, and went out.

There was a long pause after he had shut the door, then Holding pulled a pipe from his pocket and began to fill it.

I took that as a signal that we were going to be chummy and I fetched out my pack of Luckies and lit one.

"You had a talk with Captain Katchen this morning?" Holding said, not looking at me.

"You might call it that. It was a little one sided, but I managed to sound off in the end. I collected a slap in the face for my trouble, but I'm not complaining."

"Something was said about Lee Creedy," Holding said, looking up.

"Something was said about Lee Creedy," I said, watching him.

His small hard eyes searched my face.

"You mentioned his name to Katchen?"

"I did."

"You are under the impression that Creedy hired Sheppey to do a job?"

"Yes."

Holding lit his pipe, frowned, shifted in his chair and puffed smoke.

"You have no proof of that?"

"Sheppey wrote Creedy's name on his blotter while he was talking on the telephone. I know the man he was talking to hired him to come down here. Sheppey had a habit of writing on his blotter. I can't see why he should have written down Creedy's name unless Creedy was the man who hired him."

"Unless someone wanted Sheppey to work on a job connected with Creedy. I mean Sheppey's client could have asked him to get information about Creedy. Thought of that?"

"Yes, but it doesn't quite fall into line."

I went on to tell him how I had telephoned Creedy's residence and had asked for an appointment, how I had been taken in to see Creedy over the heads of six businessmen, how I had been threatened and how Fulton and I had been attacked by Hertz.

Holding listened to all this, puffing away at his pipe, his face expressionless.

"It seems to me that Creedy hired Sheppey, and now Sheppey has been murdered, Creedy is falling over backwards to hush up the fact that he did hire him," I concluded.

Holding brooded for a moment, then said, "I take it you're pretty anxious to get Sheppey's murder cleared up?"

I stared at him.

"Well, of course."

"When I heard you had come down here and had talked to Katchen," Holding said, "I called the District Attorney's office at San Francisco and made some inquiries about you. It seems your agency has been pretty co-operative in the past and you have a high rating in Frisco. You were also on the staff of the DA's office there for some years and you did a pretty good job."

I grinned.

"I bet the DA didn't tell you that."

Holding allowed himself a small smile. It didn't do much to ease the ferrety expression on his face.

"I spoke to my opposite number, the ADA. He said your rating for insubordination was high, but, given a free hand, you were a good man on an investigation."

"He told you that because he still owes me ten bucks," I said, wondering where all this was leading to.

"How would you like to have a crack at solving the Sheppey murder?"

"I'm working on it now: opposition or no opposition."

Holding nodded.

"But you won't get far without some form of protection."

"I know that. Protection is something I'm a little short of right now."

"It can be arranged." He rubbed his lean jaw. "Up to a point that is: it's not absolutely guaranteed."

"If it will hold Katchen off my neck, I'll take care of Hertz."

"Katchen can be fixed. You may find Hertz hard to handle. You don't want to under-estimate him."

"I won't."

Holding brooded some more, then said, "Well, I guess that's about it, Mr Brandon. It's getting late. It's time I was in bed."

I shook my head at him.

"Why the free hand? What chestnut am I pulling out of the fire for you?"

I saw his Adam's apple rise and fall, but otherwise his face remained impassive.

"It's not a question of that," he said carefully. "It seems to me that since your partner has been murdered and you are in the line of business, you would want to make a separate investigation."

"You'll have to do better than that if you want me to play," I said, putting an edge to my voice.

He went back to fidgeting with the pen tray, then, after taking time to find the right words, he said, "I'm not entirely convinced this is a job for the police. It could be, of course. If this girl was associated with a thug and if he found Sheppey was fooling around with her, and killed them both, then it is something the police could handle. But if it goes deeper than that, if it involves Creedy, then we're not going to make much progress."

"And that would worry you?"

He looked sharply at me.

"All right: I'll put the cards on the table. It'll be difficult for you to understand the position really unless I do."

"Let's have all the cards in view," I said. "Including the one you have up your sleeve."

He let that one ride.

"Within the next few weeks the Administration is coming up for a new term," he said, picking his words as if they were as fragile as eggshells. "The opposition is naturally looking for an opportunity to loosen the grip Creedy has on this town. If Creedy is involved in some way in Sheppey's murder, it may give the opposition the opportunity it is looking for. The Administration isn't particularly popular, but it is extremely powerful. At the moment it is balanced on a razor's edge. Any scandal that could be used on the front page of the opposition newspapers might turn the trick."

"I take it, Mr Holding, that you are a member of the opposition?"

"I believe in justice and freedom," he said, taking the pipe out of his rat-trap of a mouth and looking at it as if he were surprised to find it still alight.

"Pretty praiseworthy, Mr Holding," I said. "If the opposition gets into power, you would probably become the new District Attorney?"

That made his Adam's apple do a handspring. He looked at me from over the top of his glasses, scratched the lobe of his right ear, hesitated about looking indignant, then relaxed completely with a wide, boyish smile that was as false as a chorus girl's eyelashes.

"I suppose I would, but that, of course, has nothing to do with the issue, nothing at all."

"Who's gunning for Creedy?"

"I wouldn't call it that. This is a straight fight between the Creedy Administration and Judge Harrison, who is going to the poll on a Reform ticket."

"And this town could do with a little reforming?"

"It certainly could."

"Where does Rankin figure in all this?"

"There isn't a great deal Rankin can do if this case develops along the lines that would be detrimental to the Administration," Holding said. "The Commissioner wouldn't encourage an investigation that might embarrass Creedy. He and Creedy are good friends."

"And, of course, Rankin is hoping to become Captain and needs to keep his nose clean," I said. As Holding didn't have any remarks to make on that one, I went on, "So no one is sticking his neck out except me, is that it?"

"Judge Harrison has considerable influence. We have a newspaper with a wide circulation. You would have to be careful, of course, but providing you carry out an orthodox investigation no one would interfere."

"Except Creedy and Hertz."

Holding tapped out his pipe.

"I think you said you could take care of Hertz."

"Yes, I think I could, but I don't say that my methods would be orthodox."

"That's something, perhaps, I had better know nothing about."

I thought for a moment, then said, "Okay. I'll see what I can do. The position as I see it is that I make an investigation, present my findings to you and you persuade the Commissioner to make an arrest. Right?"

Holding went back to the pen tray again. He seemed to get a lot of comfort from pushing it around.

"Not quite. I think perhaps the best plan would be for you to make the investigation and pass the facts to the Editor of the *St Raphael Courier*. He is a firebrand who is willing to publish anything so long as it hits at the Administration. Then when it is published, the Commissioner will have to act."

I grinned.

"And you and Rankin keep out of it? So if anything goes wrong, you're right where you are, safe and happy."

He didn't like that.

"Until the Administration ..." he began, but I cut him short.

"Okay, skip it." I got to my feet. "I'll handle it. Not because I'm pulling your chestnuts out of the fire nor because I want to see Judge Harrison running for a Reform ticket. I'm doing it because my partner was killed, and a thing like that is bad for my business."

He nodded, looking wise.

"I can understand that."

"Although he was my partner and I've a sentimental feeling about turning up the killer," I went on, "I can't live on air forever. If your mob rides into office because of what I turn up, I'll expect them to meet my expenses."

He looked as if he had suddenly bitten into a quince. "That might be arranged, but we would have to be sure first that this case is connected with Creedy."

"That's understood. In the meantime do I get any help from anyone?"

"Rankin knows what I'm arranging with you. If you will contact him at his home from time to time he will let you know what progress he has made. You'll find him in the book."

"What's the name of this Editor you mentioned: the firebrand?"

"Ralph Troy. You can rely on him. Give him the facts and he'll print."

"But first I've got to find the facts." I looked at him. "Well, I'll see what I can dig up. So long for now."

He offered a limp hand.

"Good luck and be careful."

No one could say he was a ray of sunshine. I knew I would need some luck and I was certainly going to be careful.

III

On my way out I wondered if I was too late to catch a glimpse of Marcus Hahn. I was curious to get a look at him without him getting a look at me.

I asked the desk sergeant where the morgue was, explaining that I wanted a word with Lieutenant Rankin if he were still there.

The sergeant told me to follow the corridor to the rear door, turn left and I'd see the morgue light straight ahead.

I followed his directions.

The entrance to the morgue was across the yard. A blue lamp above the door made a ghostly light. Two windows of the low building showed lights and, moving quietly, I crossed the dark courtyard and looked in through one of the windows.

Rankin was standing by a table on which lay Thelma Cousins' body, covered to the neck by the sheet. Facing him was a slightly built man with a mass of corn-coloured hair and a chin beard to match. He was wearing a cowboy shirt of blue-and-yellow checks, black trousers, skin tight at the hips and that belled out around his ankles. On his feet he wore Mexican boots with high heels, and with some tricky inlaid silver work on them.

He was good looking if you could accept the long hair and the beard. He had a good nose, deep-set, intelligent eyes and a dome of a forehead.

While he listened to Rankin, he kept smacking the side of his boot with a thin riding whip.

Maybe if he had had a horse with him he would have been impressive. Without the horse, he looked just another Californian screwball.

Rankin seemed to be doing most of the talking. Hahn just nodded and uttered a word here and there. I could see from Rankin's expression that he was getting nowhere. Finally he flicked the sheet over the dead girl's face as a signal the interview was over, and Hahn started across the room for the door.

I stepped quickly back into the shadows.

Hahn came out, crossed the yard with long strides, flicking his leg with his whip. He disappeared through the doorway, leading to the street exit.

I moved around to the entrance to the morgue, pushed open the door and went in.

Rankin was just about to turn off the lights when he saw me and his hard, tight face showed his surprise.

"What do you want?"

"Was that Hahn?"

"Yeah: a phoney if ever there was one, but he does all right with his pots. He must be making a small fortune out of the sucker trade." Rankin suppressed a yawn. "Know what he told me? This will kill you." He touched the dead girl's arm. "She wasn't only religious, but she never went around with men. She hadn't even a boyfriend unless you can call her priest her boyfriend. He was the only one she went around with, and then only to help him collect for the poor. Doc says she's a virgin. I'll talk to the priest tomorrow, but I think we can believe Hahn."

"And yet she went around with Sheppey."

Rankin grimaced.

"Was he all that good? Could he have made a girl like her fall for him?"

"I wouldn't put it beyond him. He had a technique all of his own, but I don't like it a lot. He didn't go for the religious type. Maybe he and she were on the level. She might have been helping him: giving him information."

"Would they go swimming together; sharing the same cabin if it was only that?"

I shrugged.

"I don't know."

"Well, at least, it doesn't look as if we'll have to look for a boyfriend, does it?" He wandered over to the light switch and turned it off. "You playing along with Holding?" His voice came out of the semi-darkness. The light from the outside blue lamp made a silver puddle on the morgue floor.

"I said I would. He tells me I can look you up at your house if I want any information."

"He didn't tell you you could look him up at his house, did he?"

"No."

Rankin moved over to me.

"He wouldn't. He never takes chances." He put his hand on my arm. "You want to watch him: you're not the first guy he's taken for a ride. He's been in office now for four years and he hasn't got there or stayed there without a lot of help. He has a nice, well-developed talent for getting someone else to row his boat for him. He's the only punk I've ever known who hunts with the Administration and runs with the opposition and gets away with it. So watch him."

He walked out of the morgue, his hands thrust deep in his coat pockets, his shoulders hunched, his head bent.

I stood for a long moment, turning this information over in my mind. Even if he hadn't told me, I wouldn't have trusted Mr Holding. He hadn't been born with the face of a ferret for nothing.

I left the morgue, closed the door and walked quickly down the passage and on to the street.

The time was now twenty-five minutes to two o'clock. I was pretty tired, and it was nice to sink into the upholstered seat of the Buick.

I got back to the hotel as the clock was striking two.

The night clerk looked reproachfully at me as I crossed the lobby. I was too tired to bother with him. I got into the elevator, rode up to the second floor, tramped wearily down the corridor to my room. I unlocked the door, pushed it open and turned on the light.

Then I swore under my breath.

The room had been given the same treatment as Sheppey's room. The drawers in the chest were hanging out, the mattress was ripped open. The pillows were slashed. My stuff had been tossed out of my suitcases and strewn all over the floor. Even Sheppey's stuff had been thrown around too.

I went quickly to where I had hidden the match folder. My fingers slid under the edge of the carpet and I grinned.

The match folder was still there.

I hooked it out and, sitting back on my heels, I opened it. The loose match that I had wedged in between the others fell out and I had to scrabble among the pillow feathers to find it.

If someone had been looking for this folder, I thought, they had gone away without it. But suddenly I stopped feeling pleased as I turned the match over. There were no ciphers along its back! A quick check showed me that there were no ciphers on the back of the other matches either.

I straightened up.

Someone had taken away Sheppey's folder and had left another, probably hoping I hadn't spotted the ciphers on the back of the original one.

I sank down on my ripped-up bed, too tired even to care.

7

I slept until eleven-fifteen the following morning.

When I had telephoned down to the night clerk to tell him I couldn't use the room I was in and why, he had promptly called the police, and I had had yet another visit from Candy.

I didn't tell him about the match folder. I let him see for himself what had happened, and when he had asked if there was anything missing, I had said, as far as I could see, nothing was.

I then moved into another room, leaving him and his fingerprint men to check for clues. I was pretty sure they wouldn't find anything.

As soon as I got into bed I went out like a light. It was the hot sun, coming through the chinks in the blind making me uncomfortably hot, that finally woke me.

I telephoned down for coffee and toast, went into the bathroom, took a shower, shave and then lay on the bed, waiting for the coffee.

I had a lot to think about. There were a number of loose ends to this investigation that needed to be followed up.

Was there any connecting link between the Musketeer Club and Hahn's School of Ceramics? Was this link something that Sheppey had been working on? Did Marcus Hahn figure in the case? Had Creedy hired Sheppey to watch his wife, and had Sheppey stumbled on something quite away from this assignment? What had he been doing in the bathing cabin with a girl like Thelma Cousins?

The coffee arrived before I could attempt to answer any of these questions. While I was drinking it, the telephone bell rang.

It was Rankin.

"I hear you had visitors last night."

"Yes."

"Any idea who they were?"

I stared up at the ceiling as I said, "I'd have told Candy if I had. They went through Sheppey's things, now they've given me the same treatment."

"Watch out they don't give you an ice pick."

"There's that."

"I thought I'd check with you. Candy didn't find a thing. You have no ideas?"

"Not at the moment. I'm bending my brain on it now. If I come up with anything I'll tell you."

There was a pause, then he said, "I've talked to the priest. Hahn wasn't lying. This girl was just what he said she was. She didn't go out with men, and the priest said she would never associate with any strange man. He's quite convinced about that."

"She associated with Sheppey."

"Yeah. Well, I have work to do. I'm trying to get a line on that ice pick."

"I was going to ask you about that. No prints?"

"No. You can buy a pick like that at any hardware store. I have men asking around. If I get anything I'll let you know."

I thanked him. At least I was getting more co-operation from him than I had expected.

He reminded me I would have to attend the inquest on Sheppey's death that would be held in the late afternoon, then he hung up.

I finished my coffee, then called Ella at the office. I asked her how Sheppey's wife had taken the news. She said she had had a bad time with her, but she thought she would be over the shock by now.

"She'll have my letter this morning. Keep the cash box locked, Ella. It's my bet she'll be around asking for some dough before long. Tell her I'll be mailing her a cheque tonight."

Ella said she would do that.

We talked business for a few minutes. Two cases had come in: both of them sounded lucrative and interesting, but I wasn't even tempted.

"See if Corkhill will handle them on a fifty-fifty basis," I said. "I'm staying here until I've cracked this one. Can you manage?"

"Of course."

And I knew she would manage. She was as sharp and as smart as anyone I could hope to have working for me.

We talked some more, then I said I'd call her in a day or so and hung up.

By now my room was unpleasantly hot.

I still felt a little under the weather and decided I'd go down to the beach, take a swim and then plan out a campaign with the sun to inspire me.

I got dressed, dug out my swimming trunks from my bag and stuffed them into my pocket, then I took the elevator to the ground floor.

Brewer, the fat reception clerk, took my key.

"Mr Brandon," he said, looking confused, "I'm afraid that ..."

"I know: don't tell me," I said. "You have a sudden rush of business and you could use my room." I smiled at him. "I don't blame you. Okay, I'll find somewhere else. Just give me until tonight."

"I'm sorry, but we are getting a lot of complaints." He actually looked sorry. "We have had the police here four times in twenty-four hours since you've been here."

"Yes, I know. I can imagine how you feel about that. I'll move out tonight."

"That's very nice of you, Mr Brandon."

I went out to the Buick and drove down to the beach. By then it was just after twelve noon, and the beach was crowding up. I managed to find a place to leave the Buick, then I made my way to a bathing station.

The umbrellas were out. The boys and girls were already at play: some were throwing the medicine ball, some swimming, some starting on the round of before-lunch cocktails from silver flasks, some were just lying and letting the sun burn them up.

I changed into my trunks, stepped over muscular, brown bodies, picked my way past blondes, brunettes and redheads, wearing the minimum, before I could get to the sea.

I swam out for about a quarter of a mile at my fastest clip. I felt in need of the exercise. Then I turned around and came back more leisurely.

The sun was hot now, and there were even less places on the beach.

I came out of the sea and paused to look around, trying to find a place where I needn't rub shoulders with anyone else, but it wasn't easy. Then I saw a girl, sitting under a blue-and-white umbrella, waving at me.

She was wearing a white swimsuit and she had on a pair of doughnut-sized sun-goggles. I recognized her silky blonde hair and her shape before I recognized what I could see of her face.

Margot Creedy was inviting me to join her.

I picked my way over the bodies until I reached her. She looked up at me, her lovely face wearing a slightly cautious expression, and she gave me the same small smile she had given me when we had first met.

"It's Mr Brandon, isn't it?" she said, and she sounded slightly breathless. "It *is* Mr Brandon?"

"Well, if it isn't, someone has stolen my skin," I said. "Is that Miss Creedy behind those big, big goggles?"

She laughed and took the goggles off. Make no mistake about this fact: the girl was quite a dish. Apart from her shape which, in that swimsuit, was sensational, there wasn't a flaw in her.

"Won't you sit down or are you tied up or something?"

I dropped down on the hot sand right by her.

I said I wasn't tied up or anything, and went on, "Thank you for being helpful last night. I wasn't expecting you to do that for me."

"I just happened to be at the club." She hugged her knees, staring over the top of them at the sea. "Besides, I was curious. There's something intriguing as well as morbid about a murder case, isn't there?" She put on her goggles again. I was sorry because they were so big they blotted out half her face. "I was quite sure when you asked me if your friend had been to the club that he hadn't. I just had to check to see if I were right. It is very difficult now for a non-member to get in."

"Have you seen the papers this morning?" I asked, stretching out on the sand. By turning my head I could still have an exciting view of her.

"You mean the second murder? Do you know who the girl is? Was she the one who met your friend: the one he went with to the bathing cabin?"

"That's her."

"Everyone is talking about her." She reached for her big beach bag and began to hunt around in it the way women do. "It's most mysterious, isn't it?"

"Yes, but there's probably a very simple explanation." The heat of the sun was beginning to bother me a little so I turned on my face and moved my body a little more into the shade made by the umbrella. Lying that way I could look directly up at her face. It was something that I would be happy to do any time of the day or night: she really was quite a dish. Possibly the loveliest girl I've ever seen.

"Could she have committed suicide?"

"She could have, I suppose, but it is very unlikely. Why stab yourself with an ice pick? There are simpler ways."

"But suppose she killed your friend? She might have felt a need to atone for what she had done. The papers say she was very religious. She might have felt the only way to atone was to die the way he had died."

This startled me.

"For the love of mike! Did you think that up yourself?"

"Well, no. I was talking to some people. One of them said it and I thought it could be right."

"I wouldn't worry my brains how she died if I were you," I said. "That's a job for the police. She worked at this place out at Arrow Point. The School of Ceramics they call it. Have you ever been there?"

"Why, of course. I go there a lot. I'm just crazy about some of the designs that man Hahn makes. He really is wonderful. Last week I bought a statue of a little boy he made. It was enchanting."

"Did you ever see the girl there?"

"I can't remember her. There are so many girls working there."

"From what I've heard, I was under the impression the place was just a tourists' junk shop."

"Well, in a way, I suppose it is, but Hahn has a room at the back where he keeps all his newest and best work. Only his very special customers can get in there."

"So he does pretty well?"

"Of course, and he deserves to. He really is a great artist."

Watching her, I could see she meant it. Her face was alight with enthusiasm.

"I must go out and take a look one of these days. Maybe you would come with me, Miss Creedy? I'd like to look at his best stuff. I'm not a buyer, of course, but good pottery interests me."

There was a pause. I wasn't sure if she were hesitating or thinking or what.

"Yes," she said. "The next time I go I'll let you know. Will you still be at the Adelphi Hotel?"

"That reminds me. How did you know I was staying there when you called last night?"

She laughed.

She really had beautiful teeth. They were just the right size, even and as white as orange pith. And she didn't just make a hole in her face the way some girls do when they laugh. Her laugh sent a little prickle up my spine. This girl was certainly getting me worked up. I hadn't felt this way since my first serious date, fifteen-odd years back into the past.

"I asked Mr Hammerschult. You must have met him. He knows absolutely everything. I've never asked him a thing that he couldn't answer."

"That had me a little foxed. I wondered how you knew. To return to the Adelphi: I won't be there. They've asked me to leave. The police have been in and out of my room so often, the management are afraid someone will think there's a continuous raid on. I've got to find a place before tonight."

"That won't be easy. It's right in the season."

"Well, I'll have to look."

I didn't much like the idea. Usually Jack found our rooms. He had a natural talent for knowing the hotel that had a vacancy. I would call on ten hotels and be told there wasn't a room to be had. He would pick one and we'd move in straight away.

"You wouldn't know of any little place that isn't expensive?" I said, then remembered who I was talking to and laughed. "No, I guess you wouldn't. That's not quite in your line, is it?"

"How long are you planning to stay?"

"Until this case is cleared up. It could be cleared up in a week or it may take a month. I don't know."

"Could you look after yourself?"

"Why, sure. You don't imagine I go in for staff back home, do you? Have you something then?"

"It may not be what you want. I have a little bungalow out at Arrow Bay. I had to take it on a two-years' lease. I don't ever go there now. The lease has still a year to run. You could have it if you like."

I stared at her.

"No kidding?"

"If you want it, you can have it. It's furnished and there's everything there. I haven't been out to look at it for a month or so, but last time I went it was all right. All you need do is to pay the light bills. Everything else is taken care of."

"That's pretty nice of you, Miss Creedy." I was knocked back on my mental heels. "I'll take it like a shot."

"If you've nothing better to do, we could go out there tonight after dinner. I have a dinner date, but I'll be free after ten. I'll have the water and light turned on between now and then, and I'll bring the key with me."

"Honest ... you embarrass me, Miss Creedy. Such service for a stranger. Look, I don't want to trouble you ..."

"It's no trouble."

I wished I could have got a glimpse of her eyes behind those big goggles. I had a sudden idea I would like to have seen the expression in them. There was something in her voice that told me I was missing something by not seeing her eyes.

She looked at her watch.

"I must go. I'm having lunch with Daddy. He hates to be kept waiting."

"Better not tell him you're providing me with a home," I said, getting to my feet. I watched her slip a short-sleeved dress over her swimsuit. "I have an idea I'm not exactly his favourite man. He might discourage you."

"I never tell Daddy anything," she said. "Would you meet me outside the Musketeer Club at ten: then we'll go on to the bungalow."

"I'll be there."

"Then goodbye for now."

There was that small smile again that had me practically rolling on my back with my hands and feet in the air.

She moved away across the sand and I stood there looking after her.

I thought I had got long, long past the stage of being excited over a girl, but watching the way she moved, the sway of her hips and the way she held her head really did things to me.

II

After I had had a snack lunch I returned to my hotel and packed my suitcases. I told Joe, the bell hop, to arrange for Sheppey's things to be sent to Sheppey's wife. I then wrote her a brief note and included a cheque for a couple of hundred bucks, stressing that this amount would come off the amount I would finally pay her.

By then, it was time for me to attend the inquest. I had my things taken to the Buick and I settled the account.

Brewer again apologized for needing my room, but I told him I'd got something else and he needn't bother his head about me.

I went down to Greaves' office, where I found him polishing his shoes with a duster.

"You coming to the inquest?" I asked.

"I've been told to." He tossed the duster back in his desk drawer, adjusted his tie and reached for his hat. "You going to give me a ride down or do I take a bus?"

"Sure, come on."

On the drive down to the Coroner's court, I asked him if he had been along to look at Thelma Cousins' body.

"I wasn't asked," he said. "Rankin hasn't any time for me. Brewer saw her: that's a laugh, isn't it? He wouldn't be able to identify his own mother if they showed her to him on a slab. Not that it would be easy to identify the girl. That hat and the sun-goggles she wore made her just any woman in a dark wig."

I didn't tell him that he had been wrong about the wig. He wasn't the type to be told he could be wrong.

There were only nine people attending the court. Five of them were the obvious time-wasters you always see at inquests, but the other four attracted my attention.

One of them was a girl with rimless glasses with the hard, poker face of an efficient secretary. She was smartly dressed in a grey linen frock set off with a white collar and cuffs. She sat at the back of the court and took down the whole proceedings in rapid shorthand. Then there was a youngish man in a pearl-grey, loose-fitting suit. He had a lot of blond hair that had been crimped in places by a curling iron. Sunglasses completely obscured his eyes. He sat on one side of the court and looked around as if he were something pretty intellectual. Every now and then he yawned so prodigiously that I thought he would dislocate his jaws. The other two who caught my eye were a couple of glossy, smooth, well-fed men, immaculately dressed, who sat facing the Coroner. I noticed he nodded to them when he came in and again when he finally went out.

The Coroner seemed pretty bored with the whole proceedings. He hurried me through my evidence, listened with a far-away stare in his eyes to Brewer's stammering statement, didn't call Greaves and was pretty curt with the attendant of the bathing station. It wasn't until Rankin got up to say the police were still making inquiries and he would like a week's adjournment that the Coroner became remotely human. He said hurriedly that he would grant an adjournment, then whisked himself out of sight through a doorway behind his chair.

After I had given my evidence, I had returned to my seat beside Greaves. I asked him if he knew who the two glossy-looking men were.

"They're from Hesketh's office," he told me. "The biggest and smartest attorney on the Pacific Coast."

"Would he handle Creedy's business?"

"There would be no one big enough except him to handle it."

"Know who the blond dude was over there with the pencil at his nose?"

Greaves shook his head.

"Or the girl at the back?"

"No."

As soon as the Coroner had gone, the blond gentleman slid out of court with no more commotion than water makes leaving a sink.

The two glossy men went over to Rankin and talked for a minute or so before leaving. While I watched them, I missed seeing the girl in grey leave.

Greaves said he would take the bus back. He added he hoped I would keep in touch with him. We shook hands and he went off.

The two glossy men went away and that left Rankin and me alone in the court room.

I went over to him.

"Anything new?" I asked.

"No." He looked vaguely uneasy. "Not yet. I still can't get a line on that ice pick." He took out a cigarette and began to fidget with it. "We're now digging into the girl's background. She may have been a dark horse."

"Yeah? Suppose you dig into Creedy's background," I said. "That might pay off. Were those two guys representing him?"

"They just looked in to pass the time. They have a case on now, and they were a little early for it."

I laughed.

"Is that what they told you? You don't fall for that, do you?"

"Well, I can't stay here talking to you. I have work to do," he said, his voice curt.

"Did you see the blond boy in the grey suit? Know who he is?"

"He works at the School of Ceramics," Rankin said, looking away from me.

"That's interesting. What's he doing here?"

"Maybe Hahn sent him down," he said vaguely. "Well, I've got to get moving."

"If you want me, I'm staying at Arrow Point. I've got me a little bungalow out there."

He gave me a curious stare.

"There's only one bungalow out at Arrow Point. I thought it belonged to Margot Creedy."

"So it does. I've rented it off her."

Again he stared at me, started to say something, changed his mind, nodded and went away.

I gave him time to leave the building, then I went out to the Buick. The time was now half past four. I asked a policeman who was airing himself on the edge of the kerb where the *Courier's* offices were. He directed me as if he were doing me a favour.

I got over to the *Courier's* offices a few minutes to a quarter to five. I told the girl at the reception desk that I wanted to talk to Ralph Troy. I gave her my business card and, after a five-minute wait, she took me down a passage into a small office where a man was sitting behind a crowded desk, a pipe in his mouth. He was a big man with greying hair, a square jaw and light grey eyes. He pushed out a big firm hand over the litter of his desk and shook hands.

"Take a seat, Mr Brandon, I've heard about you. Holding called and said you might look in for a talk."

I sat down.

"I haven't much to talk about right now, Mr Troy," I said, "but I wanted to introduce myself. Maybe in a little while I'll have something for you. I understand that if I give you some facts, you'll print."

He showed big, strong white teeth in a wide smile.

"You don't have to worry about that," he said. "I aim to print the truth and only the truth, and that's the only reason why I'm still in business. I'm glad you looked in. I want to put you wise to this town. You've heard Holding sound off, now it's my turn." He eased himself back in his chair, puffed smoke at the ceiling, then went on. "There's an election for a new term coming along in a month's time. The old gang who have been in power now for five years have got to get back into power or sink. And when I say sink, I mean just that. The only way these boys can keep alive is to continue to keep their paws in the gravy. Take the gravy away and they're finished. St Raphael City is one of the biggest money spinners on the Pacific coast. Even without the rackets, it would still make money. It's the rich man's stamping ground. There's everything here. There's no other place outside Miami that offers so much for the millionaire who wants to relax. This town is in the hands of the racketeers. Although Creedy owns a little more than half of it, even if he wanted to, he couldn't keep the racketeers out. It so happens he doesn't give a damn one way or the other so long as his holdings pay off. He isn't a bad man, Mr Brandon. Don't get that idea into your head. I'm not saying he isn't a greedy one. He wants a return for his money. If the racketeers push up the value of his holdings as they are doing he isn't objecting. So long as the Casino, the gambling ship, the various night clubs, the five movie houses, the theatre and the opera house, all of which he has financed, pay off, he isn't worrying his brains that the racketeers, the chisellers, the con men, the dope traffickers and the vice boys don't cut into his profits, he leaves them alone, and they are smart enough to know it. This town is riddled with vice and corruption. There's scarcely an official in the Administration who isn't collecting a cut from somewhere."

"And Judge Harrison plans to put all that right?" I asked.

Troy lifted his bulky shoulders.

"That's what Judge Harrison promises to do if he gets elected, but he won't, of course. I'm not saying there won't be a token clean-up: there will be. A number of the minor vice characters will get tossed into the can. There'll be a certain amount of flag waving and a hell of a lot of talk, then, after a month or so, the big boys will flex their muscles and everything will be back as it was. The Judge will find his bank balance has suddenly mysteriously increased. Someone will give him a Cadillac. He'll find it is that much easier to let things go on without interference: for Creedy read Harrison, otherwise it will be the same old racket. It's the system, not the men. A man is honest just so far, but if the money is there, then he can be bought. I'm not saying every man can be bought, but I know damn well Harrison can."

"I was under the impression that Creedy was the boss of the rackets. If he isn't, then who is?"

Troy blew more smoke before saying, "The man who uses Creedy's money and who really runs this town is Cordez, the owner of the Musketeer Club. He's the boy. He's the one who will still be here if Creedy drops out and Harrison takes over. No one knows much about him except he is a slick operator from South America who arrived overnight and who seems to have a natural talent for making profit out of any kind of racket. If Creedy's big business, then Cordez is big rackets. But make no mistake about this: Creedy is just a song at twilight compared with Cordez. If anyone could pull the rug from under Cordez's feet, this town would be free of the rackets, but no one is big enough."

"Let me get this straight," I said. "The Musketeer Club isn't Cordez's only asset, is it?"

Troy smiled grimly as he shook his head.

"Of course not. He uses Creedy's money to make himself money. Take the Casino as an example. Creedy financed the building and gets the house stakes, but Cordez also gets twenty-five per cent as protection money. Creedy financed the gambling ship. He reckoned it would bring in the tourists. It does, but Cordez is there to pick up another twenty-five per cent. If there was no pay-off a bomb would go off in that ship. Those who run the ship and the Casino and all the other money spinners know that so they pay up."

I sat for a long moment taking a look at what he had told me. This wasn't anything new. It was happening in New York, Los Angeles, San Francisco and all over. In thirty-six hours I seemed to have moved a long way from Sheppey's sudden death in a hot little bathing cabin to this. Had he found out something that might have put Cordez on a spot? Sheppey had been a good man with a nose for finding out things like that. I thought of the ice pick that had been filed down to a razor-sharp point: a gangster's weapon.

"I wanted you to get the picture," Troy said. "That's how it is. And another thing: watch this guy Holding. You can trust him the way you trust a rattlesnake: no more, no less. So long as you play it his way, he'll be your friend, but move one step out of his way of thinking and you'll wonder what's hit you. So watch him."

I said I would, then went on to tell him about the possible hook-up between Creedy and Sheppey. I gave him all the facts and I also told him about the mysterious match holder.

"It's my bet that Creedy hired Sheppey to do a job like watching his wife or something like that and Sheppey stumbled on something big that has nothing to do with Creedy," I said. "I may be wrong, but I can't imagine a man like Creedy having anyone killed."

Troy shook his head.

"You're right. He wouldn't do that. He might have a guy beaten up if he got in his way, but killing would be out." He leaned back in his chair. "This is quite a story, isn't it? But there's nothing yet we can print. With a little digging we might come up with a real humdinger." He looked at his watch. "I've got things to do, Mr Brandon. I've got to get going. I tell you what I'll do. I'll turn young Hepple on to this set-up. He's one of my best men. You can use him when and how you like. He's got a talent for nosing out information. Don't be scared to work him hard, he thrives on it. He might dig into Hahn's background for a start. I've always thought there was something fishy about that fella."

"I'll call him tomorrow and we'll have a talk," I said. "Hepple did you say his name was?"

"That's right: Frank Hepple."

"I'll call him." I got to my feet. "You wouldn't know anyone who is a member of the Musketeer Club, would you?"

"Me?" Troy laughed. "Not a chance."

"I'd like to get in there and look around."

"You haven't a hope. Don't kid yourself. No one goes in there unless he's a member or a member takes him in."

"Well, okay. We'll keep in touch," I said. "With any luck I'll let you have something in a day or so."

"If it's anything about Creedy, it's got to be solid facts: nothing else will do," Troy said, leaning across his desk to stare at me. "I can't afford a libel suit with him. He could put me out of business."

"When I give you something on Creedy, it'll be solid facts," I said.

We shook hands and I left him.

At least now I felt I had someone I could rely on. It was a pretty comforting thought.

8

I learned from a traffic cop that the Musketeer Club was on the top floor of the Ritz-Plaza Hotel, and this came as a surprise to me. I had imagined the club would be an ornate palace standing in its own grounds.

"You mean it's just a collection of rooms on the top of a hotel?" I said. "I thought it was the Taj Mahal of this city."

The cop took off his cap, wiped his forehead and squinted at me.

"Taj who?" he said. "What are you giving me, Mac?"

"I thought it was certain to have its own grounds and be a sort of palace."

"I can't help what you thought, can I? It's way up on the twenty-fifth floor with a roof garden. But what are you worrying about? You're not going up there, Mac. Me neither."

I thanked him and went back to the Buick. I sat behind the wheel and thought for a few minutes. Then I remembered Greaves had said that at one time he had been a house dick at the Ritz-Plaza. It occurred to me he might have an idea as to how I could get into the club.

I drove to the nearest drug store and called him.

"I could use a little help if you can spare the time," I said, listening to his heavy breathing coming over the line. "How about meeting me some place? I'll buy you a beer."

He said he would meet me in half an hour at Al's Bar on 3rd Street.

I drove over to 3rd Street, left the car in a parking lot, found Al's Bar and went in.

It was one of those intimate places with booths, and I took the end one against the wall, facing the entrance, and sat down. I ordered a beer and asked the barman if he had an evening paper I could look at.

He brought the beer and the paper.

There was an account of the inquest and a photograph of Rankin looking a little like Sherlock Holmes just after he'd given himself a shot in the arm. On the back page was a photograph of Thelma Cousins. The caption said the police were pursuing their inquiries concerning the second mysterious stabbing in a Bay Beach bathing station.

While I was looking at the photograph, Greaves came in and spread his fat form on the bench seat opposite me.

After I had bought him a beer, I told him I was planning to gatecrash the Musketeer Club and had he any idea how I could do it.

He looked at me as if he thought I was crazy.

"You have as much chance of doing that as you have of gatecrashing the White House," he said.

"I'm not convinced. I hear it's on the top floor of the Ritz-Plaza. As you've worked in that hotel, you should know the layout of the club."

Greaves swallowed half his beer, set down his glass and wiped his mouth on the back of his hand.

"That won't help you. They have the whole of the top floor, and they have two private elevators. You go into the hotel, through the lobby, down a passage on the left. At the far end there's a grill guarded by a couple of guys who know all the answers. They damn well have to or they wouldn't last five minutes. Unless they recognize you they don't open the grill. It's as simple as that. If they recognize you, they open up and you have to sign the book. Then you're taken up in one of the elevators. What happens after that I wouldn't know because I've never been up there. They wouldn't recognize you so they wouldn't open up. So skip it. You're just wasting your time."

"They have a restaurant up there?"

"Sure. It's supposed to be the finest restaurant in the country. I wouldn't know. I've never fed there. What's that to do with it?"

"Don't tell me they cart sides of beef and boxes of fish through the lobby of the hotel. I just won't believe it."

He rubbed his fat nose with the beer glass.

"Who said they did? They share the hotel's goods entrance. It's around the back, down an alley. It so happens the hotel has its kitchens on the tenth floor as the restaurant is up there. I don't know what the club's system is for delivering the stuff, but I've seen goods going up there and the guys who deliver the stuff go up with it."

I smiled at him.

"I was hoping you'd say that. If I took a package up there I might get a chance to have a look around. You wouldn't know any of the staff who could be persuaded to co-operate? I'd spring fifty bucks if I had to."

Greaves thought for a long moment, then finished his beer before saying, "You're sticking your neck out, but there was one guy I knew who worked there: Harry Bennauer. I don't know if he's still there. He was fourth barman or something like that. He was always right out of dough: a sporting man. I've never known a guy to bet the way he did. It wouldn't surprise me if he mightn't be willing to help."

"Try him, will you?" I said. "See if he's still around. Ask him if he'd like to make fifty easy bucks. If he shows interest, tell him I'll be up by way of the goods elevator at seven o'clock sharp."

Greaves thought about it. I could see he wasn't too enthusiastic.

"You're taking a risk. Bennauer might sell you out. There could be a reception committee waiting for you. From what I hear the bouncers working for the club aren't a bunch of powder-puffs. You might get bounced pretty hard."

"That's my funeral. Go ahead and try him."

Greaves lifted his massive shoulders, got to his feet and went over to the row of telephone booths. While he was in one of the booths I ordered a second round of beers.

He talked for five minutes or so, then he came back and sat down.

"I got him," he said. "Right now, he tells me, he's so short of dough, he'd sell his wife for fifty bucks. It's a deal so far as he's concerned. It's up to you now. I wouldn't trust him further than I could throw him – not as far. He might go to the management and sell you out for fifty-five bucks."

"Suppose he did? They can't kill me. All they can do is to toss me out. I don't bounce easy anyway. You told him seven o'clock?"

Greaves nodded.

"He'll be waiting by the elevator. He'll probably double-cross you. You probably won't get further than the elevator doors. As soon as he gets the money, like as not, he'll kiss you goodbye."

"He won't get it until I've seen what I want to see." I looked at my watch. I had forty minutes to seven. "You wouldn't have any suggestions about what I should take up there just in case of trouble?"

He bent his brains to the problem. After turning it over for a while he said, "Stick around, I'll see what I can do." He finished his beer, then pushed his way out of the booth and left the bar.

I waited, sipping my beer, looking at the newspaper and wondering what I was walking into.

He came back within the half-hour.

He was carrying a brown-paper parcel under his arm and as he sat down opposite me he put out his big hand, palm upwards.

"You owe me twenty bucks."

I took out my billfold, parted with four five-dollar bills and asked, "What does that buy me?"

He put the parcel on the table.

"A guy I know is in the brandy trade. He wants to get his liquor into the club. He hasn't a hope, but he doesn't seem to realize it. I kidded him you could get a sample bottle of the stuff before the management. This is it." He tapped the parcel. "For the love of Mike, don't drink it. It'll raise callouses the size of tomatoes in you if you do." He felt in his vest pocket and put a card on the table. "That's his trade card. Now it's up to you to take it from here."

I picked up the card and stowed it away in my billfold.

"That's just what I'm looking for. Thanks a lot. Well, if I'm going, I'd better go."

"The hunk of beaten-up meat I'll find outside the Ritz Plaza with his brains beaten in will be you," Greaves said soberly. "You insured?"

"You don't have to worry about me," I said, and picked up the parcel. "I've been in plenty of tough spots in my time."

"But none tougher than this, brother," Greaves said with feeling. "And don't kid yourself that you have."

II

There was a fat, elderly man guarding the goods entrance to the hotel. He gave me a sour look as I came into his vision.

"This right for the Musketeer Club?" I asked, coming to rest before him.

"Could be," he said. "What's it to you?"

I poked the trade card under his nose and let him browse over it.

"I have a date with the wine waiter. Big deal, pop. You're holding up the wheels of commerce."

He sneered at me, then jerked his thumb to the elevator.

"There's the elevator. Right the way to the top."

He went back to his daydreams. They couldn't be anything to get excited about, but probably they amused him.

I got into the elevator, pressed the button marked Musketeer Club and leaned against the wall while I was hauled up into the stratosphere. It took time. This was a goods elevator: there was nothing express about it.

As I went up, I put my hand inside my coat and touched the butt of the .38 I had strapped on before leaving my hotel. The cold feel of the gun butt gave me a little comfort, but not much.

After what seemed an age, the elevator came to a stop and the doors slid back. My wristwatch showed me that it was exactly seven o'clock.

Facing me was a small lobby stacked with wooden cases, and waiting, a cigarette hanging from his thin lips, was the character Greaves had told me about: Harry Bennauer. He was a pint-size hunk of humanity, wearing a white coat and black trousers. His face was something a head-hunter from Borneo would have been proud to have added to his collection. The sunken eyes, the thin lips and the flared nostrils were arresting but scarcely beautiful.

I stepped out of the elevator and smiled at him.

"Let's have the dough, bud," he said, "and snap it up."

I produced five five-dollar bills and offered them to him. His face hardened.

"What's this? Greaves said fifty."

"Greaves also said you weren't to be trusted, bud," I said. "Half now, half later. I want to look this joint over. On my way out you collect the other half."

"You go beyond that door and you'll walk into trouble," he said, putting the bills hurriedly into his hip pocket.

"You're the boy who is going to keep me out of trouble," I said. "What do you think you're getting fifty bucks for? Is there anyone around out there?"

"Not right now, but they will be in about ten minutes. The boss is in his office."

"Cordez?"

He nodded.

"The wine waiter here yet?"

"He's in his office too."

"Well, okay, you go ahead and I'll follow you. If we run into trouble I'm here on business with the wine waiter. I've got a sample for him."

Bennauer hesitated. I could see he didn't like this set-up, but he wanted the other twenty-five bucks. I had an idea greed would win, and it did.

He went through the doorway. I gave him a few seconds' start, then I went after him. We went down a passage to another door and into a vast cocktail lounge that was really something. It was the most elaborately equipped bar I have ever been in. There was seating for about three hundred people. The bar, shaped like the letter S, ran the length of two of the walls. The floor was made of black glass. Half the room had no roof and overhead I could see the stars.

There was a terrace overlooking the sea and the ten-mile promenade. Banana and palm trees grew in enormous tubs. Flowering creepers covered the roof and the walls with a multitude of red, pink and orange blossoms.

I joined Bennauer by one of the palm trees.

"The offices are through there," he said, pointing to a door behind the bar. "The restaurant is thataway. What else do you want to see?"

"I'd like a souvenir to take away," I said. "Get me some of those match folders you hand out to the boys and girls."

He looked as me as if he thought I was crazy, but he went over to the bar, went behind it and produced a handful of the folders.

"This what you mean?"

I joined him. I took three from him, opened them and checked the back of the matches. There were no ciphers printed on them.

"This all you've got?"

"What do you mean? They're match folders, ain't they? That's what you asked for, isn't it?"

"Is there any other type: the ones the boss gives away?"

"Look, Joe, cut it out, will you?" His face was beginning to grow shiny with sweat. "I'd lose my job if you were found in here. Take your goddamn matches and beat it."

"Any chance of looking in some of the offices?" I asked. "I'd spring another fifty if I could."

I could see he was rapidly losing his nerve by now.

"You're nuts! Come on, get the hell out of here!"

Then the door behind the bar, the one Bennauer had told me led to the offices, opened, and a fat man wearing a white coat on which was a badge bearing a beautifully embroidered bunch of grapes to tell me he was the wine waiter came into the bar.

He was a Latin type with thick, heavily oiled hair and a Charlie Chan moustache. His small black eyes moved from Bennauer to me and the muscles of his face, under their covering of fat, tightened.

Bennauer didn't entirely lose his head. He said, "Here's Mr Gomez now. You've got no business to barge in here without an appointment." He turned to Gomez. "This guy wants to talk to you."

I gave the fat Latin a servile smile.

"Could you spare me a moment of your time, Mr Gomez? I'm O'Connor: Californian Wine Co."

As Gomez moved over to me, I produced the trade card and laid it on the bar. He picked it up with fat fingers and studied it: his face was as expressionless as a hole in a wall. I could smell the pomade with which he had soaked his hair: it wasn't a particularly pleasant smell.

Having read the card, he turned it on its edge and began to tap with it on the counter while he looked me over.

"I have no account with your people," he said.

"That's something we want to put right, Mr Gomez. We have several lines that would interest you. I've brought a bottle of our very special brandy for you to try."

His black eyes moved to Bennauer.

"How did he get in here?" he asked.

Bennauer had got his second wind by now. He shrugged his shoulders.

"I was here and he just walked in and asked for you."

"I came up in the goods elevator. The guy on the door downstairs told me to come up," I said. "Did I do wrong?"

"I don't see any salesman without an appointment."

"I'm sorry, Mr Gomez. Maybe you could give me a date for tomorrow." I put the parcel on the counter. "If you could look at this in the meantime, we might be able to talk business tomorrow."

"We'll talk business now," a voice said behind me.

Both Gomez and Bennauer became as rigid as marble statues. Okay, I admit my heart did a back flip. I looked over my shoulder.

A dark man in a faultless tuxedo, a white camellia in his buttonhole, stood about twenty feet from me. He had the face of an eagle, narrow with a big, sharp nose, a thin mouth and black restless eyes. He was thin and tall; the South American type that women rave about and men watch uneasily when they are raving.

I was pretty certain this was Cordez. These other two wouldn't be behaving as if they were in the presence of a real hot shot unless he was.

The tall man moved up to the bar, held out a brown, thin hand for the card Gomez was holding. Gomez gave it to him. He stared at it, then with no change of expression he bent it in two and flicked it behind the bar.

"That ..." he said, and pointed to the brown-paper parcel on the counter.

Gomez hurriedly stripped the wrapping off the bottle and laid the bottle on the counter so Cortez could read the label.

He read it, then he turned sleepy black eyes on me.

"I said no to this a month ago," he said. "Don't you know what 'no' means?"

"Why, I'm sorry," I said. "I'm new to this territory. I didn't know someone had shown it to you before."

"Well, you know now. Get out of this club and stay out!"

"Why, sure. I'm sorry." I made out I was pretty confused. "Maybe if I leave the bottle ... it's pretty good brandy. We could supply it on very favourable terms."

"Get out!"

I stepped away from the bar, turned and started across the vast acreage of black glass. I hadn't taken six steps when I became aware that three men in tuxedos had appeared. They stood in a semicircle, blocking the way out.

Two of them I had never seen before. They were big, beefy Latin-Americans. Their faces were hard and expressionless.

The third man, standing between them, a snarling grin on his broken face, made me feel suddenly a little weak at the knees.

It was Hertz.

III

For a long moment Hertz and I stared at each other. His tongue came out and went over his thick lips, the way a snake flicks out its tongue before it strikes.

"Hello, peeper," he said softly. "Remember me?"

I remembered him all right.

I hadn't reckoned on being bounced by Hertz. I had been prepared to be roughed up a little and shot out on my tail on the hard, cold sidewalk, but having Hertz in it as well hadn't come into my calculations.

I did some rapid thinking. I moved sideways so I could see Cordez while at the same time I could watch Hertz.

Cordez said, in his flat, bored voice, "What is this?"

"The creep's name is Brandon," Hertz said. "He's a shamus. He's that punk Sheppey's sidekick."

Cordez stared at me, his eyes completely impersonal, then he lifted his shoulders, walked around the bar and made for the door leading into his office. There he paused looking at Hertz.

"Get him out of here."

Hertz smiled.

"Sure," he said. "Give me a little room, boys, I want to take this baby on my own."

He waved the other two hunks of beef aside, and still smiling, his close-set eyes glittering, he came across the glass floor towards me.

There were five against one; that's if Mr Cordez would condescend to join in, and that seemed to me overlong odds.

I equalized the situation by sliding my hand inside my coat and throwing my .38.

"Relax," I said, and let the gun sight swing in a semicircle to cover Hertz, the two roughs, Gomez, Bennauer and Cordez. "Don't let's have any rough stuff or there could be some damage around here."

Hertz came to an abrupt stop as if he had walked into a brick wall. He stared at the gun as if it were the last thing he expected to see.

Cordez paused, his hand on the doorknob, his eyes on my face.

The two muscle-men remained motionless. They were professionals, and they were quick to realize I would shoot if I were crowded.

Cordez moved back to the bar and leaned against it. "I told you to get out, didn't I?" he said. "Well, get out!"

"Keep this ape out of my way and I will," I said, nodding at Hertz.

Then the lights went out.

Maybe that was Gomez's contribution to the tableau. I shall never know. I heard a quick patter of feet and I squeezed the trigger. An orange spurt of flame came from the gun and the bullet smashed a mirror somewhere ahead of me. Then a wave of bodies rolled over me, taking me to the floor. Hands groped for my throat, my arms, my wrists. I was squeezing the trigger again as the gun was wrenched out of my hand. A fist that felt more solid than a lump of pig-iron smashed against the side of my head. A boot thumped into my side as someone fell over me. I hit out blindly. My fist hit a face, and there was a grunt. Something whistled past my face and made a dull thud on the glass floor. Hands found me. I fought, kicked out and mentally cursed, then a fist slammed me on the side of the jaw and that was that.

Lights came on again.

I lay on my back staring up at the two thugs and Hertz. One of the thugs had my gun which he held down by his side.

My jaw ached and my head felt as if it were bursting. I heard the sound of footsteps across the glass floor. Cordez joined the happy band. His thin face was still indifferent, still without expression.

I pushed myself to a sitting position, my hand holding my aching jaw.

"Take him away and dump him," Cordez said. "Make sure he doesn't come back."

He turned and walked away. It was then that I saw he was wearing very high-heeled shoes: just another phoney who wanted to look better than he was.

Neither Hertz nor the two thugs moved until Cordez had gone through the doorway at the back of the bar. Gomez and Bennauer had already faded out of sight.

Hertz held out his hand for my gun and the thug who was holding it gave it to him. I watched Hertz slide the gun through his fingers until he was holding it by the barrel. All the time he stared at me, a meaningless smile on his moronic, battered face.

I had shaken off the effects of his punch by now. The movement he was making to hold the gun by its barrel told me I was in for a pistol whipping. He was aiming to club me with the gun. An expert pistol-whipper knows how to handle the gun. He hits you in every spot except a vital one. You're out of action for months by the time he has finished with you. The gun, used by a vicious thug like Hertz, can do a lot of damage, but it needn't be lethal.

I had served five years as a special investigator to the DA's office in San Francisco. If you think there is any tougher place than San Francisco's dockland, tell me and I'll keep clear of it. For five years I had rubbed shoulders with thugs like Hertz. So long as he didn't get behind me, I wasn't all that scared of him.

But I let him think I was.

As he swung the gun in his hand, I squirmed away, horror on my face.

"Let me out of here," I whined. "I won't make any trouble. Just let me out of here."

Hertz's grin widened.

"You're going, pally," he said in his soft, moronic voice. "And you're going my way."

He gave me time to squirm further from him. He even gave me time to get to my feet. Then he came dancing in, his ruined face alight with fiendish happiness as he swung the butt of the gun towards my head.

I timed it right. Just when we should have connected I shifted. The gun-butt flashed past me, his arm thumped on my shoulder and that brought him close to me. I grabbed hold of his coat lapels, bent my knees, leaned against him and heaved. He sailed over my head with the grace of an acrobat, arrived on his mouth and his nose on the glass floor with a crash that rocked the bottles on the shelves behind the bar, and slid along the floor to land with his head squarely connecting with the bar counter.

I went for one of the thugs the way a fighting bull goes for a matador. He swerved aside, his eyes bulging. But I wasn't after him. That was just a feint. I was after his pal. He was standing close by, and he was totally unprepared. My fist caught him on the side of his jaw: a beautiful punch with all my weight behind it, and it lifted him off his feet and sent him sliding along the glass floor to take a toss that ended up with his head hammering against the wall. The contact between his head and the wall made such a mellow, lovely sound, I knew he would be out of action for some time.

That left the other thug.

He came at me like an enraged elephant. It was good to see the startled fear in his face. I slid under his right lead and thumped him in his ribs, sending him backwards. Then I dived for his ankles, grabbed them and jerked him upwards. The bang his skull made on the floor made even me wince. He gave one spasmodic heave of his body and then stiffened out cold.

I paused and looked over at Hertz. He was still counting stars, huddled up against the bar counter. I went over to him, took my gun out of his limp grasp, shoved it into my holster, than taking him by his ears, I lifted his head and connected it with the floor. He flopped around for a brief second like a landed trout, then went limp.

I stepped back and surveyed the wreckage. All this had taken about eighty seconds, no more; and I felt quite pleased with myself. I hadn't had a rough house like this for four or five years. At least it showed me that I hadn't lost my grip.

I now had two alternatives: I could either get out fast or I could remain on the premises, out of sight, in the hope of picking up some worthwhile information.

Up to this moment I hadn't found anything worth the risk of getting my neck broken. I decided, as I might never again get the chance of crashing this club, I had better stick around.

But where to hide?

I ran across the glass floor out on to the terrace. I could see a row of lighted windows to my right. Unless my geography had gone awry, these would be the windows of the club's offices. I saw there was a wide ledge running below the windows. I looked up. The roof sloped gently away into the darkness. I could just make out a small flat roof at the top. It seemed to me if I could get up there, I would be out of trouble for a while, and when the club got busy, I had a chance of exploring without attracting attention.

I heard one of the thugs groan softly, and I knew I hadn't much time. I stepped up on to the balustrade of the terrace, reached up for the narrow coping running along the edge of the roof, got a grip, then pulled myself upwards.

I have a pretty good head for heights, but while I was dangling in mid-air, I did think of the long, long drop far below.

I got my leg up on the roof, heaved upwards and slid my body on to it. For a long moment I remained there, clutching on to the tiles and wondering if I made one more move I'd start a slide I wouldn't be able to stop.

I made the move, got up on hands and knees, and then, very cautiously, I stood up. My crêpe-sole shoes afforded a good grip. Bending low, I walked up the tiles to the flat roof and sat down.

There was no skylight. If anyone came after me, he would have to come the way I had, and with a gun in my hand, that made my position for the time being impregnable.

I had a magnificent view over the whole of St Raphael City and I sat admiring it.

Around eight o'clock I heard the club suddenly come to life. Far below big Cadillacs, Packards and Rolls-Royces pulled up outside the hotel entrance. A very slick dance band started up: lights came on on the terrace. I judged it safe to light a cigarette. I decided to wait an hour and then see what I could see.

By nine o'clock the rush was on. Above the precision slickness of the band, I could hear a great buzz of voices and laughter. Now was the time and I stood up.

Going down the sloping roof was a lot more dangerous than going up: one slip and I would shoot over the edge and down on the sidewalk some three hundred feet below. I moved an inch at a time, squatting on my haunches, digging my heels into the tiles and checking myself with my hands. I reached the edge, got a grip on the coping, got my legs over the edge, twisted off and swung into space.

Away to my right I could see the brilliantly lit terrace with its tables, its elegantly dressed men and women and the regiment of waiters milling around them. I was just in the shadows, and unless anyone came right to the end of the terrace, I couldn't be seen.

My feet touched the wide ledge that ran below the windows of the offices. I let myself drop: a dangerous move, and as I landed I nearly lost my balance and toppled backwards. But by dropping my head forward I just managed to correct my balance, then I hooked my fingers into the coping and held on while I got my breath back.

The rest was pretty plain sailing. All I had to do was to walk along the ledge and look in the windows as I passed.

The first two rooms I came to were empty. They were furnished as offices with desks, typewriters and filing cabinets: everything on the de luxe scale. The third window was much larger. I paused beside it and looked in.

Cordez sat in a high-backed chair before a big glass-topped desk. He was smoking a brown cigarette in a long holder and was checking figures in a ledger.

The room was big and done over in grey and egg-shell blue. All the desk fitments were of polished steel. Three big filing cabinets, also of steel, stood along the wall. Near where Cordez was sitting was a big safe.

I kept just out of the stream of light that came through the open window, bending forward so I could peer into the room.

Cordez worked quickly. His gold pencil travelled up the rows of figures, casting them with the practised ease of an accountant.

I remained watching him for perhaps ten minutes, and then, just when I was beginning to think I was wasting my time, I heard a knock on the door.

Cordez looked up, called, "Come in," and then went back to his casting again.

The door opened, and a fat, white-faced man in a well-fitting tuxedo entered. He had a red carnation in his buttonhole and diamonds glittered at his shirt-cuffs. He closed the door as if it were made of something very brittle and stood still, waiting, his eye on Cordez.

When Cordez had finished casting a column, he noted down the total, then looked up.

His expression was coldly hostile.

"Now look, Donaghue," he said, "if you haven't any money, get out. I've had about all I'm going to take from you."

The man fingered his perfectly set tie. Sullen hatred showed in his eyes.

"I've got the money," he said, "and don't give me any of your damned impertinence." He hauled out a roll of bills from his hip pocket and threw them on the desk. "Here's a thousand. I'll have two this time."

Cordez picked up the roll, straightened it and counted the bills. Then he opened a drawer in his desk and dropped the roll into it. He got to his feet and walked over to the safe. Standing squarely in front of it so his body hid the combination from Donaghue and myself, he twirled the dial and pulled the door open. He reached inside, took something out, closed the safe door and came back to the desk.

He flicked two match folders across the glass top of the desk so they came to rest before Donaghue.

Donaghue snatched them up, opened them and examined them carefully, then slid them into his vest pocket. He went out without a word, and Cordez returned to his desk. He sat for a long moment staring at the opposite wall, then he picked up his gold pencil and began casting again.

I remained where I was, watching.

During the period of forty minutes, two other people came in: a fat, elderly woman and a young fellow who looked as if he were still at college. They each parted with five hundred dollars for a match folder. Each time Cordez treated them as if he were doing them a favour.

By now it was ten minutes to ten, and I remembered my appointment with Margot Creedy.

I leaned forward and looked down. Ten feet below and to my left I could see a balcony to one of the hotel bedrooms. No lights showed from the window. I decided that would be my safest and easiest way out.

Crouching, I slid past Cordez's window and arrived immediately above the balcony. Then I sat on the ledge, turned, caught hold of the coping, let myself hang, then dropped.

The French doors were easy enough to force, and a few minutes later I was in the bedroom. I groped my way to the door, opened it and looked cautiously out into a wide, deserted corridor.

Then I set off down the corridor in search of the elevator. It was as easy as that.

9

At five minutes after ten o'clock, I saw Margot Creedy come through the hotel's revolving doors and pause under the brightly lit canopy.

She was wearing an emerald green dress made of sequins, with a plunging neckline, that fitted her like a second skin.

Around her throat was a string of big, fat emeralds. She glittered as she stood there, and she was pretty breathtaking.

I was acutely aware of the Buick's shabbiness as I edged it up to the hotel entrance. I pulled up, slid across the bench seat and got out.

"Hello there," I said. "I want to be personal and tell you you look wonderful. That's just for the record. My real opinion is a little too intimate for expression."

She gave me her small smile. Her eyes were very alive and sparkling.

"I put this on specially for you," she said. "I'm glad you like it."

"That's an understatement: it's a dazzler. Have you your car here?"

"No. I'll show you the bungalow, and then perhaps you wouldn't mind driving me back?"

"Of course I'll drive you back."

I held the door open and she got in. I had a brief glimpse of her slender ankles as I shut the door. I went around the car, got in and drove down the drive.

"You turn right and go to the far end of the promenade," she told me. There were a lot of cars idling along the promenade. It wasn't possible to do more than twenty miles an hour and then only in short bursts.

The moon was up, the night was warm and the sea and the palms made a nice setting. I was in no hurry.

"From what I hear this Musketeer Club is quite a place," I said. "Do you go there often?"

"It's the only place you can go to that isn't crammed with tourists. Yes, I go there quite a lot. Daddy owns half of it, so I don't have to pay the bills. I wouldn't go there so much if I did."

"All you'd have to do is to hock one of those emeralds and you could move in there for good."

She laughed.

"It so happens they don't belong to me. Daddy allows me to wear them, but they are his. When I want a change, I take them back and he lends me something else. I don't own anything. Even this dress I really can't claim as mine."

"There's the bungalow you have on lease," I said, looking at her out of the corners of my eyes.

"It's not my lease. Daddy bought it."

"He'll love his new tenant. I think maybe I'd better skip this idea and not move in."

"He won't know. He still thinks I use it."

"It would come as a surprise if he drops in for a cup of tea, wouldn't it?"

"He never drops in for anything."

"Well, if you're sure about that. So you're the genuine poor little rich girl?"

She lifted her lovely shoulders.

"Daddy likes to control everything. I never have any money. I have to send him the bills and he settles them."

"No one ever settles my bills."

"But no one tells you you shouldn't have bought this or that, and you can do without these or those, do they?"

"You know if you go on like this, I'll begin to feel sorry for you, and you wouldn't want that, would you?"

She laughed again.

"I don't see why not. I like sympathy. No one ever gives me any."

"You listen carefully: the drip, drip, drip you hear is my heart bleeding for you," I said.

We were reaching the quieter part of the promenade now and I was able to increase speed. I shifted into top, and moved up to forty miles an hour.

"You don't believe me, do you?" she said. "Sometimes I'm quite desperate for money."

"So am I. Now look, you don't ever have to be desperate for money: not a girl like you. You could make a small fortune as a model. Ever thought of that?"

"Daddy wouldn't allow me to do it. He is very careful about the dignity of his name. No one would employ me if he told them not to."

"You're just stalling. You don't have to live here. New York would love you."

"Do you think it would? Turn, left here, down that road."

The headlights picked out a rough, sandy road that seemed to be running right into the sea. I swung the car off the broad promenade and reduced speed. We went down the sandy road into darkness. The headlights cut a white path ahead of us.

"I was just talking: it's easy to talk," I said. "You can't lead other people's lives. You've managed so far. You'll go on managing."

"Yes, I suppose I will."

"This is a little off the beaten track, isn't it?" I said, as the car bumped over the uneven road. Palm trees on either side blocked out the moon and there was only darkness each side of the headlight beams.

She opened her bag and took out a cigarette and lit it. "That's why I wanted it. If you had lived in this town as long as I have, you would welcome a little seclusion. Don't you like being alone?"

Thinking of a possible visit from Hertz and his thugs, I said with reservation, "Within reason."

We drove for a quarter of a mile in silence, then the headlights picked out a squat bungalow within twenty yards of the sea.

"Here we are."

I pulled up.

"Have you a flashlight?" she asked. "We'll need it until I can find the light switch."

I got a big flashlight out of the door pocket. We both got out and together we walked up the path to the bungalow's door.

The moon was brilliant and I could see a mile-long strip of empty sand, palm trees and the sea. In the distance I could see lights of a house that was built up on a rocky hill, projecting into the sea.

"What's out there?" I asked as Margot opened her bag and hunted for the door key.

"That's Arrow Point."

"Those lights from Hahn's place?"

"Yes."

She found the key, pushed it into the lock and turned it. The door swung open. She groped, and then a light sprang up on a big luxuriously furnished lounge with a small cocktail bar in the distant corner, a radiogram and television combination, plenty of comfortable lounging chairs, a three-foot-wide padded window-seat that ran the length of one of the walls and a blue-and-white mosaic floor.

"This is quite something," I said, walking in and pausing in the middle of the big room to look around. "Are you sure you mean me to move in here?"

She walked over to the double French doors and threw them open. She touched a light switch and lights came up on a thirty-foot-long terrace that had a magnificent view of the sea and the distant lights of St Raphael.

"Do you like it?"

She came back to stand in the doorway and she again gave me her small bewitching smile. Just to look at her got my blood running around in my veins like a car on a roller-coaster.

"It's terrific."

I was looking at the bar. There was an assortment of bottles on the shelves. It seemed to me there was every drink you could want there.

"Are those bottles the property of your dad or are they yours?"

"They're his. I took them from the house. Four bottles at a time." She smiled. "He has everything. I don't see why I shouldn't help myself sometimes, do you?"

She went behind the bar, opened the door of a refrigerator and took out a bottle of champagne.

"Let's celebrate," she said. "Here, you open it. I'll get the glasses."

She went out of the lounge. I broke the wire around the cork of the bottle and, as she returned with two champagne glasses on a tray, I eased the cork out. I poured the wine and we touched glasses.

"What do we celebrate?" I asked.

"Our meeting," she said, her eyes sparkling at me. "You're the first man I've met who doesn't care if I'm rich or poor."

"Now wait a minute ... what makes you think that?"

She drank the champagne and flourished the empty glass.

"I can tell. Now go and look at your new home and tell me what you think of it."

I put my glass down.

"Where do I begin?"

"The bedroom is through there to the left."

We looked at each other. There was an expression in her eyes that could have meant anything.

I went to look at the bedroom, finding I was a little short of breath. I told myself I was letting my imagination run away with me, but the feeling that she wasn't here merely to show me the bungalow persisted.

It was a nice bedroom: a double bed, closets and a mosaic floor. The closets were full of her clothes. The room was decorated in pale green and fawn.

The bathroom was right next door and looked as if it had been built for a Cecil B de Mille movie with a sunken bath and a shower cabinet in pale blue and black.

I returned to the lounge.

Margot was lying full length on the window-seat, her head supported by two cushions. She was staring out across the expanse of moonlit sea.

"Do you like it?" she asked, without looking at me.

"Yes. Are you quite sure you want me to have it?"

"Why not? I don't use it now."

"You have your things here still."

"There's nothing I want immediately. I'm a little bored with them. Later, I'll use them again. I like giving clothes a rest. There's plenty of room for your things."

I sat in a lounging chair by her. Having her alone in this bungalow gave me a feeling of acute excitement. She turned her head and looked at me, then she said, "Are you making any progress with your murder?"

"I don't think I am, but you can't expect me to keep my mind on my job with this sort of thing happening to me, can you?"

"What is happening to you?"

"This – the bungalow. And of course, you ..."

"Am I so disturbing then?"

"You could be. You are."

She looked at me.

"But then so are you."

There was a long pause, then she swung her long legs off the window-seat.

"I'm going to have a swim. Coming?"

"Why sure." I got up. "I'll get my bag. It's in the car."

Leaving her, I went out into the darkness, got my bag out of the car and came back.

I carried the bag into the bedroom where I found her standing before the full-length mirror. She had taken off her dress and she had on now a white négligé. She was looking at herself, her hands lifting her hair off her shoulders.

"You don't have to do that," I said, setting down the bag. "I'll do it for you."

She turned slowly. There was that look in her eyes I've seen from time to time in the eyes of a woman who is making a proposal.

"You think I'm beautiful?"

"More than that."

I felt myself sliding over the edge. I made a poor attempt to stop this from developing into something I could be sorry about in the morning, by saying, "Maybe we'd better skip the swim and I'll take you home." I was aware of feeling suddenly short of breath. "We might be sorry ..."

She shook her head.

"Don't say that. I'm never sorry for anything I do."

Still looking at me, she walked slowly towards me.

II

"Give me a cigarette," Margot said from out of the darkness.

I reached for my pack on the bedside table, shook one out, gave it to her, then flicked my lighter alight.

In the tiny flame, I could see her with her golden head resting on the pillow. There was a relaxed, peaceful expression on her face and she looked at me, our eyes meeting above the flame and she smiled.

I snapped out the flame, and all I could see of her was the faint outline of her nose as she drew on the cigarette, making the spark burn redly.

"I wonder what you think of me?" she said out of the darkness. "I don't want to make any excuses. I'm not all that free and easy, but sometimes it happens, and then it's a must. The moment I saw you I felt something I haven't felt for months, and this is the result. I don't expect you to believe me, but it's true. One of those mad, uncontrolled impulses, and I am shamelessly glad." She reached out her hand and took mine. "I want to say you are nicer than I hoped you would be, and a better lover than I dreamed you would be."

I was still pretty confused and surprised at the sudden way this had happened. Her words pleased me, but at the same time I was aware that I had fallen for her too easily. I had imagined I had got beyond the point where I could be swept off my feet. It disturbed me to know I hadn't.

I lifted myself on my arm and bent over and kissed her. "And you were wonderful," I said, letting my lips browse over her face, "and you are wonderful."

She ran her fingers through my hair.

"So long as both of us are pleased with each other."

Then she slid away from me and, getting off the bed, she went out of the room.

I reached for my dressing-gown, put it on and went after her.

I found her standing by the open French doors looking out at the silvery beach and the sea. She made a picture in the light of the moon: like a statue by the hand of a master.

"What now?" I said, coming up by her side. "What's going on in that pretty head of yours?"

"Let's swim now," she said, taking my hand. "Then I must go. What is the time?"

I led her out on to the terrace so I could read my watch in the light of the moon.

"It's after two."

"A quick swim, and then I really must go."

She ran ahead of me down to the sea and I went after her, throwing aside my dressing-gown. We swam out for two hundred yards or so, then turned and headed back to the beach. The water was warm and around us there was a complete stillness as if we were the only two people left on earth.

We walked across the sand towards the bungalow, hand in hand.

As we reached the bungalow steps, she stopped suddenly, turned and lifted her face. I slid my hands down her long, slender back, over the curve of her hips and pulled her to me. We stood like that for a long moment, then she pushed me away.

"It's been lovely, Lew," she said. "I'm coming again. Will you mind?"

"What a question! Can you imagine I'd mind?"

"I'll get dressed. Will it bore you to take me back?"

"I'd rather you stayed the rest of the night. Why don't you?"

She shook her head.

"I can't. Don't think I don't want to, but I have a maid whom Daddy pays. If I stayed out all night, Daddy would hear about it."

"You certainly seem to have your old man in your hair," I said. "Well, all right. Let's go in."

It didn't take me more than a few minutes to get dressed. While she was fixing her hair, sitting before the dressing-table mirror, I sat on the bed, waiting for her.

"You know I think I should pay you rent for this place," I said. "I could rise to thirty dollars a week, and it'd give you some pin money."

She shook her head and laughed.

"That's very sweet of you, but I don't want pin money: I want spending money. No. I'm glad for you to have it, and I'm not going to be paid for it." She stood up, smoothed down her glittering dress over her hips, looked at herself and then turned. "Now, we must go."

"Well, all right, if you're absolutely sure."

She came over to me and touched my face with her fingertips.

"Yes, I'm sure."

We went through the rooms, turning off the lights, then I locked the front door and dropped the key into my pocket. We walked down to the car.

As we drove back over the uneven road, my mind was busy. It seemed to me this was a good opportunity to ask questions. I felt she must be in a receptive mood, and there was one question that I really wanted answered.

So I said casually, "Can you think of any reason why your father would want to hire a private detective?"

She was sitting low down, her head resting against the top of the bench seat. She stiffened a little, turned to look at me.

"Now you have had your way with me," she said, "you are hoping I will be compliant."

"No. You don't have to answer the question. I won't hold it against you if you don't."

She was silent for a long moment, then she said, "I don't know, but I could make a guess. If he did hire your partner, then it was because he wanted him to watch his wife."

"Has he any reason to have her watched?"

"I should imagine he has every reason. It surprises me he hasn't done it long ago. She has some gigolo always hanging around her. She has this horrible man Thrisby at the moment. Perhaps Daddy is getting tired of it. I wish he would divorce her. Then I could go home."

"Would you like to do that?"

"No one likes to be turned out of their home. Bridgette and I just can't live together."

"What's the matter with Thrisby?

"Everything. He's the complete home wrecker: a horrible man."

I let the subject hang for a few moments then, as I drove off the beach road on to the promenade, I said, "Your father wouldn't have hired Sheppey to check on you, would he?"

She flicked her cigarette out of the window.

"He doesn't have to pay a detective to do that. My maid does all the necessary spying. It was a condition he let me have the apartment that I should have her with me. No, unless it's something I know nothing about, I think you can be fairly sure he hired him to watch Bridgette."

"Yes, that's what I think."

We drove in silence for a mile or so, then she said, "Do you plan to watch Bridgette?"

"No: there's not much point in that. I don't imagine she had anything to do with Sheppey's death. What I think happened was that while he was watching her, he came across something that had nothing to do with her. It was something important, and he was smart enough to realize it, so he got killed. This is a gangster town. Take the Musketeer Club. Sheppey could have found out something going on there. Although it is only used by the blue-blood trade, it is run by a gangster."

"Oh, you really think that?"

"I'm guessing. I may be wrong, but until I've found out more I'm going to stay with the idea."

"If Sheppey got evidence that would give Daddy a divorce, Bridgette would be without a dime. She hasn't any money of her own, or practically none. If Daddy divorced her, she would be out in the cold and she wouldn't like that."

"You're not suggesting that she killed Sheppey?"

"Of course not, but Thrisby could have. I've seen him; you haven't. He's utterly ruthless, and if he thought he wasn't going to get any money out of Bridgette because of something Sheppey had found out, he might have killed him."

That was a line I hadn't thought of.

"I think I'll take a look at him. Where do I find him?"

"He has a little place up on the Crest. It lies at the back of the town. He calls it the White Château. It isn't a château, of course. It's just a flashy, nasty little love nest."

The bitterness in her voice made me look quickly at her.

"Bridgette isn't the only woman he entertains up there," she went on. "Any woman with money is welcomed."

"Well, at least, he isn't the only one," I said. "This coast line is full of them."

"Yes." She pointed. "You take the first on the right now. It'll bring you straight to the Franklyn Arms."

I turned off the promenade and saw ahead of me the lighted sign of her apartment block.

I drove to the entrance and pulled up before the revolving doors.

"Well, good night," she said, and her hand touched mine. "I'll call you. Be careful of that man Thrisby."

"You don't have to worry about me," I said. "I'll handle him. I'll be waiting to hear from you."

As I made to get out, she said, "No, don't. My maid is probably watching from the window. Good night, Lew." She leaned against me and I felt her lips touch my cheek, then she opened the car door, slid out and walked quickly under the lighted canopy and disappeared through the revolving doors.

I drove away.

When I reached the promenade, I pulled up by the kerb to light a cigarette then, setting the car moving, I drove slowly back to the bungalow.

On the way, I did some thinking. I switched my mind from Margot and concentrated on Cordez. For some reason or other the folder of matches that I had found in Sheppey's suitcase appeared to be worth five hundred dollars. Cordez had parted with three of these folders to three different people and in each case they had paid him that sum. It was safe to assume that Sheppey had either found the folder or had taken it from someone. That someone had ransacked both Sheppey's and my room at the hotel. He had failed to find it in Sheppey's room, but had found it in mine, and had substituted another folder, probably in the hope I hadn't noticed the ciphers at the back of the matches. Therefore it was safe to assume that the ciphers meant something. It could also mean that this mysterious folder of matches was the cause of Sheppey's death.

I felt I was moving in the right direction, but I had still a lot more information to collect before I could get further than guesswork.

I arrived back at the bungalow at a quarter to three. I was pretty tired by then. I unlocked the front door and, turning on the light, I entered the lounge.

I had in mind to give myself a small whisky and soda before turning in, and I was crossing the lounge towards the bar when I saw something lying on one of the small occasional tables that made me pause.

It was Margot's evening bag: a pretty thing in black suede in the form of a scallop shell. I picked it up, idly pushed open the gold clasp and opened the bag. In it was a built-in powder compact in gold. A silk pocket contained a handkerchief. I pushed the handkerchief aside and saw beneath it a match folder in red water-silk.

For a long moment I stared at it, then I picked it out, set down the bag and turned the fold over between my fingers.

I opened it. There were only thirteen matches: the others had been torn out of the folder. Bending the matches back I saw a row of numerals printed on the back of them. The numerals ran from C451148 to C451160.

I knew then this was the match folder I had found in Sheppey's suitcase; the one I had hidden under the carpet in my hotel bedroom; the one that had been stolen.

As I stared at it, the telephone bell began to ring, making a loud, strident sound in the silent bungalow.

I slid the folder into my pocket and walked over to the telephone and picked up the receiver.

"Hello, yes?" I said, fairly certain who was calling.

"Is that you, Lew?"

Margot's voice. She sounded a little out of breath.

"Hello again: don't tell me: I know. You've lost something?"

"My bag. Did you find it?"

"It's right here on one of the tables."

"Oh, good. I didn't know if I had left it at the club or in your car. I'm always leaving things in places. I'll pick it up tomorrow morning unless you are passing and can leave it for me. Could you?"

"That's all right. I'll leave it some time during the morning."

"Thank you, darling." There was a pause, then she said, "Lew ..."

"I'm still with you."

"I'm thinking of you."

I put my hand in my pocket and fingered the folder.

"I'm thinking of you too."

"Good night, Lew."

"Good night, beautiful."

I waited until I heard her hang up before I replaced the receiver.

III

I awoke around ten o'clock the following morning. For some minutes I lay in the big double bed, staring up at the patterns made by the sun on the ceiling. Then I ran my fingers through my hair, yawned, threw off the sheet and got out of bed.

A long, cold shower brought me fully awake.

Wearing only my pyjamas, I went into the kitchen and made some coffee. When it was made, I carried it out and drank it on the terrace.

From where I sat I could see the building that housed the School of Ceramics perched on its rocky peninsula: a low rambling building that had a blue-tiled roof and white walls.

I decided as soon as I was dressed I'd go out there and mix with the tourists and see what there was to see.

When I had finished the coffee, I returned to my bedroom, put on a pair of swimming trunks and then went down to the sea. I spent half an hour proving to myself that I was still as husky and athletic as I liked to think I was. After I had swum out about a quarter of a mile, I found myself getting slightly short of breath, so I turned around and made for the shore, with a longer stroke and at a slower speed.

I went back to the bungalow, dried off, put on a pair of slacks and an open-neck shirt, then, locking up the bungalow, I got in the Buick and set course for Arrow Point.

By then the time was twenty minutes past eleven. If there were going to be tourists, this was the time when they would begin their visit.

I had to get back on to the promenade, and after a five minute drive, I came upon a branch road which had a sign that said: *This way for the School of Ceramics: the Treasure House of Original Design.*

As I turned on to the road I saw in my driving mirror a big blue-and-white rubber-neck bus loaded with eager beavers with the usual brick-red faces and awful hats and making the usual over-happy noises.

I pulled to one side and let the rubber-neck get ahead of me. It went past with a roar and a stream of dust that kept with me all the way up the long road and through the double gates leading to the blue-tiled building.

There were already six cars in the parking lot as I pulled up. An elderly man wearing a white coat, the pocket of which had a design of two fishes floating in a wine-red sea on it, came over and gave me a parking ticket.

"One dollar," he said with an apologetic smirk as if he knew it was robbery, but there was nothing he could do about it.

"I bet they hate anyone who has the strength to walk," I said, giving him the dollar.

He said no one ever walked.

I was killing time by talking to him. I wanted the bunch from the bus to get themselves sorted out. I planned to walk in with them.

By the time I had crossed the parking lot, they had got out of the bus and were moving towards the entrance to the building. I tagged along with them.

The courier, a busy, worried little man, bought tickets at the door and shepherded his flock through a turnstile into a big hall. I paid out another dollar, was given a ticket by a hard-eyed man in a white coat with the fish symbol showing on his pocket.

He told me if I bought anything I'd get a refund on my ticket.

"Heads you win, tails I lose," I said.

He lifted his shoulders.

"If you knew the number of jerks that come in here out of the sun before we began to charge them entrance and never bought a damn thing, you'd be surprised."

I could see his point.

I went through the turnstile, and was in time to join up with the last straggler as he moved after his party into a big room crammed with pottery of all shapes, sizes, colours and designs. The overall effect was pretty horrible.

The room was around fifty feet long and twenty feet wide. On each side were long low counters which held more specimens of pottery. Girls, wearing white coats with the fish symbols on the pockets, stood behind the counters. They watched the bunch come in with bored eyes. I found myself thinking that Thelma Cousins had probably stood behind one of these counters and had probably watched a similar bunch of tourists with the same bored look only a few days ago.

There were about twenty girls in the big room, all dressed alike, all shapes and sizes, all ready to sell something the moment anyone paused or was unwise enough to handle the ugly specimens of pottery on show.

At the far end of the room was an open doorway across which hung a wine-red curtain. A hard-faced blonde sat on the chair by the curtain, her legs crossed, her hands folded in her lap. She looked as if she had been sitting like that for a long time.

I tagged along in the rear of the tourists, pausing when they paused, shuffling on when they shuffled on. It surprised me the amount of stuff they bought: the prices were high and the stuff was pure junk.

I kept my eye on the curtained doorway. I had an idea that it was beyond that curtain the real business was done. A fat old woman, her wrinkled fingers loaded with diamond rings, carrying a wheezing Pekinese, suddenly came out from behind the curtain. She nodded to the hard-faced blonde, who gave her an indifferent stare. The old woman walked down the centre aisle and went out. Through one of the big windows I saw her heading for a Cadillac where a chauffeur was waiting.

I caught the eye of one of the girls behind one of the long counters: a pretty little thing with a pert nose and a cheeky expression.

"Haven't you anything better than this junk?" I asked. "I'm looking for a wedding present."

"Isn't there anything you like here?" she asked, and tried to look surprised.

"Take a look yourself," I said. "Is there anything here you'd want as a wedding present?"

She cast her eye around the room, then she pulled a little face.

"You could be right. Will you wait a moment?"

She left the counter and went over to the hard-faced blonde and spoke to her. The blonde looked me over. She didn't appear to be impressed. I had no diamond rings, nor a Pekinese. I was just another jerk on vacation.

The girl I had spoken to came over to me.

"Miss Maddox will look after you," she said, and indicated the hard-faced blonde.

As I moved over to her, she stood up. She had one of those hippy, bosomy figures you see in the nylon ads, but rarely in real life.

"Was there something?" she asked in a bored voice, her eyes running over me and not thinking much of what they saw.

"I'm looking for a wedding present," I said. "You don't call this muck a treasure house of original design, do you?"

She lifted her plucked eyebrows.

"We have other designs, but they come a little pricey."

"They do? Well, you only get married once in a while. Let me see them."

She drew aside the curtain.

"Please go in."

I moved past her, through the doorway into a slightly smaller room. There were only about sixty specimens of Mr Hahn's art on show there; each had its own stand and was shown off to its best advantage. A quick look told me that this must be the stuff Margot had raved about. It was unlike the junk in the other room as crystal is unlike a diamond.

Miss Maddox flicked long fingers at the exhibits.

"Perhaps something like these?"

"Better," I said, looking around. There was another curtain covering another doorway at the far end of the room with a redhead guarding it. "Can I wander around?"

Miss Maddox took a few steps away from me and rested her elegant hips against one of the counters. Her bored eyes told me I wasn't kidding her for one moment.

The exhibits in this room were certainly good. A bronze statue of a naked girl about ten inches high, with her hands covering her breasts, held me entranced. I could feel life flowing out of her. It wouldn't have surprised me if she had suddenly jumped off the pedestal on which she stood and had run out of the room.

"That's nice," I said to Miss Maddox. "What's it worth?"

"Two thousand dollars," she told me in that indifferent voice a car salesman will tell you the price of a Rolls.

"As much as that? It's a little high for me."

A small sneer came and went, and she moved a few more paces away from me.

The curtain of the doorway through which I had come moved aside and a fat, white-faced man came sliding in. He was wearing white flannel trousers, a natty blazer with an elaborate crest on its pocket and a six-inch cigar between his fat, white fingers.

I immediately recognized him.

It was the man Cordez had called Donaghue: the man who had handed over a thousand dollars for two match folders the previous night when I had been looking through Cordez's window.

10

I moved across the room and came to rest before the model of a matador with his cape extended and his sword in his hand. I moved slowly around it while I watched Donaghue out of the corner of my eye as he came to an abrupt stop at the sight of me.

He was as nervous as a flustered hen. He took two quick steps back towards the doorway through which he had come, changed his mind and came forward with a little rush, paused again to look at me, then took three steps sideways. I could see he couldn't make up his mind whether to run or stay.

I said to Miss Maddox, "Would this item be a little less expensive?"

"That is three thousand, five hundred dollars," she said, not even bothering to look at me.

Donaghue started off across the room towards the redhead, who watched him come, her face expressionless.

I moved on to a group of children that was even better than the matador.

Donaghue paused beside the redhead, fumbled in his pocket, took something from it and showed it to her. I saw something small and red in his hand. I didn't have to be a detective to guess it was a Musketeer Club match folder.

The redhead pulled aside the curtain and Donaghue disappeared through the doorway. I caught a glimpse of a passage before the curtain fell into place.

I began to move around the room, looking for something that was small and modest, but there wasn't anything. I felt the blonde and the redhead were watching me. I finally came to rest before a model of a poodle, again executed with the same brilliance of the other models. This put me near the curtained door where the redhead was sitting. I took my time while I examined the poodle.

After five minutes or so, Miss Maddox said, with an edge to her voice, "That is seventeen hundred dollars."

"As cheap as that?" I said, smiling at her. "It's almost alive, isn't it? I must think about it. Seventeen hundred dollars: almost giving it away, isn't it?"

She pursed her lips and stared at me, her eyes now plainly hostile.

The curtain pulled aside and Donaghue slipped out. He gave me a startled stare, his eyes bulging, then he scuttled across the floor and out through the other doorway.

I decided I couldn't continue to hang around like a heist man casing a joint. I told myself I'd better see what the match folder I had found in Margot's bag would buy me. I hoped it wouldn't buy me trouble.

I looked over at the redhead and caught her staring at me. I gave her a toothy smile and advanced on her.

She watched me come suspiciously. I dipped my fingers into my trousers pocket and let her see the match folder. Her mouth tightened, and she looked over at Miss Maddox with an exasperated expression on her face as she leaned forward and pulled the curtain aside.

"Thanks," I said. "I just wanted to be sure no one was watching me."

Her blank, frozen stare told me I had said the wrong thing, but as she still held the curtain aside I didn't try to make matters worse or better. I stepped through the doorway and entered a long passage, lit by strip lighting and decorated in wine-red and blue.

I moved cautiously down the passage. The something inside me that works overtime when I am heading for trouble began to nudge me, starting an alarm bell going in my mind. I wished now I had brought a gun with me.

At the end of the passage, facing me, was a door. It had a cut-away panel in it which was closed, a shelf and a bell push. On the shelf was one of Marcus Hahn's lesser works: a large pink-and-green earthenware bowl.

Moving soundlessly on my crêpe soles I reached the door and peered into the bowl. Lying in the bottom of it were about a dozen red paper matches. They were the companions of the matches I had in my folder. Each one of them had a row of ciphers printed on them; each one had been torn from a match folder and all the heads had been burned. The matches had been struck alight, and then immediately extinguished.

I felt this was probably an important discovery if I knew what it meant. I looked over my shoulder. At the far end of the passage the curtain hung in place: neither the redhead nor Miss Maddox were peeping at me.

I decided not to press my luck further. I was tempted to ring the bell on the door to see what happened, but as I wasn't equipped for trouble at this moment, I decided against it. At least I had found out that there was a definite hook-up between the Musketeer Club and Marcus Hahn's so-called Treasure House. People paid out big money for a folder of matches to Cordez, then came here and parted with a match at a time: for what?

I turned around and went very quietly back down the passage. I pulled aside the curtain and stepped out, trying to look as flustered and as guilty as Donaghue had done.

The redhead was using a buffer on her nails. She didn't bother to look up as I passed her. I walked into the outer room.

The party of tourists were through spending their money now. They were being herded towards the exit, most of them carrying neatly packed parcels.

I tagged along on their heels, and as soon as I had passed through the turnstile, I side-stepped them and walked over to where I had left the Buick.

Leaving the School of Ceramics, I drove fast along the promenade to the Franklyn Arms. I took Margot's bag from the glove compartment, put the match folder in it, then, leaving the car, I entered the lobby of the apartment block.

I asked the reception clerk to send my name up to Margot, asking her to see me. After he had called her, he told me she would meet me in the bar in five minutes. He showed me where the bar was and I went in and sat down at a corner table.

It was a good ten minutes before Margot appeared. By then the time was a quarter past twelve. The bar was fairly full, but there was no one sitting close to my table.

She came towards me. She was wearing a short beach coat over a swimsuit and sandals. Her hair was tied back with red ribbon and she carried her big beach bag.

Most of the men turned and stared at her. She was worth staring at: I stared myself.

I got up as she reached the table and pulled out a chair for her.

"I can't stay more than ten minutes, Lew," she said, smiling at me. "I have a lunch date the other side of the town."

I asked her what she would drink and she said a gin gimlet. I had one too.

"I'd like to tell you, you look wonderful," I said as soon as the waiter had gone away. "I expect you get tired of being told that."

She laughed.

"It depends who says it. Did you bring my bag?"

I had it lying on a chair beside me and I lifted it into sight and laid it on the table.

"I'll claim the reward for it later," I said.

Her eyes sparkled.

"And I'll willingly pay the reward. Thank you. Lew. I'm terribly careless with my things." She picked up the bag and began to put it in her beach bag.

"Wait a moment. You'd better check to see there's nothing missing."

She looked inquiringly at me.

"What could be missing?"

Her mauve black eyes were entirely without guile and that pleased me.

"Margot, there's a folder of matches in that bag that interests me."

"Is there?" She looked surprised. "A folder of matches? Why does it interest you?" She opened the bag, pushed aside the handkerchief and took out the match folder. "You mean this?"

"Yes. Where did you get it from?"

"I have no idea. I didn't even know it was in here. Why, Lew? Why so much interest?"

"I have reason to know that's the folder I found in Sheppey's luggage. Later someone ransacked my room, found it and substituted another folder for it. Now it turns up in your bag."

"Are you quite sure it's the same folder? I've seen dozens like this in the club."

"Look at it. On the back of the matches you'll find a row of numbers. They are the same numbers that were on the matches in Sheppey's folder."

She opened the folder and bent back the matches and frowned at the numbers.

"It's odd, isn't it? Perhaps all the matches in all the folders have these numbers on them."

"They haven't. I checked that. Where did you get that folder from?"

"I must have got it from the club last night. I was dining there." She thought for a moment, frowning. "Yes, that's right. I remember I had forgotten to bring my lighter with me. I never use matches unless I forget my lighter. I suppose I must have picked up the folder from the tray on the hat-check counter."

I shook my head.

"You didn't do that. This is a special folder, Margot. Someone committed a murder for it. It wouldn't be in any tray."

She was beginning to look worried.

"I don't know then. Unless I asked someone for a light and they gave me the folder."

"I can't imagine anyone doing that. Who did you dine with?"

"There was a party: there were five people and myself. Bridgette and Thrisby, a man called Donaghue, Harry Lucas, who I play tennis with sometimes, and Doris Little, a friend of mine."

"Any of these people could have put the match folder absent-mindedly on the table and you could have picked it up?"

"I suppose so. I just can't remember picking it up, but, of course, it's the sort of thing one could do without thinking."

"I don't like it a lot. This folder is worth money. I can't imagine anyone laying it on the table for you to pick up."

"They might have been under the impression it was an ordinary match folder. The waiters leave them on every table."

"Maybe. Well, okay. I want the folder, Margot. I'll have to show it to Lieutenant Rankin."

Her eyes widened.

"But, Lew, if you do that you'll mix me up in this," she said. "I mustn't get mixed up with the police, darling. Daddy would be livid."

"I'll have to tell Rankin. He'll want to know where I got it from. You don't have to worry. He's far too scared of your father to involve you."

"But, darling, suppose he does? You mustn't do it. Don't you see that? He'll want to know how you found the folder in my bag. You're not going to tell him what happened last night for heaven's sake!"

I thought for a moment.

"Okay, I'll handle it myself. I'll go and talk to Thrisby before I see Rankin. Maybe I can get a line on it from Thrisby."

She handed me the match folder.

"Please don't involve me, Lew. If the newspapers thought I was mixed up in this ..."

I patted her hand.

"Relax. I'll keep you out of it. Between now and the next time I see you, will you think very hard and try to remember how you did get hold of the folder? If you do remember, will you call me, Margot? It's important."

"Of course." She looked at her watch. "I must fly. I'm late already." She got to her feet. "Are you going to see Thrisby now?"

"I think so. It might be a good time to catch him in."

"You know how to get there? Take Franklyn Boulevard, go right to the top and turn right on to the mountain road. It's about five miles up. You'll see a signpost saying The Crest." She gave me her small smile. "I'll be seeing you soon, Lew."

"You bet."

I watched her hurry across the bar lounge, and mine weren't the only eyes that stared after her. Her long brown legs were the focal point of every male eye in the bar.

I snapped my fingers at the waiter and, after the inevitable wait, he came over and gave me the check. I paid, waited for my change, then got up and went out into the sunshine where the Buick stood.

I drove up Franklyn Boulevard, not hurrying and enjoying the hot sunshine while my mind turned over the bits and pieces of information I had collected. At the moment the problem was in a state of flux. It was like when you begin to work out the bits and pieces of a jigsaw puzzle. At the moment there was no picture, but I did have a number of pieces that I felt pretty sure would make up into a picture reasonably soon.

At the top of the wide boulevard I turned right and came immediately to a very steep mountain road. A mile further on I came to a signpost which pointed encouragingly upwards and said, "The Crest".

Halfway up the road which had climbed steeply all the way, I pulled into a lay-by to look at the view.

Far below me I could see St. Raphael City. To my right was the big Casino, the miles of glittering sands, the palm trees, the luxury hotels and the swarms of people on the beach. I could see Creedy's estate with the blur of red, yellow and white of the massed rose beds, and along the drive I could see a Rolls moving swiftly towards the barrier where two ant-like figures stood guard.

My eyes shifted to the snake-back road below me: the road on which I had come up, leading from Franklyn Boulevard.

In the mid-morning heat of the sun the white road was deserted of traffic. I seemed to be the only one using the road, and it gave me a feeling of isolation to be up here, looking down at this rich, gangster-ridden town.

I hunched my shoulders, then started the engine, shifted into drive and continued on my way up the twisting road.

II

The White Château was at the end of a side road that cut sharply away from the mountain road and went down three hundred yards to an open tarmac just wide enough for a car to turn. There was a freshly painted sign at the head of the road announcing this was a private road and parking was forbidden.

There was a convertible Cadillac standing on the tarmac; a glossy thing of pale blue with dark blue nylon upholstery and glittering chromium. I parked the Buick beside it, got out and looked towards the house. It was screened by flowering shrubs and palm trees. I could just see the overhanging roof of green tiles but no more.

I walked to the wooden gate on which was written the name of the house. I pushed open the gate and walked up a path bordered on either side by a neatly clipped hedge, then I came to a stretch of lawn and to the house.

It was a small, chalet type of building with green shutters, white walls, a wide verandah, window-boxes with begonias in them under each window and a bright creeper climbing over the front entrance with a red-and-white, bell-shaped flower I had never seen before.

French doors stood open on to the verandah. A Siamese cat lay in the sun on the balustrade of the terrace. It lifted its head and its blue eyes stared without interest in my direction, then it laid its head once more on the hot stone and went off into its Valhalla of dreams.

I walked across the lawn and up on to the verandah. The front door was to my left: a green, neat affair with chromium fitments and a pull-down bell.

As I moved towards it, a man's voice, coming from the open French doors said, "Well, if you don't want a drink, I do."

I paused.

"For heaven's sake, don't start drinking now, Jacques," a woman said. "I want to talk to you."

"And that, darling, is exactly why I must have a drink. Do you imagine I can sit here listening to you unless I do have a drink? Be reasonable, please."

"You're a bit of a swine, Jacques."

The note in the woman's voice was ugly to hear. I moved quietly along the hot verandah and paused just outside the French doors.

"I suppose I could be called that, but it shouldn't bother you, my pet," the man said lightly. "You should be used to swine by now, surely."

The sound of a siphon hissing told me he was mixing a drink. I moved another few inches closer and that allowed me to get a sight of the room.

It seemed, from where I stood, the room was over large. There was a pale blue fitted carpet on the floor and the furniture was of light oak. There were plenty of lounging chairs and two enormous settees.

Sitting in one of the lounging chairs was a woman of around thirty-six or seven. She had silky hair dyed a warm apricot colour, and she was beautiful in the way movie stars are beautiful without character in the face that gives interest. She was wearing a bikini swimsuit that revealed a lot of sun-tanned flesh, just going a little soft and losing its first elasticity of youth. She was stacked well enough, but it wasn't the kind of body that made me want to look twice: maybe ten years ago it would have done, but not now.

She was wearing openwork sandals and her toenails were painted silver. She wore white coral earrings and a white coral choker around her sun-tanned throat.

I didn't have to guess who she was. I immediately recognized her. This would be Bridgette Creedy, ex-movie actress, Lee Creedy's wife.

Jacques Thrisby moved into sight. He was just what I expected him to be. A big hunk of glamorous beef, heavily sun-tanned with dark curly hair, blue eyes, a hairline moustache and a handsome face. He was wearing a white singlet, dark red shorts and sandals. In his right hand he carried a highball and between his full, sensual lips hung a cigarette.

"Where were you last night, Jacques?" Bridgette asked, looking at him, her face set and hostile.

"My dear pet, how many more times? I told you: I was right here watching the fights on TV."

"I waited two hours for you at the club."

"I know. You've already said that at least five times. I've said I'm sorry. Do you want me to pour ashes on my head? Our date wasn't definite. I simply forgot."

"Our date was definite, Jacques. I telephoned you and you said you would be there."

He drank from his glass and put the glass down on an occasional table.

"Yes, you are quite right. You did telephone and I still forgot. I'm still sorry." He yawned, putting his hand before his mouth. "Must we go over all this again?"

"You weren't watching the fights, Jacques. I telephoned here and there was no answer."

"I don't always answer the telephone, Bridgette, darling. It's so easy for some bore to trap me on the telephone. I heard the bell and I didn't answer it."

Her nostrils flared out.

"Am I a bore then?"

He smiled.

"You mustn't jump to conclusions. You know as well as I do how easy it is for some bore to call up and trap you."

"That doesn't answer the question."

He studied her, his smile remaining fixed, a meaningless thing.

"You are being a bore right now, darling," he said at last. "I have told you what happened last night. I was here watching the fights. I heard the telephone bell ring. I ignored it, and when the fights were over, I went to bed. I just forgot our date. And I'm very, very, very sorry."

She sat up abruptly in her chair: her eyes smouldering.

"You're lying! You weren't here! I came out here and found the place in darkness and your car wasn't in the garage. How dare you lie to me! What were you doing?"

His fixed smile suddenly went away and his face hardened. He was no longer the handsome playboy. The smooth veneer of his polish suddenly slid off him, showing the hard, unscrupulous man that lay below the surface.

"So you came out here, did you? Just how cheap are you going to make yourself, my pet? First, you hire a private dick to watch me, then when he gets murdered, you do your own spying. I've had enough of this. Let's cut it out, shall we? I'm fed to the teeth if I may say so with all of it."

She placed her silver-tipped fingers on her bare knees and squeezed. Her long thin fingers looked like claws.

"Who was the woman?"

He finished his drink and stubbed out his cigarette.

"I guess that will be all for today," he said. "I've things to do even if you haven't. So let's break it up, shall we?"

"Was it Margot?" The hate in her voice was ugly to hear. "Have you started with her again?"

"Just because Margot is better looking than you and at least ten years younger, it doesn't follow she means anything to me," he said. "Between you and me, I find the Creedy women a drug on the market right now." His smile widened. "If the truth must be told they are both over-sexed, too possessive and utter bores. Now, would you mind very much running along, my pet? I have a lunch date."

"It was Margot, wasn't it? She's still in love with you, isn't she? She's determined to take you away from me," Bridgette said, her voice shaking.

"Look, don't let's have a scene," Thrisby said, and he moved out of my view. I heard the sound of a cork being twisted from a bottle. "Will you please go away now, Bridgette?"

"I'm not going until I know who the woman is you were with last night!"

"All right. If you must know she was a little blonde, very cute and young and fresh, I found on the promenade who happened to be lonely. You should know by now, Bridgette, that lonely women are utterly irresistible to me." He came back into view with another highball in his hand, his smooth veneer back in place. "So out of the kindness of my heart I had to console her, and I was agreeably surprised by her enthusiastic response."

"You rotten swine!" Bridgette said, her voice harsh. Her face had suddenly become pinched-looking and her glittering eyes seemed to have sunk into their sockets. "You're lying! It was Margot!"

"Well, if you won't go, then I must," Thrisby said, and smiled. "Never let it be said I throw my ex-mistresses out of my house. Make yourself at home, my pet. Don't drink too much of my liquor. I hope I find you gone when I come back."

"So we're through for good, is that it?" Bridgette asked.

"My dear, that is really brilliant of you. I've been saying that for the past ten minutes, and now you tell me. Yes, Bridgette, we're through for good. We've both had a lot of fun, and now it is better for us to go our ways."

She leaned back in her chair: her expression wasn't pleasant to see. She seemed to have grown older during the past minutes: her near nakedness now was an embarrassment.

"All right, if we're going to part for good, Jacques, you'd better settle up your debts," she said in a cold, flat voice. "You haven't forgotten you owe me some money, have you? Thirteen thousand dollars to be exact."

His smile widened.

"Is it as much as that?" He picked up his glass, looked into it with lifted eyebrows and drank a little of the whisky. "I suppose you have it all written down in a leather-bound book?"

"I have kept an account. I want the money."

"I dare say you do. Your elderly husband isn't over generous, is he? I'm afraid you will have to wait for it. I haven't got thirteen thousand dollars: nothing like it. It has

179

cost quite a lot to take you around and amuse you. I'll let you have it when I can, but you must make up your mind to the dismal fact that it will be a long, long wait."

"I want it now," she said tonelessly.

"So sorry. Well, I must be running along. Shall I see you to your car?"

"I said I want the money now," she said, raising her voice.

"Well, of course, if you insist, then you will have to sue me." His smile broadened. "I'm quite sure your husband will advise you how best to set about it. Of course, he'll probably divorce you when he hears that you have given me so much money. After all, he is a man of the world, and he will realize that a man like me wouldn't get money out of you unless I gave something in return. But never mind, you are possibly as tired of him, my beautiful pet, as I am of you."

She studied him for a long moment. There was an expression in her eyes that would have worried me, but it didn't seem to worry him.

"I don't think you are fit to live," she said finally. "I must have been out of my mind to have ever had anything to do with you."

"I wouldn't put it as strongly as that," he returned. "You were an unsatisfied woman and I supplied your need. It's something you must expect to pay for. We have had fun, now it's time for us to part. Be sensible, Bridgette; don't let's part on an unpleasant note. There are plenty of other guys as good-looking as I am, and as big and as strong. You won't have any trouble in finding someone to replace me. Think of the fun you will have breaking in a new lover as you tried to break me in. I never did quite toe the line as you wanted, did I? But, never mind, you might find someone who will. In a few weeks you will have forgotten all about me."

She stared at him for a long moment, then she reached down by her side and lifted into view a big beach bag that was a little like the one Margot carried around with her. She opened it and began to hunt around in it, reminding me of the way Margot had hunted around in her bag.

Thrisby watched her, his eyebrows lifted, his fixed smile in place.

She looked up, her hand still out of sight in the bag and said, "You really mean this, Jacques? We really are through?"

He ran his fingers through his hair in a movement of exasperation.

"Yes," he said, his voice suddenly harsh, "how many more times do I have to tell you?"

"We don't ever meet again?" she said, still watching him, her eyes glittering.

"All right, if you want it the hard way, you can have it," he said, leaning forward to glare at her. "Get the hell out of here. I'm sick to death of the sight of you! Now get out or I'll damn well throw you out!"

She smiled at him, a tight, spine-chilling grimace.

Then she said, "I'm going to kill you, Jacques. If I'm not having you, no one else is."

From the bag she pulled out a .38 automatic and pointed it at him.

11

It was suddenly very quiet on the verandah and the sun felt over hot. Somewhere in the distance I could hear the sound of the sea breaking on the shore: a whisper of sound that seemed loud in the silence around me.

There was also a sudden silence in the big lounge. I looked at Thrisby, who was standing motionless, staring at the gun, his eyes startled, his smile sliding from his face.

Bridgette slowly stood up. With the gun in her hand, she looked incongruous in the skimpy bikini swimsuit. Her face was the colour of marble under her tan and her skin had a mottled look. Her silver-tipped finger was curled around the trigger of the gun.

"Yes, Jacques," she said softly. "I'm going to kill you. I've suffered enough from you: now it's your turn to share a little of the hell you've given me."

"Don't be a mad fool," Thrisby said, speaking each word slowly and breathlessly. "Put that gun down. It won't get you anywhere. The police will arrest you. Everyone knows I'm your lover. The first person they will think of is you."

"Do you think I care? Do you think I'll want to go on living after I've killed you, Jacques? Oh, no. When I have shot you, I'm going to shoot myself. That's how I feel about it. I'm not afraid to die as you are."

He passed his tongue over his lips.

"Put the gun down, Bridgette, and let's talk about this. Maybe I've been a little hasty. We could pick up the threads. I was only fooling when I said ..."

"You miserable, rotten coward," she said contemptuously. "I thought that's how you would talk once I had you cornered. It's too late now. I have as much mercy for you as you've had for me."

Very slowly he began to back away, his eyes starting out of his head, his face beginning to sweat. Equally slowly, she moved forward, stalking him across the big lounge.

Softly I stepped through the French doors into the lounge.

Thrisby, who was facing her, saw me at once. She had her back to me. He lifted his hands and half-turned away. I could see he was terrified that I might startle her into shooting him. I jumped forward, my hand slamming down on her wrist, forcing the gun to point to the floor.

The gun went off with a bang that rattled the windows and the slug made a neat hole in the fitted carpet.

I twisted the gun out of her hand as she spun around, her green eyes opening wide. For a long moment she stared at me, her face old, drawn and frightened. Then she moved to one side, walked past me, snatched up her beach bag and ran out on to the terrace.

Thrisby sat down abruptly on the settee. He hid his face in his hands.

I laid the gun on one of the cocktail tables, took out my handkerchief and wiped off my face and wrists.

The sound of a car starting up made a loud noise in the silence of the lounge.

For a long moment I didn't say anything. I just stood looking at Thrisby.

"I doubt if she was going to kill you," I said mildly. "She was probably only going to put a bullet in your leg."

He made a tremendous effort to get hold of himself and he stood up abruptly, his mouth working, his eyes still dark with fright.

"These damned neurotics," he said. "How the hell did she get hold of that gun?"

"Very often it's the only way a woman can level the score," I said. "Men are getting themselves shot every day all over the world by women who haven't any other way of coping with certain situations. You should have thought of that before you planned to ditch her."

He stared at me.

"Who are you and where did you spring from?" he demanded.

I dug out one of my business cards and offered it to him. He peered at it, not taking it. I was pretty sure he didn't want me to see how badly his hands were shaking.

"Well, I'll be damned!" he said, after he had read what was on the card. "The Star Agency ... that's the agency the fellow who ..." He stopped abruptly, moved away from me, an alarmed, puzzled expression in his eyes.

"That's right," I said. "Sheppey was my partner."

"Is she employing you to watch me?" he asked, not looking at me.

"No. I just happened along. I wanted to talk to you."

He took out a handkerchief, mopped his face, then carried his glass over to the bar.

"Have a drink?"

"Thanks, I think I will."

He gulped down the drink left in his glass, then made two very strong highballs, carried them over to a table, set them down and dropped into a lounging chair. He took a cigarette from an ebony box, set fire to it and dragged smoke down into his lungs.

"She had me rattled for a moment. Did you see the expression in her eyes? She meant to kill me," he said, picked up his drink and took a long pull. "If you hadn't walked in when you did ..." He let it hang, while he grimaced.

"Oh, I don't know. She probably only intended to scare you," I said, knowing she meant to kill him. "You must lead quite an eventful life."

He smiled crookedly.

"That's taught me a lesson: no more middle-aged neurotics for me. I'm going to stick to the young ones in future. They don't take it so hard." He leaned forward to stare at the .38 lying on the table where I had put it. "Now where do you imagine she got this from?"

"Anyone can get a gun these days." I scooped up the gun and shoved it into my hip pocket. "Is that right she hired Sheppey to watch you?"

His face suddenly became expressionless.

"Did she? I wouldn't know. I wouldn't put it past her to hire a flock of dicks to watch me. She looked on me as her special possession."

"Quite an expensive one if you owe her thirteen thousand bucks."

He shrugged his broad shoulders.

"She's crazy. I didn't borrow anything like that amount from her. I dare say during the six months we've been around together it cost her something, but I was spending it on her, and that's not quite the same thing as owing it to her, is it?"

"You said to her she had hired a private dick to watch you. That was Sheppey, wasn't it?"

"Did I say that? I tell you I don't know who it was."

"If you're bothered about getting mixed up with the police you can relax," I said. "I'm carrying out my own investigation. You tell me what I want to know and I'll keep it away from the police."

He thought for a long moment then asked, "Just what do you want to know?"

"Did Mrs Creedy hire Sheppey to watch you?"

He hesitated.

"This isn't going to get me a cop in my lap?"

"No."

"Well, okay. Yes, she did."

"Why?"

"Because she imagined I was running around with her step-daughter."

"Were you?"

"Good grief, no! I'd had enough of her months ago."

I took a pull at my glass, then I lit a cigarette.

"Then who was the girl you were running around with?" I asked, staring at him.

He grinned. By now he had got his nerve back, and also he was getting a little drunk.

"That would be telling. Just a girl."

"Did Sheppey get on to her?"

Thrisby nodded.

"Yeah; he told Bridgette. She went along and tried to put the fear of God into her."

"Did she succeed?"

"She must have done. I didn't see her again."

"Then what happened?"

"I let Bridgette put the ring back in my nose and lead me around again. Then a couple of nights ago I decided I'd had more than enough and the rest you know."

I had a feeling I was only getting half the truth, certainly not all of it.

"This is important, Thrisby," I said. "Was this girl Sheppey was watching Thelma Cousins?"

I saw his eyes flicker as my words gave him a stab of surprise.

"Look, brother. I'm not getting snarled up in any police inquiries. I've told you: she was just a girl."

"You'll have to do better than that," I said. "You've already said too much. Was she Thelma Cousins?"

"Okay, okay, so she was," he said impatiently. "Now are you happy?"

I stared at him, feeling a little prickle of excitement run through me. At last I was really getting somewhere.

"From what I've been told, she never went around with men."

He grinned.

"Those are the easy ones. When they fall, they fall hard. I had her eating out of my hand in a couple of days. We were all set for the big night when your pal Sheppey barged in."

"How did you meet her?"

"At the pottery place. Bridgette took me there and I spotted this little thing. I saw she had fallen for me and when a girl falls for me I like to be obliging."

He was beginning to sicken me, and it was only with an effort I kept from showing it.

"How did you find out Sheppey was watching you two?" I asked.

"Thelma told me. She called me up and said he'd been around to her place and had warned her to keep clear of me. I guessed Bridgette had slicked him on to me so I told Thelma we'd better pack it up. I knew Bridgette would start trouble if I didn't give the girl up."

"I thought you said Bridgette went to see her?"

He lit a cigarette.

"She went to see her after Sheppey had seen her. At least that's what she told me."

I had liked it fairly well up to now, but I began not to like it. There was something wrong with this story. I couldn't quite put my finger on it, but I had a growing feeling I wasn't getting all the truth.

"Who killed them, Thrisby?" I asked, watching him.

"I wouldn't know," he said, his eyes meeting mine. "I've been wondering why she went with Sheppey to that bathing cabin. All I can think of is she took up with him after I had dropped her."

That was possible, I thought. Sheppey had a way with women. If this girl had imagined she was going to have her first affair with Thrisby and then had been let down, she might well have rebounded into Sheppey's arms.

"You have no idea who killed her?"

He hesitated, then said, "Well, I've thought about it. It seems to me it's possible the killer wasn't after Sheppey, but after the girl. Sheppey might have tried to protect her and got killed instead of her. That would explain why she had left her clothes there. She probably was so scared she bolted for her life."

"Then why didn't she tell the police?"

"Well, ask yourself. She was a religious kid: it says so in the newspapers. How was she going to explain what she was doing with a man in a bathing cabin meant for a married couple? I think she bolted down to the sand dunes and hid there. The killer, after fixing Sheppey, went after her, caught her and took her some place. Later she was killed and her body brought back to the cabin. That's my idea, but I could be wrong."

"And you think Bridgette killed Sheppey and the girl?" I asked.

He stiffened, frowning at me.

"I didn't say that. I can't see Bridgette sticking an ice pick into Sheppey, can you?"

I thought about it and decided I couldn't either.

"But she could have hired someone to do it: one of her husband's thugs: Hertz, for instance."

Thrisby grimaced.

"That thug! Yes, she could have done that. It wouldn't surprise me if she doesn't slick him on to me. That would be her idea of levelling scores." He began to look worried. "Maybe I'd better get out of this town. It might not be safe to stay here."

Then I had a sudden idea.

I took a cigarette from my pack, put it between my lips, then took from my hip pocket the Musketeer Club match folder. I held it between my fingers so he could see it as I said, "What do you know about Hertz?" I bent one of the matches, tore it out of the folder and laid the head against the scraper.

I didn't take my eyes off him.

His reaction was immediate. He made a movement as if to stop me lighting the match, but checked it. His face was suddenly tense and his eyes stared fixedly at the folder.

I struck the match, lit my cigarette, flicked the flame out and laid the match in the ashtray, being careful to lay it cipher side up.

His eyes went to the row of ciphers and he drew in a quick, sharp breath.

"Anything wrong?" I asked, slipping the match folder into my hip pocket.

He got hold of himself.

"No. I – I didn't know you were a member of the Musketeer Club."

"I'm not. You mean the match folder? Just something I picked up."

"I see." He took out his handkerchief and wiped his face. "Well, I've got to be moving. I have a lunch date." And he stood up.

"You didn't answer my question. What do you know about Hertz?"

"Only that Creedy uses him for his rough stuff. I don't know a thing about him except that. Well, thanks for walking in when you did. I've really got to be going. Do you mind seeing yourself out? I'm late as it is."

"That's okay." I got to my feet. "I'll be seeing you."

Nodding to him, I crossed the lounge and went through the French doors on to the verandah.

The jigsaw pieces were beginning to fall into shape, I thought, as I started across the verandah.

The Siamese cat raised its head to stare at me. I paused to tickle its tummy. Its paw with the claws out made a quick dab at my hand, but I got it out of reach just in time.

"Take it easy," I said to the cat. "You don't have to be neurotic too."

I set off across the lawn, aware that Thrisby was watching me from behind the curtains.

II

I drove slowly back to St Raphael City, my mind busy. There now seemed a reasonable possibility that I had two separate investigations on my hands: Sheppey's murder and the mystery of the match folder. It was possible that neither of them had any direct bearing on the other.

Thrisby's theory that Sheppey had been killed by mistake seemed to me to be an acceptable one. Having seen the murderous, uncontrolled expression on Bridgette Creedy's face, I couldn't now rule out the possibility that she had hired someone to kill the girl who was taking Thrisby away from her. Sheppey might have tried to protect the girl and had got killed instead.

I decided it was time to have a talk to Bridgette Creedy, but before doing so I had to make up my mind what line to take with her.

The time was now half past one and I was hungry. I pulled up outside a small seafood restaurant, left the car and went in.

I gave myself a nice meal and took my time over it. The food was good, even though the bill, when it came, made me look three times to be sure the waiter hadn't added in the date by mistake. By the time I had left the restaurant, it was close on half past two. I drove over to a drug store, shut myself in a telephone booth and called Creedy's residence.

The butler answered. His adenoids were no better nor, come to think of it, no worse. I asked for Mrs Creedy.

"I'll put you through to her secretary," he said, and after a few clicks and pops a cool efficient voice said it belonged to Mrs Creedy's secretary.

"I want an appointment to see Mrs Creedy," I said. "I met her this morning. I have something that belongs to her. Will you ask her when she can see me?"

"What is your name, please?"

"The name doesn't matter: just tell her what I've told you."

"Will you hold on, please?"

There was a longish pause. I looked through the glass door of the booth and admired a blonde girl, wearing a French swimsuit, who came into the drug store, climbed up on a high stool and ordered a hamburger with onions. I was glad I wasn't going to be the boy to be taking her out this night.

The cool, efficient voice said, "Mrs Creedy will see you at three o'clock if that will be convenient."

I smiled into the receiver.

"I'll be there," I said, and hung up.

I walked out of the drug store, got into the Buick and, driving slowly, I drifted along the crowded promenade, packed with glittering Cadillacs and Clippers, until I was within sight of the Creedys' residence. I pulled into a space between two cars, lit a cigarette and let the sun, coming through the open car window, add another layer to my sunburn.

At five minutes to three, I started the engine and drove along the private road leading to the Creedy estate.

The two guards came over as I pulled up before the barrier.

"Mrs Creedy," I said to one of them.

He looked me over. I could see my rolled-up shirtsleeves and slacks were causing him pain, but he decided against making remarks. He walked over to the barrier and raised it. There was no list to be consulted, no telephoning the house, no nothing. Mrs Creedy wasn't important, but ask for her husband and then see the trouble you'd buy yourself.

I drove up the now-familiar drive, past the massed rose beds and the Chinese gardeners who had just finished the third bed of begonias and were sitting on their haunches, staring at the begonias as if willing them to remain on their best behaviour and produce large and continuous blooms.

I parked the car next to a big black Rolls-Royce, got out and walked up the steps, along the terrace to the front door.

The butler opened the door two minutes after I had rung the bell. He gave me his steady, searching stare, said, "Mr Brandon?" But not in the way an old friend greets another.

"Yes," I said. "I have an appointment with Mrs Creedy."

He took me down a passage, through a door, up some stairs, along another passage, then opened a door and stood aside.

"You should buy yourself a Vespa," I said, as I moved past him. "It would save your legs."

He went away smoothly as if he were on wheels, not looking back and with no change of expression. Frivolous remarks were a sprinkle of rain in a desert to him.

I walked into a small room, fitted as an office with filing cabinets and a desk. At the desk was the girl I had seen at the inquest. She was wearing the same grey linen frock, set off by white cuffs and a white collar, and, of course, the rimless glasses.

"Mr Brandon?"

"How did you know?"

"I recognized you."

"Oh, yes: we were at the inquest together."

She flushed a little and looked pretty and slightly confused.

"Will you sit down? Mrs Creedy won't keep you long."

I sat down on an upright chair and tried to look less like a tourist than I knew I looked. I decided I should have gone back to the bungalow and put on my best suit: a shirt and slacks were scarcely the right attire to be in in a place like this.

The girl busied herself with a typewriter. Every now and then she looked over the top of her glasses at me as if to assure herself she was seeing a man in shirtsleeves and slacks and wasn't just imagining it.

At a quarter past three, I decided not to be pushed around any longer.

I got to my feet.

"Well, thanks for the chair," I said, with a wide, friendly smile. "It's been nice breathing the same air as you. It's been nice too to see how quick you are on the typewriter. Tell

Mrs C any time she would like to talk to me I can be found in the bungalow out at Arrow Point." And I started towards the door.

I thought that would get some action and it did.

"Mr Brandon ..."

I paused, turned and looked pleasantly inquiring.

"Yes?"

"I think Mrs Creedy will see you now. Please let me go and ask her."

She looked flustered and worried. In spite of her rimless glasses she was a pretty thing and I didn't want to distress her.

"Sure, go ahead," I said, and looked at my watch. "I'll be out of here in two minutes, so let's snap it up."

She crossed the room, opened the door, went into a room and closed the door behind her.

She was gone fifty-five seconds by my watch, then she appeared, holding the door open.

"Mrs Creedy will see you now."

As I passed her to enter the room I gave her a quick wink. It may have been my imagination, but I fancied her eyelid flickered in return.

Bridgette Creedy was standing in the bay window that overlooked the rose garden. She was wearing a pale green shirt and yellow slacks. She had the figure for slacks and she knew it.

She turned slowly the way they are taught to turn in Hollywood and gave me a careful, cold stare. This was scene 234 of a heart-throb movie directed by Cecil B de Mille, complete with the ornate room, rose beds seen through the window and the slightly fading actress who, in the past, has won a number of Oscars and is still considered pretty sound, but possibly slipping.

"You wanted to see me?" she asked, her eyebrows lifting as she took in the rolled-up sleeves and the slacks. "Isn't there some mistake?"

I went over to a lounging chair and sat down. I was a little tired of neurotic women. I had had dealings with them in the past. They run to type. In some ways they are pathetic; in other ways they are a plain pain in the neck. This afternoon I was completely out of sympathy with them, and that went for Mrs Creedy too.

"I didn't tell you to sit down," she said, drawing herself up and giving me the standard Hollywood freeze.

"I know you didn't," I said, "but I'm tired. I have had too much excitement for one day and excitement always makes me tired. I've brought your gun back." I fished the .38 from my pocket, removed the magazine, shook the slugs into my palm, put the magazine back and offered the gun to her.

She hesitated for a brief moment, then took the gun.

"I suppose you now want money," she said disdainfully.

"Well, you haven't much else to offer, have you?" I said, and smiled at her.

That really got her mad, as I intended it to. I was glad I had removed the slugs from the gun, otherwise I believe she would have shot me.

"How dare you talk to me like that!" she said, almost spitting at me. "If you think you can blackmail me ..."

"Of course I can blackmail you," I said. "Stop kidding yourself and stop acting like a 1948 Oscar winner. Sit down and listen to me."

She stared at me as if she couldn't believe her ears.

"My husband ..." she began, but I cut her short with a wave of my hand.

"Don't throw your husband in my face," I said. "Even if he is the hot shot of this town, he couldn't keep this set-up out of the *Courier*."

She put the gun down on a table and then moved over to a lounging chair away from me and sat down.

"What exactly do you mean by that?" she said, steel in her voice.

"You know what I mean. If I hadn't happened along this morning when I did, Thrisby would be dead by now. A murder attempt by Creedy's wife would hit the headlines of every newspaper in the country."

"They wouldn't dare print!" she said furiously.

"Don't be too sure about that."

She controlled her anger, and for a long moment she studied me.

"Well, all right: how much do you want?"

"I'm not another of your boyfriends, Mrs Creedy, looking for money. I want some information out of you."

Her eyes narrowed.

"What information?"

"I understand you hired my partner to watch Thrisby."

She stiffened, her silver fingernails like claws on her knees.

"If Jacques told you that, he is lying. I did nothing of the kind!"

"He says you did."

"He is and has always been a liar," she said fiercely. "It's a lie! I didn't hire anyone to watch him!"

"Did you hire Sheppey to watch anyone?"

"No!"

"Did you know Thrisby was going around with a girl named Thelma Cousins?" I asked.

Her mouth tightened and I saw her eyes flinch.

"No."

"Did you see Thelma Cousins and warn her to keep away from Thrisby?"

"No. I've never heard of the woman!"

"You can't kid me to believe that. She was found murdered yesterday. It was in the papers with her photograph."

"I tell you I've never seen nor heard of her," she said, and I could almost hear her heart beats as she glared at me.

I stared at her for a long moment and she met my gaze, her eyes smouldering. I could see I had come up against a wall of resistance I wasn't going to penetrate. She had plenty of nerve, and she must have realized that I had no proof except Thrisby's word.

"You would have no objection if I told Lieutenant Rankin what Thrisby has told me?" I said. "If you didn't hire Sheppey and you know nothing about the girl you would have nothing to worry about if I did tell him, would you?"

Her eyes flickered and I thought for a moment she was going to lose her nerve, then she snapped, "You can tell him what you please, but I warn you if you start trouble for me I'll sue you out of existence, and don't imagine I can't do it: I'm not listening to any more of this rubbish, so please go!"

I played my last card. I took out the match folder.

"Is this yours, Mrs Creedy?"

I was watching her closely, but she gave no sign of surprise nor of tenseness as Thrisby had done.

"I don't know what you mean."

"I think this belongs to you. Do you want it?"

She looked at me as if she thought I was out of my mind.

"I think you had better go now."

She got up and went over to the bell push and pressed it. Her secretary appeared, her rimless glasses glittering as she held the door open for me.

"We'll probably meet again, Mrs Creedy," I said.

She turned her back on me.

I went into the other room, and her secretary closed the door and stood looking at me.

I said, "I didn't seem to make much of a hit in there, did I?"

She crossed the room and opened the other door. "If you will please go down the passage, Hilton will show you the way out."

"Thank you," I said, then I paused to look at her. I asked, "Do you have to wear those glasses?"

She flushed and took a quick step back.

"Why, no. I – I ..."

"I'd ditch them if I were you. They make a barbed-wire fence around your personality, and that's a pity."

Leaving her staring blankly after me, I walked down the passage, opened the door at the far end and found Hilton, the butler, sitting on a straight-backed chair, waiting for me.

He got to his feet the way an elderly stork will get out of its nest.

"Mr Creedy is asking for you, Mr Brandon," he said.

"Asking for me?" I said, startled. "Are you sure?"

"Yes, Mr Brandon."

"Did he say what he wanted?"

"No, Mr Brandon. He told me to ask you to see him when you had finished talking to Mrs Creedy."

"Do I go right in or do I have a five-hour wait?"

"I understand Mr Creedy is waiting for you."

"Well, that makes a change: okay, let's go then."

He started off down the passage, out through the patio, through open French doors, along another passage, past the waiting-room, down another passage, past the small lobby, through the green-baize door to the massive door of solid polished mahogany, with me trailing along at his heels.

He paused outside the door, rapped, turned the handle and pushed the door open.

"Mr Brandon, sir," he said, and stepped aside.

I started off on the sixty-foot journey towards Creedy's desk.

Creedy sat at the desk, polishing his glasses. He watched me come. His face was as blank as a stone wall, and apart from his moving fingers, his body was as lifeless as the Great Sphinx and nearly as impressive.

I arrived at his desk and gave him a meaningless smile to show him I was no longer impressed with his little show. Then, without being told, I folded myself into an armchair near by and waited.

He finished polishing his glasses to his satisfaction, examined them, and then put them on. He stared at me through them, then lifted them to rest them on his forehead.

"What are you doing in my house, Mr Brandon?" he asked mildly.

"Paying a social call," I said.

"Who were you calling on?"

"I don't want to be offensive, Mr Creedy, but I don't really think that is your business," I said.

He pursed his lips. I don't suppose anyone had ever spoken to him like that before.

"Were you seeing my wife?"

"I should ask her if you are all that interested," I said. "Is that all you want to see me about? If it is I must be running along. I have my living to make and time presses."

He studied me for some seconds, then picked up a sharp letter opener and studied it with lifted eyebrows as if he had never seen it before.

"I have been making inquiries about your agency," he said, not looking at me. "I learn that you are solvent, that you have a reasonably profitable business and your assets are worth three thousand dollars."

"They are worth more that that," I said, smiling at him. "That's what they are worth on paper. Personality and goodwill are the backbone of a business like mine. I have the goodwill and I am cultivating a personality. Three thousand isn't a fair estimate."

"I'm interested in buying a going concern," Creedy said, suddenly staring at me. His eyes went through me like twin bullets through chiffon. "I'm prepared to take over your agency. Shall we say ten thousand dollars to include the goodwill and what there is of the personality?"

"And what happens to me if sold you the business?" I asked.

"You carry on, subject to my supervision, of course."

"I don't supervise easily, Mr Creedy: not on an offer of ten thousand dollars."

"I might be prepared to raise the purchase price to fifteen thousand dollars," he said, and began to puncture holes in his snowy blotter with the letter opener.

"I take it I wouldn't be encouraged to continue to investigate my partner's death?"

He pursed his lips and did more damage to his blotter.

"That is a police matter, Mr Brandon. You are not getting paid to investigate your partner's death. I think it would be reasonable, if I bought your business, to expect you to exert your talents on something that made a profit."

"Yeah." I rubbed the back of my neck. "I'm sorry. Thanks for the offer. I appreciate it, but I'm solving this case, profit or no profit."

He laid the letter opener down, placed his fingertips together and rested his chin on them. He stared at me the way you might stare at a spider that has dropped into your bath.

"I intend to buy your business, Mr Brandon. Perhaps you will name your price."

"On the theory that every man has his price providing the price is big enough?"

"That is an accepted fact. Every man does have his price. Don't let us waste time. I have a lot to do today. What is your price?"

"For my business or for not going ahead with the investigation?"

"For your business."

"It amounts to the same thing, doesn't it?"

"What is your price?"

"I'm not selling," I said, and got to my feet. "I'm going ahead with this investigation and no one is stopping me."

He leaned back in his chair and began to drum gently on the desk with his fingertips.

"Don't be hasty about this," he said. "I have made inquiries about your partner. I am told he was an utterly worthless person. I am told that if you hadn't worked with him the business wouldn't have survived for very long. I am told he was a womaniser, if I may use the term. He wasn't even a good investigator. Surely you are not going to pass up a very good opportunity because of a man like that. I want your business, Mr Brandon. I'll give you fifty thousand dollars for it."

I stared at him, not believing I had heard aright.

"No," I said. "I'm not selling."

"A hundred thousand," he said, his face intent.

"No," I said and I felt my hands turn moist.

"A hundred and fifty thousand?"

"Cut it out!" I said, and I put my hands on his desk and leaned forward to stare into his expressionless eyes. "You are bidding too cheap, Mr Creedy. A hundred and fifty thousand isn't much to keep your name out of the biggest scandal on this coast, is it? A million would be more like it, but don't offer it to me because I wouldn't take it. I'm going through with this investigation and you and your money won't stop me. If you're all that anxious to keep me from finding out the truth why don't you give your lackey Hertz a couple of hundred bucks and tell him to fix me? Probably he would do it for less. Sheppey was my partner. I don't give a damn if he was a good or a bad partner. In my racket no one kills an investigator and gets away with it. We feel the same way about it as the police feel when a cop gets killed. Get that into your money-riddled mind and stop trying to buy me off!"

I turned around and started my long walk towards the exit. The silence I left behind me was painful.

12

I drove back to the bungalow with plenty on my mind. I put the car in the garage to be out of the blazing sun, unlocked the front door of the bungalow and went into the bedroom.

I stripped off, put on a pair of swimming trunks, collected a towel and then walked down to the sea.

I had a twenty-minute swim, then returned to the bungalow and sat down on the verandah in the shade, put my feet up on the rail and considered the various points I had discovered.

I had to make up my mind if it was Thrisby or Bridgette Creedy who was lying. Thrisby's story was acceptable to me and Bridgette had every reason to lie, but I wasn't absolutely sure she had been lying.

What I had to decide was whether Thelma Cousins was being dangled in front of me to take my attention away from something else. I was quite sure the match folder meant nothing to Bridgette, but it meant a lot to Thrisby.

I wondered if it would pay off to go to his place, wait until he went out then search the house. I might turn up something that would give me the key to the mystery. I wondered if he had a servant living with him. I thought it would be a good idea to go out there this night.

I was lighting a cigarette when I heard the telephone bell ring. I got up and went into the lounge, lifted off the receiver and said, "Hello."

"Is that you, Lew?"

Margot's voice.

"Why, I wasn't expecting to hear from you," I said. "Where are you?"

"I'm in my apartment. I've been thinking about that match folder."

I sat on the arm of a lounging chair, holding the telephone on my knee.

"I'm pretty sure it belongs to Jacques Thrisby," she went on.

I didn't say I thought it might too.

"What makes you say that, Margot?"

"I remember now that he was sitting opposite me at the table. I remember he took out his cigarette case. It had a lighter attached and the lighter wouldn't work. He took this match folder out of his pocket, then a waiter came up and gave me a light. He left the match folder and the cigarette case lying on the table beside him. He left them there when he danced with Doris. I am pretty sure now I took the folder to light my cigarette. It's quite possible I put the folder into my bag without thinking. I can't say definitely that I did so but I am sure Jacques put a folder of matches on the table."

"It adds up," I said. "I let him see the folder when I went out there this afternoon. He reacted like a man who has sat on a tack."

"Did you talk to him, Lew?"

"Bridgette was there. I arrived at the dramatic moment when she was about to shoot him."

"Shoot him?" Margot's voice went up. "Oh, Lew, surely not!"

"She may have been planning to scare him, but I had the idea she meant to give him the full treatment. He had just handed her a pretty brutal brush-off."

"She must be out of her mind! What are you going to do about it, Lew? You haven't told the police?"

"No. I doubt if Thrisby would admit she tried to kill him. I'd only be landing myself into more trouble, and I can't imagine the police filing a charge against her. Did you know she had a gun?"

"No."

"I think she was the one who hired Sheppey. Thrisby said so. I talked with her this afternoon, but she says Thrisby is lying. He told me he was going around with Thelma Cousins, the girl who was murdered. Bridgette found out and hired Sheppey to watch them. That's his story, but she denies it."

"This is fantastic. Will the police find out about it?"

"They could do. It's something you'll have to face up to, Margot. This is a murder case."

"Do you think Bridgette had something to do with Sheppey's death?"

"I don't know what to think at the moment."

"What are you going to do?"

I could hear a note of alarm in her voice.

"Tackle Thrisby again. Do you know if he has a servant at his place, Margot?"

"Yes: a Filipino, but he doesn't sleep there. He comes in early, and leaves around eight o'clock."

"I'll go out there tonight and take a look around."

"What do you expect to find there, Lew?"

"I don't know, but it's surprising what you can dig up if you take the trouble to look. When am I seeing you again, Margot?"

"Do you want to?"

"You mustn't ask trifling questions. You wouldn't like to come out here after half past ten? I might be able to tell you what I've found in Thrisby's place."

She hesitated, then said, "Well, I might be able to."

The thought of seeing her again this night sent a hot wave of excitement through me.

"Then I'll expect you around ten-thirty."

"All right. Be careful, Lew. Don't go near the house unless you're sure he's out. Don't forget what I told you: he's dangerous and ruthless."

I said I wouldn't forget and she hung up.

I sat and thought, then after a while I called St Raphael police headquarters. When I got a connection, I asked if Lieutenant Rankin was in.

After a pause, Rankin came on the line.

"What do you want?" he growled when I told him who was talking.

"Traced that ice pick yet?" I asked.

"What do you think I am – a miracle worker? You can buy those picks anywhere in town. There must be hundreds of them lying around."

"Sounds to me as if you're making no progress."

"I'm not, but it's early days yet. This isn't going to be a fast job. Have you got anything?"

"Only a pain in the neck for you," I said. "I'm beginning to think it wasn't Creedy who hired Sheppey. It looks as if his wife did."

"Why do you say that?"

"From the odd talk I have picked up. Would you know if she has a gun permit?"

"What are you getting at, Brandon?" There was a rasp in his voice. "Don't you know you're fooling around with dynamite with the Creedys?"

"I know that, but dynamite doesn't scare me. Has she a gun permit? It's important, Lieutenant."

He told me to hold on. After a long delay, he came back on the line.

"She has a permit for a .38 automatic: serial number 4557993. She's had the permit now for three years," he told me.

I reached for a scratch pad and jotted down the number.

"Thanks, Lieutenant. One more thing: did you get anywhere with your digging into Thelma Cousins' background?"

"No. She just hasn't any background. We've asked around. Hahn seems to be right. She didn't go with men. It beats me what she was doing with Sheppey."

"You have her last address, Lieutenant?"

"She had a room at 379 Maryland Road. The landlady's name is Mrs Beecham. You won't get anything out of her. Candy spent an hour with her. She had nothing to tell him."

"Thanks," I said. "If anything new turns up, I'll call you." And I hung up.

I went into the bedroom, put on a suit, shoved the .38 in my shoulder holster, then left the bungalow, locked the door after me and got the Buick out of the garage.

The time was now a quarter past five. There was still plenty of heat in the sun, and as I drove along the promenade I could see the long stretch of beach was crowded. I pulled up by a cop who was resting his feet on the edge of the kerb and asked him where Maryland Road was. He gave me directions. The road lay at the back of the town and it took me some twenty minutes of fighting traffic to get there.

Mrs Beecham was a fat, elderly body with a friendly smile and an inclination to gossip.

I told her I was connected with the St Raphael *Courier* and could she give me some information about Thelma Cousins.

She invited me into a room full of plush-covered furniture, a canary in a cage, three cats and a collection of photographs that looked as if they had been taken fifty years ago.

When we had sat down I told her I was writing a piece about Thelma and I was interested to know if she had a boyfriend.

Mrs Beecham's fat face clouded.

"The police officer asked that. She hadn't. I often told her she should have some nice young man, but she was so bound up in the church ..."

"You don't think she had a secret boyfriend, Mrs Beecham?" I asked. "You know how it is. Some girls are shy and they don't let on they have someone."

Mrs Beecham shook her head emphatically.

"I've known Thelma for five years. If there had been anyone, she would have told me. Besides, she very seldom went out. The only time she did go out after she had finished her work was on Tuesdays and Fridays. It was then she went to the church to help Father Matthews."

"She might have told you she was going to the church but she could have been going out with a boyfriend. That's possible, isn't it?"

"Oh, no," Mrs Beecham said, and looked shocked. "Thelma wasn't like that at all. She wouldn't do anything like that."

"Did she ever have visitors here, Mrs Beecham?"

"She had her friends from time to time. Two girls from the School of Ceramics and a girl who did church work."

"No men?"

"Never."

"Did a man ever call on her here?"

"No. I wouldn't have encouraged it. I don't believe in young girls having men in their rooms. Besides, Thelma wouldn't have done such a thing."

I took out my billfold and produced a photograph of Sheppey.

"Did this man ever call on Miss Cousins?"

She studied the photograph and then shook her head.

"I've never seen him before. No man ever called on her."

"Did a blonde, smartly dressed woman ever call on her? A woman of about thirty-six … wealthy?"

She began to look bewildered.

"Why, no. Just her three friends and Father Matthews; nobody else."

It looked then to me as if Thrisby had been lying when he had said both Sheppey and Bridgette had gone to Thelma's place.

"On the day she died, did anything unusual happen? Did anyone come to see her, did she get a letter, or did someone call her on the telephone?"

"The police officer asked that. Nothing happened out of the way. She left as usual at eight-thirty to get to the School at nine. She always came back here for lunch. When she didn't come back as usual, I got worried. When she didn't turn up at her usual time after work I first called Father Matthews, and then the police."

Rankin was right. It was like digging into concrete. I thanked the old girl, said she had helped me and got away with difficulty.

As I walked back to the Buick, I was feeling a little depressed. I realized I hadn't made the progress I thought I had. It seemed pretty certain to me now that Thrisby had been lying.

II

Around nine o'clock I drove out to the White Château. It was growing dusk as I got on to the mountain road, and as the sun set, the sky and the sea turned an orange red. From the height of the road, the view of St Raphael City was magnificent.

But I wasn't in much of a mood to admire the view. I had too much on my mind, and I couldn't help thinking from time to time that in an hour and a half I would have Margot with me in the isolation of the bungalow.

I drove fast, using my spotlight to warn traffic coming in the opposite direction that I was on my way.

I reached the branch road down to the White Château soon after nine-thirty. Leaving the Buick on the roadside, I walked down the road until I came to the wooden gate. I pushed this open and walked quietly up the path. By now the sun had set, and it had grown suddenly very dark.

I had brought with me a flashlight and a couple of tools for opening a window or a locked drawer. I paused at the edge of the lawn to look at the house, which was in darkness.

Crossing the lawn and moving silently, I walked around the house. No lights showed anywhere, but before attempting to break into the place, I walked over to the double garage and tried one of the doors. It slid back at my touch, and I was surprised to see a Packard Clipper in there.

I touched the hood and found it cold. It obviously hadn't been out all day.

Moving even more cautiously, I crossed the lawn again and went up on to the terrace. I walked to the front door, and rang on the bell.

For three minutes I waited. Nothing happened. No one answered the bell. I moved along to the French doors. Out of the darkness the Siamese cat suddenly appeared and walked along by my side. I paused outside the French doors, tried the handles but found the doors locked. The cat took this opportunity to twine itself around my legs. I bent to rub its head, but it moved quickly away, jumped up on to the balustrade of the terrace and watched me warily.

I took a flat jemmy from my pocket, inserted it between the French doors, exerted pressure while I pulled steadily on the door handle. There was a sudden clicking sound and the door swung open.

I pushed the door further open and stood listening, but I heard nothing. The room was in darkness. I took out my flashlight and shot the beam into the room.

I was a little uneasy about the Packard being in the garage. It might be that Thrisby hadn't left the house – but why the darkness? I told myself it was more than likely that someone had picked him up in their car, and that was the reason why his Packard was in the garage.

I stepped into the lounge, crossed to the light switch and turned it on. Then I got a shock. Standing across one of the corners of the big room was a desk. All the drawers hung open, and a mass of papers, letters, old bills, lay scattered on the top of the desk and on the floor. Across the room was a cupboard containing a nest of drawers: these drawers hung open too and more papers were scattered on the floor.

It looked as if someone had beaten me to it, and I swore softly under my breath.

I crossed the lounge to the door, opened it and stepped into a big hall. Facing me were stairs leading to the upper rooms. Across the way were two more doors. I opened one and looked into a fair-sized dining-room. Here again the drawers of the sideboard hung open and tableware had been bundled out on to the floor.

I tried the other door and looked into a luxury equipped kitchen that hadn't been disturbed.

I returned to the hall and stood at the foot of the stairs, holding the beam of the light on the stairs while I listened. Somewhere in the house a clock ticked busily, but otherwise there was an oppressive silence.

As I stood there, I wondered what it was the intruder had been looking for and if he had found it. I wondered too, how Thrisby would react when he returned and found the disorder. It would be interesting to see if he called the police or if he did nothing about it.

I would be in an unpleasant position if he suddenly walked in on me, and for a moment I hesitated about going up the stairs. I was pretty sure that anything that might have interested me in this house had already been taken.

But I finally decided to have a quick look over the rest of the house and then get out fast. I mounted the stairs two at a time and arrived on a broad, dark landing.

Then I got a shock that pretty nearly lifted me to the ceiling.

As I swung the beam of my flashlight around, I saw in a far corner of the landing the figure of a crouching man. He looked as if he were about to spring on me.

My heart did a somersault. I jumped back and the flashlight fell out of my hand. It rolled across the floor and then went bumping down the stairs sending the beam flashing against the wall, then the ceiling, then the banisters until it landed in the hall below, leaving me in total darkness.

I stood rooted, my breath whistling between my teeth, my heart slamming against my side.

Nothing happened. The clock downstairs continued to tick busily, making an enormous sound in the tomb-like silence of the house.

I slid my hand inside my coat and my fingers closed around the butt of the .38. I eased it out of the holster and my thumb slid the safety catch forward.

"Who's there?" I said, and I was annoyed to hear that I sounded like a flustered old maid who finds a man under her bed.

The silence continued to press in on me. I listened, standing motionless, my eyes staring into the darkness ahead of me where I had seen the crouching man.

Was he creeping towards me? Would I suddenly have him on top of me with his fingers searching for my throat?

I suddenly remembered how Sheppey had died with an ice pick driven into his throat. Was this Sheppey's killer facing me? Had he an ice pick in his hand?

Then something moved across my leg. My nerves leapt practically out of my body. My gun went off with a bang that rattled the doors and I sprang back, sweat starting out on my face.

I heard a low growling sound and a scuffle, and I knew the cat had come up in the dark and had rubbed itself against my leg.

I stood still, my back pressed against the banister rail, cold sweat oozing out of me, my heart hammering.

I put my hand in my pocket, and took out my cigarette lighter.

"Stay where you are," I said into the darkness. "One move and you'll get it!"

Pushing the .38 forward, I lifted my left hand above my head and flicked the lighter alight.

The tiny flame gave me enough light to see the man in the corner hadn't moved. He still crouched there on his heels: a little, dark man with a brown wrinkled face, slit eyes and a big, grimacing mouth that showed some of his teeth.

There was a stillness about him that gave me the creeps. No one could stay so completely still unless he were dead.

The lighter flame began to fade.

I moved to the head of the stairs, then went down them to where the flashlight lay, its beam pointing across the hall to the front door.

I picked up the flashlight, turned around and forced myself up the stairs again. When I reached the head of the stairs, I swung the beam of the flashlight on to the crouching man.

I guessed he was Thrisby's servant. Someone had shot him through the chest and he had crawled into the corner to die.

There was a puddle of blood by his feet and a dark patch of blood on his black linen coat.

I walked slowly over to him, pushing the gun back into my holster. I touched the side of his face with my fingertips. The cold skin and the board like muscles under the skin told me he had been dead for some hours.

I drew in a long slow breath and swung the beam of the flashlight away from the dead face. Two big sparks of living light lit up in the beam of the flashlight as the cat paused at the head of the stairs, crouching and growling the way Siamese cats do when they disapprove of anything.

I watched the cat cross the landing, walking slowly, its head held low with the sinister wild-cat movement, its tail trailing.

It passed the Filipino without even pausing and stopped outside a door, facing me. It reached up, standing on its hind paws and tapped the door handle with its front paw. It tapped three times, then let out its moaning growl and then tapped again.

I moved forward slowly, reached the door, turned the handle and gave the door a little push.

It swung wide open.

Darkness and silence came out of the room. The cat stood on the threshold, its ears pricked, its head slightly on one side. Then it walked in.

I stood where I was, my heart hammering, my mouth dry.

I turned the beam of the flashlight on the cat. The beam held it in its clear-cut circle of light across the room to the foot of the bed.

The cat jumped up on the bed.

I shifted the circle of light and my heart skipped a beat.

Thrisby lay across the bed. He was still in his white singlet, his dark red shorts and his sandals.

The cat moved over to him and began to sniff inquiringly at his face.

In the beam of the flashlight I could see the terrified, fixed grimace on his face, the clenched hands and the blood on the bed sheet.

There was no sign of a wound or of blood on the white singlet, but I was sure if I turned him over I would find the wound.

Someone had shot him in the back as he had tried to get away. As he had died, he had fallen across the bed.

III

I swung the flashlight beam around until I found the light switch, then I turned on the lights.

I turned again to the bed.

Thrisby looked a lot more dead in the shaded lights than he had done in the beam of the flashlight.

The cat moved slowly around his head, crouching, its tail outstretched, its ears flat. It stared angrily at me over the dead man's face.

I looked around the room.

It was in disorder. The closet doors stood open. Clothes had been bundled on to the floor. The drawers of the chest hung open: shirts, socks, ties, collars and scarves spilled out of the drawers.

Stiff-legged, I walked over to the bed.

The cat spat at me as I came and crouched down; its eyes wide. I reached out and touched Thrisby's hand. It was hard and cold: at a guess, he had been dead five to six hours.

As I stood over him, my foot kicked against something lying just under the bed: something hard. I bent, pushed aside the sheet and lifted into sight a .38 automatic.

It was the gun I had returned to Bridgette Creedy. I was sure of that, but to make absolutely certain, I carried it over to one of the lamps and looked for the serial number. I found it under the barrel: 4557993.

I slid out the magazine. Four shots had been fired: at least two of them had been fatal.

I stood for a moment, thinking. The whole set-up was a little too good to be true. Why leave the gun where the police would find it? I thought. Bridgette would know the police would have the serial number logged. I tossed the gun from hand to hand, frowning. Too pat, I kept thinking; then on a sudden impulse I dropped the gun into my pocket, crossed the room, turned off the lights and walked down the stairs.

I went into the lounge. Crossing over to where the telephone stood on the bar, I dialled Creedy's number.

As I waited for a connection I glanced at my watch. The time was a quarter to ten.

Hilton's voice came over the line.

"This is Mr Creedy's residence."

"Connect me with Mrs Creedy."

"I'll put you through to her secretary if you will hold on, sir."

A few clicks, then the cool efficient voice I now recognized said, "Who is calling, please?"

"This is Lew Brandon. Is Mrs Creedy there?"

"Yes, but I don't think she will speak to you, Mr Brandon."

"She's got to speak to me," I said, "and I'm not fooling. Put me through to her."

"I can't do that. Will you hold on? I'll ask if she will come to the telephone."

Before I could stop her, she went off the line. I waited, holding the receiver against my ear with unnecessary pressure.

After a long pause, she came back on the line.

"I'm sorry, Mr Brandon, but Mrs Creedy says she doesn't wish to talk to you."

I felt my mouth form into a mirthless smile.

"Maybe she doesn't want to, but she's got to. Tell her an old friend of hers has just died. Someone shot him in the back and the law could be on its way to talk to her."

I heard a faint gasp over the line.

"What was that?"

"Look, give me Mrs Creedy. She can't afford not to talk to me."

There was another long pause, then there was a click on the line and Bridgette Creedy said, "If I have any further trouble from you, I'm going to speak to my husband."

"That's fine," I said. "He'll love it. If that's the way you feel about it, you'd better speak to him now because you're heading for a whale of a lot of trouble and it's not of my making. Right at this moment, Jacques Thrisby is lying on his bed with a .38 automatic slug in him. He's as dead as your last year's tax return and your .38 automatic is right by his side."

I heard her draw in a long, shuddering breath.

"You're lying!"

"Okay, if you think I'm lying, sit tight and wait until the law descends on you," I said. "I couldn't care less. I'm sticking my neck out calling you. I should be calling the cops."

There was a long pause. I listened to the hum on the line and to her quick, frightened breathing, then she said, "Is he really dead?"

"Yeah; he's dead all right. Now listen, where were you between five and six this evening?"

"I was here in my room."

"Anyone see you?"

"No. I was alone."

"Didn't your secretary see you?"

"She was out."

"What did you do with the gun I gave you?"

"I put it away in a drawer in my bedroom."

"Who could have got at it?"

"I don't know – anyone. I just left it there."

"Did anyone come to see you?"

"No."

I stared at the wall, frowning. Then I said, "I don't know why I'm doing this for you, but I'm taking the gun away. They might be able to trace the gun through the bullet; if they do, you'll be in trouble, but there's a chance they won't. I think someone is fingering you for Thrisby's murder, but I could be wrong. Sit tight and pray. You have a chance of sliding out of this, but not much of one."

Before she could say anything I dropped the receiver back on to its cradle.

Then I turned out the lights in the lounge, lit my way to the French doors with the aid of my flashlight, pulled them shut behind me and then walked quickly down the path, through the gateway up the road to where I had left the Buick.

No cars passed me as I started down the mountain road. I could see the bright lights of St Raphael City every time I turned into a bend: it looked deceptively lovely.

It was nudging ten-fifteen when I pulled up outside the dark, quiet bungalow. As I got out of the car I saw a convertible Cadillac standing under the palm trees, its lights out. I stared at it for a moment, then walked up the steps leading to the front entrance of the bungalow, took out my keys, then, on second thoughts, turned the handle first. The door swung open and I stepped into the dark hall.

I thumbed down the light switch and stood listening, my hand on my gun butt.

For a long moment there was silence, then Margot said out of the darkness, "Is that you, Lew?"

"What are you doing in there in the dark?" I said, moving to the doorway.

The light from the hall made enough light for me to see her shadowy outline. She was lying on the long window-seat, her head outlined against the moonlit window.

"I came early," she said. "I like to lie in the moonlight. Don't put on the light, Lew."

I stepped away from the doorway and shed the two guns. I slid them into the drawer of the hallstand that stood just by the front door, then I took off my hat and dropped it on to the hall chair.

I walked into the lounge, picked my way past the various pieces of furniture until I reached her.

From what I could see of her, she was wearing only a dark silk wrap. I could see her bare knee through the opening of the wrap. She reached out her hand.

"Come and sit down, Lew," she said. "It's so lovely here, isn't it? Look at the sea and the patterns of the moonlight."

I sat down, but I didn't take her hand. Thrisby's dead face still haunted me. It spoilt the mood for intimacy. She was quick to sense that. "What is it, darling? Is there something wrong?"

"Margot ..." I paused, then went on. "You were once in love with Thrisby, weren't you?"

I felt her stiffen. Her hand dropped to her side.

"Yes," she said after a long hesitation. "I was once. It was one of those inexplicable things. I think I fell for his vitality and his colossal conceit. I didn't last long, thank goodness. I'll never forgive myself for being such a fool."

"We all do things we regret," I said, and groping for a cigarette, I lit it. In the light of my lighter I saw she had raised her head from the cushions and was staring at me, her eyes wide.

"Something has happened, hasn't it? You've been out there? Something has happened to Jacques?"

"Yes. He's dead. Someone shot him."

She dropped back on to the cushion and covered her face with her hands.

"Dead?" She gave a strangled little moan. "Oh, Lew! I know he treated me shamefully, but there was something about him ..." She lay still, breathing quickly, while I stared out of the window. The only light coming between us was from the red glow of my cigarette. Then she said, "It was Bridgette, of course."

"I don't know who it was."

She sat up abruptly.

"Of course it was Bridgette! She tried to shoot him this afternoon, didn't she? If you hadn't stopped her she would have killed him. You said so. Did you let her have the gun back?"

She swung her legs off the window-seat.

"She went out there and killed him! She's not going to get away with it this time!"

"What are you going to do then?"

"Tell my father, of course. He'll get the truth out of her!"

"Suppose he does ... what then?"

She turned her head. Although I couldn't see her face in the darkness I knew she was staring at me.

"Why, he'll throw her out! He'll divorce her!"

"I thought you wanted to keep the police out of it?" I said quietly.

"The police? Why, of course. The police mustn't know. Daddy wouldn't call the police. He would throw her out and then divorce her."

Through the window I saw the headlights of a car coming fast over the rough beach road and my eyes went to the red lamp on the hood.

"You may not be able to keep them out of it, Margot," I said, getting to my feet. "They're here now."

13

In the hard light of the moon I saw Lieutenant Rankin, followed by Sergeant Candy, climb out of the police car. The uniformed driver remained at the wheel.

I walked out on to the verandah to meet them as they came towards the verandah steps.

I stood squarely in Rankin's path so that he had to stop on the second step from the top.

"I want to talk to you," he said. "We're coming in."

"Look behind you, Lieutenant," I said softly, so Candy couldn't hear, "then change your mind."

He turned his head and saw the convertible Cadillac. He looked more to his right and saw the Buick, then he turned and stared at me.

"Should that mean anything?"

"I'll give you one guess who owns the Caddy," I said. "You haven't got your promotion yet, Lieutenant. You walk in there, and it's a fair bet you won't get it."

He took off his hat, stared into it, ran his fingers impatiently through his hair, put on his hat and took three steps back.

"Come on," he said. "We'll talk in the car. We're going out to Thrisby's place."

"You go, Lieutenant, I'm busy." I said. "I'm not all that worked up about Thrisby. I have a Cadillac owner to take care of."

"Are you coming the easy or the hard way?" he said, a sudden bite in his voice.

Candy moved forward, his hand sliding inside his coat.

"Okay, if you put it like that," I said, and started down the steps. "What's on your mind, Lieutenant?"

"Don't give me that crap," Rankin said, his voice savage. "You've just come from Thrisby's place, haven't you?"

"That might be difficult to prove," I said, and got into the back seat of the police car. Rankin joined me and Candy got in beside the driver.

"Let's go," Rankin said.

The car moved off.

I looked back at the bungalow wondering what Margot was thinking. I didn't see any sign of her. In a few minutes she would be dressed and away from the bungalow. I wished now I hadn't gone up to the White Château.

"Give me your gun," Rankin said abruptly.

"I haven't got it on me."

Rankin told the driver to stop. As the car pulled up, he said, "Where is it?"

"In the bungalow."

"Go back," Rankin said, an exasperated note in his voice.

The driver reversed the car and drove fast down the road until we reached the bungalow.

"Go with him," Rankin said to Candy. "I want his gun."

I got out of the car and, with Candy plodding at my heels, I walked up the steps, pushed open the door, turned on the light and crossed over to the hallstand.

I tried to block Candy away from the drawer, but he shoved me aside, opened it and took out my .38.

"This it?" he asked.

"Yes."

I was looking into the now-empty drawer, feeling a little prickle run up my spine: Bridgette's gun had vanished!

Candy broke open my gun and looked down the barrel. Then he sniffed at it, grunted and dropped the gun into his pocket.

"Who owns the Caddy out there?"

"You'd better ask the Lieutenant," I said.

He looked at me, grimaced and shrugged his shoulders.

"Let's go."

"What is all this?" I said, wondering if Margot were listening.

"Who do you imagine you're kidding?" he said, disgust in his voice. "We saw you go into Thrisby's place and we saw you come out."

"You did? Then why didn't you arrest me, Sergeant?"

"We had no orders to arrest you," Candy said, "but we have now."

"Whose orders?"

"The Captain's."

"Does Holding know?"

Candy shifted his gum around in his face.

"You can forget Holding. Situations change from hour to hour in this city. Come on. We don't want to keep the Captain waiting."

We went back to the car.

Rankin said as we got in, "Did you get it?"

"Yeah." Candy slid my gun to Rankin. "It's been recently fired."

"I can explain that," I said. "You're not trying to make out I killed those two, are you?"

"I'm not trying to make out anything," Rankin said in a tired, flat voice. "Just shut up, will you? I've been told to bring you in, and I'm bringing you in."

"What's this about Holding?"

"You'll find out." Rankin settled back in the corner of the car. "Just shut up."

Nothing further was said during the fast run up to the Crest.

During the run, I did some thinking. Then I suddenly realized I might have the key to the whole case: I couldn't be absolutely sure, but all of a sudden the bits of the jigsaw that had made no sense, suddenly meant something. It was one of those sudden flashes one gets when one mentally steps back and looks over all the bits and pieces and suddenly sees a connecting link which before hadn't meant anything.

I hadn't time to get excited about this discovery because we arrived at the White Château.

We got out.

Rankin said to Candy, "Take the car and go back to the bungalow. Take Jackson with you. Search the place. Bring anything you find back here. Get moving."

Candy looked surprised, but he got back into the car and the driver slid under the driving wheel.

"Think she'll be gone by now?" Rankin asked as the police car drove off.

"Yeah. What's happened to Holding?"

"You're way out on a limb, Brandon. Creedy's done a fast deal with Judge Harrison. Holding is back with the Administration. There's no opposition just now."

That really set me back on my heels.

"Come on," Rankin said. "We don't want to keep the Captain waiting. Don't let's have any trouble. You were told not to push this thing so you can't say you weren't warned."

"Holding told me to go ahead."

"Couldn't you see the kind of rat he is?" Rankin said impatiently. "Come on."

We walked up the path, across the lawn to the house. All the lights were on. Three uniformed policemen were pacing up and down on the terrace.

We walked through the open French doors into the lounge. A squad of fingerprint men and photographers were at work. None of them bothered to look at me.

Rankin said to one of them, "Captain here?"

"Upstairs, Lieutenant," the detective said as he peered at a fingerprint he had discovered on the edge of one of the cocktail tables.

We went out into the hall.

Two men in white coats were bringing down a stretcher on which lay a body covered with a sheet. From the size of the body I guessed it was the Filipino's.

We stood aside and I watched the two men tramp across the hall and out through the French doors.

"Come on," Rankin said. "You first."

I climbed the stairs, and at his nod I walked into Thrisby's bedroom.

Thrisby still lay across the bed. Standing, looking out of the window was the enormous figure of Captain Katchen. Two plain-clothes men were going through the various drawers in the room. There was no sign of the Siamese cat.

I moved into the room and stopped by the foot of the bed. I didn't look at Thrisby.

Rankin leaned against the doorpost, his hands in his pockets, his eyes on Katchen's broad back.

Katchen didn't turn. He continued to stare out of the window. Cigar smoke drifted from his mouth and crawled across the room in a small grey cloud, passing close to me. It smelt rank and strong.

Nothing happened for two long, unpleasant minutes, then Katchen growled, "Got his gun?" He still remained with his back towards me. The old technique of breaking down nerves and softening-up resistance.

As Rankin left the doorway, one of the other detectives moved over to take his place. It was a hint that they didn't expect me to make a sudden dive for the stairs.

Rankin put my gun into Katchen's hand. His hand was so big the gun looked like a toy. He took the gun, sniffed at the barrel, broke open the gun, looked at the barrelling, took out the magazine and then checked the slugs. He lifted his massive shoulders and held the gun in Rankin's direction.

As Rankin took the gun, Katchen said, "Got the cuffs on him?"

I saw Rankin's face muscles tighten.

"No, Captain."

"Why not?" The snarl in his voice would have chilled anyone's blood. It didn't warm mine.

"I didn't think it was necessary."

"You're not paid to think! Put 'em on!"

Rankin produced a pair of handcuffs from his hip pocket and came over to me. His set face was expressionless. I held out my wrists and he snapped the handcuffs on.

"They're on, Captain," he said, moving away from me.

Slowly Katchen turned. His big brutal face was dark with congested blood: his small eyes were as restless and as savage as the eyes of a rogue elephant.

"So you imagined you could get away with it, shamus," he said, glaring at me. "You thought your pal Holding could keep me off your neck. Well, I'm going to show you just how wrong you are." While he was speaking he moved slowly towards me and I could see little red flecks in his eyes. "I've been waiting for another session with you, shamus," he went on, "but I'll be damned if I thought I was going to nail you on a double murder charge."

"You can't pin that one on me," I said, watching him. "They've been dead five or six hours and you know it."

For a man of his size he certainly could throw a quick punch. I saw his left coming towards my head and I shifted just in time. I felt his iron knuckles graze my ear, but I hadn't a chance of blocking his right with my hands handcuffed. His fist slammed into me with the force of a mule's kick.

I went down and lay with my knees drawn up, trying to get breath into my lungs. For a long minute I held on to myself, trying to get my breath. Then I heard Katchen snarl, "Stand him up!"

One of the detectives got hold of me and dragged me to my feet. I swayed against him, bent double, and he shoved me from him and moved away.

There was a heavy silence while I got hold of myself. After a while I managed to straighten up. I found Katchen facing me, a sneering grin on his face.

"You're going down to headquarters, shamus," he said, biting off each word, "and you're going to be locked in a cell, but you'll have company. I've got three or four boys who like softening beetles. After they're through with you, you'll be glad to confess to four murders, let alone two."

I knew if I said anything he would hit me again and, taking one full-blooded punch from him was all I wanted to take. I stood there, looking at him.

"And if I can't pin a murder rap on you, shamus," he went on, "we'll put you away for breaking and entering. You'll get three months, and every day of those three months one of the boys will bounce you around. I told you to keep your snout out of this, now you're going to be sorry you didn't."

He turned to Rankin.

"Okay, take him down to headquarters and book him on a charge of murdering Thrisby and the Filipino. That'll hold him until I can look the evidence over. We should be able to nail it on him."

Rankin, his face expressionless, moved over to me and took hold of my arm.

"Come on," he said.

Katchen came up to me and dug me in the chest with a finger the size of a banana.

"I'm going to make you wish you were dead, beetle," he snarled and, drawing his hand back, he clouted me across the face so violently he sent me staggering against Rankin. "Get the punk out of my sight," he snarled, "and throw him in a cell!"

Rankin grabbed hold of my arm and jerked me out of the room. We went down the stairs together, out on to the terrace, down the path to where three police cars were parked. Neither of us said anything. As we moved beyond the gate, the police car that had collected me from the bungalow came down the road and pulled up.

Candy got out and came over to us.

"Find anything?" Rankin asked.

"Another gun: recently fired with four slugs out of the magazine: a .38," Candy said, and took Bridgette's gun out of his pocket.

"Where did you find it?" I said.

He looked at me.

"Under your bed ... where you put it."

I shook my head.

"I didn't put it there, but I don't expect you to believe me."

Rankin was frowning at me.

"I'm taking him to headquarters," he said to Candy. "I'll get the gun checked. There was nothing else?"

"No."

"Take one of the other cars and get off home," Rankin said. "The Captain's got all the men he wants here."

"Okay. You taking Brandon in on your own?"

"Yeah."

They looked at each other. I thought Candy's left eyelid flickered, but I could have been mistaken. He went off into the darkness.

Rankin waved me to one of the police cars.

"You drive."

"Come again?" I said, surprised.

"You drive."

"In handcuffs?"

He took his key out and took the handcuffs off.

I got in under the driving wheel and started the engine. He slid in beside me, took out his pack of cigarettes and lit one.

"Go ahead," he said.

As I drove up to the mountain road, I said, "You'll be careful what you do with that gun, Lieutenant." I slowed, looked to right and left, then got on to the highway. "It belongs to Mrs Creedy."

"I'll be careful."

"What's the idea of taking me in this way?" I asked. "This must be the first time on record a prisoner has driven himself to jail with a cop smoking at his side."

"I'm not taking you to jail," Rankin said. "This is Katchen's idea of acting smart. He thinks by now you've had such a scare thrown into you, you'll get out of town and stay out. I'm supposed to give you a chance to escape."

I was so surprised I didn't say anything for the next two hundred yards, then I began to think again and I suddenly laughed.

"Well, he certainly threw a scare into me," I said, "but not big enough to make me run away. Were you supposed to tell me this?"

"I was supposed to look the other way while you ran for it," Rankin said, his voice bored. "It occurred to me you might not run."

"I wouldn't have. I'm not risking a bullet in the back. This is Creedy's idea, of course. Having tried to buy me off with a hundred and fifty thousand bucks, now he's trying to frighten me off." I blew out my cheeks. "How did you know I had been to Thirsby's place?"

"Creedy's got one of his stooges watching the place," Rankin said. "The stooge called him, told him he'd seen you go in and Creedy called Katchen and told him to slap a breaking and entering charge on you. He told him to scare you silly, give you the treatment and then run you out of town. We just missed you and found Thrisby. Katchen decided to scare you with a murder charge."

"Not giving a damn who really killed Thrisby?"

Rankin shrugged.

"Oh, he'll get around to it in his own time," he said indifferently.

"Didn't the stooge see the killer?"

"No. He only comes on duty at night." He took Bridgette's gun from his pocket and turned it over in his hand. "This the gun that killed Thrisby?"

"Yes."

"Did she kill him?"

"You'd better ask her. I'd say no."

"You don't ask Creedy's wife questions like that. You don't ask Creedy's wife any questions come to that if you want to keep your job in this town."

"No man should have that amount of power. So Creedy has done a deal with Judge Harrison?"

"Yeah. It wasn't so hard. The Judge hasn't a dime to call his own and an extravagant wife. Creedy paid him off so he's ready to pull out of the political racket. It'll be in the newspapers tomorrow."

"The *Courier* will be pleased."

"Nothing they can do about it. You can drive back to the bungalow. Then you'd better pack, take your car and beat it."

"I'm not ready to go yet," I said, coming off the mountain road on to Franklyn Boulevard. "I'm leaving when I've cleared up Sheppey's death and not before."

"You'd better clear off tonight, Brandon. Katchen has given orders about you. If you're not out of town within two hours you'll be in trouble. Katchen's prowl boys are expert at staging an accident. You could lose a leg in the kind of smash they can manufacture."

I stared at him.

"Are you kidding?"

"I've never spoken a truer word," he said soberly. "Be out of St Raphael within two hours or you'll be a hospital case. There's nothing you can do about it. These boys come up on you so fast: we have thirty prowl cars in this town, and any one of them could nail you. Just don't kid yourself. You wouldn't have a chance for a kick back. You'd be lucky to survive. They are professionals at the job."

I thought about that while we bumped over the uneven road that led to the bungalow.

As I pulled up and got out of the car, I said, "You want that gun, Lieutenant? I might be able to make use of it whereas you possibly won't."

"You still after Creedy?" Rankin asked, turning his head to look at me.

"I'm after Sheppey's killer. The gun could have a connection. I'll let you have it back."

He hesitated then shrugged.

"Okay: it's not much use to me. Katchen would lose it as soon as he found out it belongs to Mrs Creedy."

"Well, thanks, Lieutenant. You've been quite a pal. Here's hoping you will get your promotion," and I offered my hand.

He shook hands, gave me the gun, then slid under the driving wheel.

"You can't buck this system, Brandon," he said seriously, looking at me through the car window. "These punks are too big, too strong and too well organized for a loner to tackle them. I know. I've given up trying. Get out fast and stay out."

He nodded, then he turned and drove rapidly away into the darkness.

II

As I turned towards the bungalow I saw the headlights of a car coming fast down the rough road. Rankin's car swerved aside and the other car passed it, and came on towards me.

I put Bridgette's gun into my empty shoulder holster and waited. I was suddenly tired, the muscles in my stomach ached dully from Katchen's punch and I didn't feel like anything now except some sleep.

The car pulled up and a tall, thin man got out. He came over to me. I couldn't see much of him in the moonlight except he seemed reasonably young and he was wearing a slouch hat at the back of his head.

"Mr Brandon?"

"Yeah."

"I'm Frank Hepple of the *Courier*. Mr Troy told me to contact you. Is it too late for a talk?"

It was too late and I didn't feel like talking, but Troy had said this guy was good and I needed help so I said for him to come on in.

"How did you know I was here?" I asked, as we walked over the sand towards the bungalow.

"I called Lieutenant Rankin this afternoon and he told me," Hepple said. "I've got something for you. I thought I'd better get out here and let you have it right away."

The bungalow was silent, and there was a feeling of emptiness about it. I could smell Margot's perfume that still hung in the hot, stale air. I thumbed down the switch and led the way into the lounge, turning on the lights as I entered.

The clock on the mantelpiece showed twenty minutes past eleven. I thought a little sourly that if Rankin hadn't come to drag me to Thrisby's place, I would be lying in Margot's arms by now.

I went over to the bar, found a full bottle of Vat 69 and I made two large highballs. I carried the drinks to a table and then sat down.

I looked over at Hepple, who was standing with his back to the fireplace, watching me.

He was around thirty, with a thin, pleasant face, shrewd eyes and a jutting jaw. He looked the kind of man that would want a lot of stopping once he got going.

"Help yourself," I said, waving to the glasses, then I put my hands on my aching stomach and tried to relax.

He came over and picked up one of the glasses, took a long drink, then as I reached for my glass he said, "Mr Troy told me to take a look at Hahn. I've been digging into his past and I've struck gold."

"In what way?"

"I went out to his place and asked him if he'd give me an interview," Hepple said. "He jumped at the chance of getting some free publicity. Make no mistake about this guy. He's an artist and he knows his stuff. I persuaded him to do me a rough model in clay, and he let me take the model away. It was only a rough thing, but on it was a perfect set of his fingerprints." Hepple grinned at me, delighted with his strategy. "This morning I took the model to the FBI headquarters in Los Angeles. They checked the prints and out came the story." He picked up his drink, took another pull at it and waved the glass excitedly. "Hahn's real name is Jack Bradshaw. He served two years for drug smuggling back in 1941. When he came out, he went to Mexico and the FBI lost sight of him. He turned up again four years later and was caught crossing the border with two suitcases loaded with heroin. This time he drew eight years. When he came out, the FBI kept tabs on him, but this time he seems to have settled down and become legitimate. They know all about his School of Ceramics and they have even looked the place over, but they say there is nothing shady going on there." He leaned forward and pointed a finger at me. "Now this is the part that's going to interest you. While Hahn was serving his last sentence, he palled up with a guy called Juan Tuarmez, who was another drug operator. They left jail together. I had a hunch about Tuarmez and got the FBI to show me his photograph, and guess who?"

"Cordez?"

Hepple nodded.

"That's right: Cordez of the Musketeer Club. How do you like that?"

"Does the FBI know he's here?"

"Oh, sure, but there's nothing they can do about that. He's served his sentence and on the face of it, he's running a successful club. They drop in every now and then and take a look around, but they are satisfied he isn't up to his old tricks."

"Do they wonder where the money came from to start the club?"

"They've gone into that. Cordez told them a group of financiers backed him."

"And Hahn?"

"The same story."

"Any idea who the financiers are?"

"Creedy, of course."

"Doesn't the FBI think it fishy that these two jail birds should have set up business in the same town?"

"They put a tail on them for some time. Cordez never goes to the School nor does Hahn go to the club. They haven't met since they moved into St Raphael."

I thought for a moment, then said, "I hear Judge Harrison has quit politics."

Hepple grimaced.

"The old snake. Creedy bought him out."

"Are you printing that?"

"Not on your life. We have no proof, but that's what has happened. It's going to take some time to find anyone to take his place. In the meantime there'll be no opposition and the present bunch will romp home. Looks as if we're in for another term of rackets."

"Maybe: maybe not. You heard about the shooting out at the White Château?"

Hepple nodded.

"But that hasn't any connection with Cordez and Hahn, has it?"

"I don't know yet. I'm working on it now. Have you a good safe in your office?"

"Sure." Hepple's face showed his surprise.

"I have something I want you to take care of," I said, and took Bridgette's gun from my holster. "Will you put this in your safe and keep it until I ask for it?"

"Sure."

He took the gun, looked at it, lifted the barrel to his nose and sniffed at it. Then he looked sharply at me. "This couldn't be the gun that killed Thrisby?"

"It could be. That's something I've got to find out. I don't want to lose it and I think your safe is the place for it."

"Shouldn't the police have it?"

I shook my head.

"No. They might lose it."

He tossed the gun from hand to hand as he asked, "Would you know the owner?"

"I have an idea, but that doesn't mean the owner shot Thrisby."

He dropped the gun into his pocket.

"Well, okay. I hope you know what you're doing."

"You don't have to worry about that. If I have any luck I'll have a story for you by tomorrow. That gun may be the star turn of the story."

"Is there anything else you want me to do?"

"Stay in the office all day tomorrow. I may want you in a hurry, and I want to know where I can find you."

He looked earnestly at me, a worried expression on his face.

"I have an idea you know more about this set-up than you're telling me. You could be on thin ice, Brandon. How would it be if you told me what you know now so we could both work on it?"

I shook my head.

"I'm not ready yet. I have a fistful of theories, but no real facts."

"Why not give me the theories? Suppose before you're ready to talk, you run into trouble? There are plenty of ways in this city for anyone with an inquiring mind to get into trouble. Suppose you were silenced before you can talk? That's not going to help us, is it?"

I was tempted to tell him what was going on in my mind, but I knew I wasn't ready. If I were going to pull the rug from under Creedy's feet, I had to be absolutely sure of my facts.

"I'll call you tomorrow," I said. "That's the best I can do."

"Well, look, don't stay out here on your own tonight. You're a good mile from anyone and anywhere. Anything could happen to you out here and no one would be the wiser. Why don't you come back to my place for tonight? You can doss down on my settee."

I shook my head.

"Don't worry about me," I said. "I'm all right here. Nothing's going to happen to me until tomorrow. By then I hope it'll be too late for anything to happen."

He shrugged his shoulders.

"Well, okay. But it seems to me you're taking an awful chance." He produced his wallet and found a card and gave it to me. "That's my home telephone number. If you want me I'll be there until eight o'clock tomorrow morning, and from then on I'll be at the office."

"Take care of that gun."

"I'll go to the office now and park it. Be seeing you."

"Some time tomorrow."

"And watch out."

"Oh, sure."

I watched him walk down the steps, across the sand to his car. He turned and waved his hand, then he got in the car and drove away.

I stood on the verandah watching his red tail-lights until I lost sight of them.

14

The moon rode high over the palm trees casting long black shadows. The sea was like a silver mirror. There were only the distant sounds of the traffic passing along the promenade and the gentle movement of the sea.

Standing there on the verandah, looking at the lights of St Raphael, I had a sense of complete isolation, and I wondered if I shouldn't have gone with Hepple.

If anyone was planning to wipe me out, this lonely bungalow was the place in which to do it.

I put my hands on the verandah rail and hunched my shoulders. I was feeling tired, and it was an effort to drive my mind. I could see the lighted windows of the School of Ceramics away to my right, and I wondered what Hahn or, to give him his real name, Jack Bradshaw, was doing at this moment.

I now knew the mystery behind the match folder, but knowing that still didn't make me absolutely sure of Sheppey's killer. I had a feeling I was right on the brink of knowing who killed him, but there was one piece in the jigsaw puzzle to fall into place before the picture was complete.

There was no point standing out there in the dark. I told myself I might just as well go to bed. There was nothing further I could do until tomorrow.

I turned around and went into the lounge. I shut the French doors and locked them, took the two glasses Hepple and I had used over to the bar and put them down.

I looked around to make sure no cigarettes were burning in the ashtrays, then I walked over to the light switch by the door. As my hand reached for the switch, I heard a very faint sound that told me instantly that I was no longer alone in the bungalow.

For a full second I remained motionless, aware that I was frightened and that my mouth had suddenly turned dry. I remembered that I had no gun: Rankin had taken mine, and I had given Bridgette's gun to Hepple. I recalled what Hepple had said: *You're a good mile from anyone and anywhere. Anything could happen to you here and no one would be the wiser.*

The sound had been of someone in the bedroom: the distinct sound of someone's foot on a loose board: someone moving stealthily.

I snapped off the light and the room turned to darkness.

Through the big window I could see the moon: its light made a big puddle of whiteness on the carpet at the far end of the room, but where I stood was shrouded in darkness.

I stood tense, listening, my heart thumping.

I heard the movement again, still in the bedroom, and then I heard the door creak slightly as it began to open.

"Stay right where you are," I said, a snarl in my voice, "or you'll get a slug in your guts!"

As soon as I had spoken, I dropped down on one knee, expecting a blast of gunfire, but instead I heard a quick, scared gasp.

"Lew?"

Margot's voice.

"For crying out loud!" I exclaimed.

I straightened up and snapped on the light.

Margot stood in the doorway, her eyes wide and scared, her face tense. She had on a nylon nightdress that was as transparent as a sheet of glass. She looked more than lovely: she looked out of this world.

"Oh, Lew! You frightened the life out of me!"

"Out of you? What do you think you did to me? I nearly had a heart attack. Margot: what are you doing here?"

"I came back. I was so worried about you, darling. I didn't know what to do. I drove the car to the promenade and walked back. I waited out there in the darkness. The police came, then they went away. I got cold out there so I came in to wait for you. I've only just woken up."

I took out my handkerchief and wiped my face.

"I'm sorry I scared you," I said. "You certainly made me hit the ceiling. I thought my last hour had come."

"I'm so sorry. I've been asleep. I woke up just in time to see the light go off. I thought it might be you, but I was afraid to call out just in case it wasn't. So I crept to the door to listen. When you called out in that awful voice, you terrified me."

"That makes two of us."

She came swiftly to me and slid her arms around my neck. The feel of her soft, yielding body against mine set my heart hammering. My hands moved down the length of her long back, over the curve of her hips and I pulled her close to me.

"Kiss me, Lew ..."

My mouth found hers and she moaned softly, pressing herself against me.

"Oh, darling ..."

It needed a lot of will-power to push her away, but I did it.

"Get into bed, Margot," I said. "You'll catch cold ..."

She put her head on one side as she looked at me. Her face was slightly flushed, her lips were parted and there was that look in her eyes I had seen before. She looked the most devastatingly desirable woman in the world.

"I won't catch cold, but I'll go back to bed. And you?"

"What do you think? Let me have a shower first. Then I'll be right with you."

"Oh, Lew, you haven't told me ... what happened? Why did the police ...?"

I lifted her and carried her across the lounge and into the bedroom.

There was an impression where her head had lain on the pillow and the sheet had been thrown back as she had slid out of bed. I laid her on the bed, covered her with the sheet and looked down at her. I thought how beautiful she looked.

"The police? I have orders to get out of town right away," I said. "They think I'm getting too close to Sheppey's killer, Margot."

Her dark eyes opened wide and she reached out and touched my face.

"You're going away, Lew?"

"I guess so. It won't be healthy to stay, but before I go I'm going to close up at least one racket here. I've found out what that match folder means."

"You have? What does it mean then?"

I sat on the side of the bed and took her hands in mine.

"The matches are drug vouchers."

"Drug vouchers? What do you mean?"

She stared up at me: her eyes puzzled.

"It's simple enough. Cordez and Hahn are dope peddlars. They are well known to the Narcotic Squad and they are being constantly watched. They've already served a sentence for drug smuggling, and they know their next sentence will be for life. They entered into partnership and worked out what seemed to them to be a safe scheme. This is what they did: they moved into one of the richest cities in the country. They got financial backing to open a club and to open a ceramic shop: both legitimate businesses. The Narcotic Squad investigated and found nothing suspicious. Hahn and Cordez were watched, but they didn't meet nor did they appear to have any association of any kind together. But, of course, they were still in the drug trade together and this is how they worked it: Hahn got the drugs and Cordez supplied the customers. A lot of rich people used Cordez's club; some of them wanted to buy drugs. Cordez sold them a folder of matches. They then went over to Hahn's place – safe enough because there's always a steady flow of people going in and out – and in exchange for a match the customer received so many ounces of drug. Hahn returned the matches to Cordez who then paid him his share of the take. In this way everyone is happy and safe. Cordez gets the money, the customer his regular supply of drugs and Hahn gets paid for supplying the drugs."

"It's fantastic, Lew."

"Not all that fantastic. Drug operating is a tough racket, Margot. The Narcotic Squad knows nearly all the answers. A successful peddlar has to be one jump ahead all the time, and Cordez and Hahn were one jump ahead with this idea until now. Hahn's place is ideally situated to receive supplies of drugs. A boat can come in at night and no one would be any the wiser. Well, there it is. I'll bet my last buck that's the mystery of the match folder." I reached in my hip pocket and took the folder out. "Each customer probably has a different set of ciphers so he or she can be identified. If the folder is lost, no one else can use it. It is like a season ticket to hell. Sheppey got hold of one of these folders.

That's why he was killed and that's why his room and mine were searched."

"Then Jacques took drugs?" Margot asked, staring at me.

"It's possible. Anyway, he knew about the folder. When I set fire to a match he nearly gave himself away. He knew I was throwing away so many ounces of drugs." I put the folder back into my hip pocket. "Well, tomorrow finishes it. I'm turning the folder over to the Los Angeles Narcotic Squad, and they'll handle it."

"And then you'll go away?" she said, her hand closing over mine. "I don't want you to go, Lew."

I smiled at her.

"I can't stay here. I have my work to do in Frisco. That's where my roots are. What's to stop you coming to Frisco?"

"Daddy, of course. He wouldn't let me."

I stood up.

"You know what the trouble with you is, don't you? You want your fun and your dollars. Think about it. It might be an idea for you to forget your old man and see what it's like to earn your own living."

She lay back, her eyes suddenly bright and inviting.

"I might try, darling, but what about that shower you said you wanted to take?"

"I'll be right with you."

I stripped off my coat, slid out of my trousers and shirt and dropped them on a chair, then, clad only in my shorts, I went into the bathroom.

I closed the door, turned on the shower and stood by the door, my heart beginning to thump.

I waited for perhaps ten seconds, then I took hold of the door handle and turned it very gently. I inched the door open so I could see into the bedroom.

Margot was out of bed, standing by the chair on which I had thrown my clothes. Her hand was in the hip pocket of my trousers and, as I watched her, she took out the folder of matches. There was an expression of terror and relief on her face that made me feel pretty bad.

I reached out, cut the shower, opened the door wide and moved into the bedroom.

Margot spun around, her eyes widening, and she caught her breath in a tight little scream.

I didn't even look at her. I walked across to the bed and caught hold of the pillow that still held the impression of her head. I jerked it on to the floor.

Lying on the sheet where the pillow had hidden it was a yellow-handled ice pick.

II

In a silence I could almost feel, I looked over at Margot, who stood as if turned to stone, the folder of matches in her hand, her eyes enormous.

"Did you really imagine you could get away with it, Margot?" I said. "Did you really imagine it would be third time lucky?"

Her lips moved, but no words came.

I picked up the ice pick and turned it over in my fingers. The point of the blade had been filed and it looked as sharp as a needle. A little chill snaked up my spine as I realized what a close escape I had had.

"You were good, but not quite good enough," I said, watching her. "As an actress you were superb, but you were only a second-rate liar. You were doing fine until you tried to sell me the idea that Thrisby owned the match folder. That dinner you described never took place. Thrisby was fooling around with a new girl friend on that particular night and Bridgette was up at his house. That was a clumsy lie, Margot, and it led me right to you."

She sat down abruptly and hid her face in her hands.

"I was puzzled why you should have lent me this bungalow," I went on. "It was so out of character, but now I can see you were taking precautions. If I got to be a nuisance you might have to get rid of me. This is a conveniently lonely place to kill a man in, isn't it?"

She looked up then, her face white and her eyes glittering. She still looked beautiful, but it was a hard, dangerous beauty.

"And you had this under your pillow," I said, holding up the ice pick. "It explains why Sheppey's killing appeared to be so expert and Thelma Cousins' death so clumsy. When you have a man in your arms, Margot, it is easy to reach under your pillow, take out the pick and drive it into the back of his neck. That's what you planned to do to me, wasn't it? Thelma, of course, would have been standing when you struck her, and in that position it would be much more difficult to kill cleanly." I looked at her. "Well, say something. You killed Sheppey, didn't you?"

She shook her head.

"You don't understand," she said, the words spilling out of her mouth. "He was blackmailing me. He found the folder and he stole it from me. He said he wouldn't give it back to me unless I submitted to him. He forced himself on me. I killed him in self-defence."

"You'll have to lie better than that, Margot. Sheppey wasn't a blackmailer. He had lots of faults, but he wouldn't go as low as that. It's much more complicated than that. Let me tell you what I think happened," I said, and sat on the edge of the bed. "Thrisby and you were short of money. You were in love with him and he appeared to be in love with you. He got money out of Bridgette, and you two spent it. But Bridgette was no fool. She began to suspect what was going on. She probably got someone like Hammerschult to hire Sheppey to watch you. It must have been fun for Sheppey to follow you around. I bet he fell for you a lot faster than I did. You persuaded him to double-cross Bridgette and not tell her you were Thrisby's mistress. I am quite sure you rewarded him. Unfortunately for him, he stumbled on the match-folder racket. He got hold of your folder. You had to get it back. You can't live without your regular shot, can you? So you decided to kill him."

"No!" she exclaimed, beating her fists together. "It didn't happen like that! He attacked me ..."

"And you had an ice pick handy? You planned it, Margot."

"I didn't! You've got to believe me ..."

"Then why did you go to his hotel in an elaborate disguise? The black wig, the sunglasses and the get-up made you feel safe when you lured Sheppey to that bathing cabin. You had to be sure no one at the hotel could identify you. The hotel dick was smart enough to see through your disguise, but I was mug enough not to listen to him. Because Sheppey was double-crossing Bridgette, he accepted your disguise. You had only to point out to him that Bridgette mustn't see you two together for him to accept the wig and the dark glasses. Anyway, you probably gave him that look of invitation you gave me. He wouldn't care what colour your hair was so long as you made good on that invitation. You got him to the beach cabin and you killed him. When you found he hadn't the match folder on him, you took the key of his room, went to the hotel and hunted for the folder there, but you didn't find it."

She crossed her arms over her breasts and shivered.

"I don't want to hear any more of this," she said. "It's not true."

"Of course it's true. And I'll tell you something else. You discovered Thrisby was making a play for Thelma Cousins. He was getting bored with you and an innocent girl like Thelma would amuse him. You knew the police would hunt for the girl who had been seen with Sheppey. You saw your chance of confusing the investigation, and at the same time of getting rid of a rival. You went regularly to Hahn's place for your drugs so you must have known Thelma. It wouldn't have been difficult for you to persuade her to go for a swim with you. Probably you said you wanted to talk to her about Thrisby. You took her to the bathing station where you had killed Sheppey. The police had closed the place so you two were alone there. You stabbed her and left her for dead. You only just had time to get back to your apartment and change before I called on you. You hid your panic pretty well, Margot, but when I had gone you began to wonder just how much I knew. So you called me to tell me that Sheppey hadn't been to the Musketeer Club and like a mug, I told you I had the match folder. You went around to my hotel and found it, and you were smart enough to substitute one of the ordinary folders in the hope I wouldn't know the difference."

She shook her head wildly.

"No, Lew ... you're wrong! I swear I didn't ..."

"Thrisby knew you were a drug taker," I went on. "He knew you had the motive for getting rid of Thelma. You realized he might give you away. When I told you Bridgette had threatened to kill him, you saw your chance to silence him and get rid of Bridgette. I'll say this for you, Margot: you're certainly a great opportunist. It was easy enough for you to get hold of Bridgette's gun. You went out to Thrisby's place and you shot him. His servant was still in the house so you had to silence him too. I don't know how you felt when you discovered you had left your bag here and I had your match folder again, but you must have been pretty desperate. That was when you decided to get rid of me, too, wasn't it?"

She lifted her head and stared at me, her eyes dark with hate.

"You can't prove any of this," she said hoarsely. "I'm not afraid of you."

"Yes, you are, Margot. The guilty are always afraid."

She stood up.

"There's nothing you can do to me! There's nothing you dare do!"

"I'm sorry, Margot, but you can't be allowed to get away with this thing. Four people died because of you."

"My father won't let you do anything to me," she said breathlessly.

"There's nothing your father can do now," I said. "I'm going to tell Rankin. Even this corrupt administration can't hush up four murders."

While I talked, she slowly backed away until she reached the chest of drawers, then she spun around, pulled open a drawer, dipped her hand into it as I started across the room towards her. I stopped abruptly as she turned a .25 in her hand.

"Now ..." she said, her eyes glittering. "I'll show you I'm not afraid."

A soft, effeminate voice said from the doorway, "Don't act like a fool, Margot."

She gave a faint scream as she spun around. I looked quickly over my shoulder.

Lee Creedy stood in the doorway. He was wearing a tuxedo: a white camellia in his buttonhole. His horn glasses rested on his forehead: a cigar burned evenly between his thin lips.

"Give me that gun," he said, holding out his hand.

Without hesitation, she went to him and gave him the gun. Her face was chalk white and she was shaking.

"Put some clothes on," he said. "You look like a whore in that thing."

She went quickly to one of the closets, jerked open the door, snatched out a dress and then ran into the bathroom and slammed the door after her.

Creedy's expressionless eyes moved to me.

"You get dressed too," he said. "I'll wait in the lounge," and he walked out of the bedroom.

I slid into my clothes. As I was putting on my jacket, Margot came out of the bathroom, smoothing the dress over her hips.

"He won't let you do anything to me," she said breathlessly. "I know he won't."

She ran past me into the lounge and I followed her.

Creedy was pacing up and down. He still held the gun in his hand. His face was completely expressionless.

"Sit down," he said to Margot, waving to a chair. Then, looking at me, he went on, "And you sit down too."

We sat down.

He continued to pace up and down for several seconds, then he said, without pausing in his prowling, "Bridgette told me you had a man here. I thought I'd come down to see who it was. You are a disappointment to me, Margot, but most children are disappointments to their parents. I dare say I haven't been much of a father to you and your mother was a thoroughly rotten woman, but that doesn't entirely excuse you." He stopped as he came close to her. "I heard what Brandon was saying to you. Is it true?"

She couldn't meet his cold, steady gaze.

"No, of course it isn't," she said, clenching and unclenching her fists. "He's lying!"

"Then tell me why that ice pick was under your pillow."

She started to say something and then stopped. She suddenly lost her beauty. She looked older, defeated and completely lost.

"There is no answer to that, is there?" he said. "Now listen to me, Margot. I control this town. The police do what I tell them. Brandon has no power here. You have nothing to fear from him. All I want from you is the truth, then I will be able to cope with the situation. Did you kill this man Sheppey?"

She looked up at him; her eyes suddenly trusting.

"I had to, Daddy – there was no other way."

His mouth tightened, but otherwise his expression didn't change.

"What do you mean – there was no other way?"

"He was going to tell the police about Cordez," she said. "I couldn't let him do that."

"Why not?"

She made a helpless little movement.

"You wouldn't understand ..."

"You are trying to tell me you are a drug addict: that's it, isn't it?"

"I suppose so."

He took his glasses off, stared at them, put them back on and pushed them up on to his forehead.

"This woman Thelma Cousins." He began to move around the room again. "Did you stab her as he says you did?"

"I had to, Daddy."

"And Thrisby?"

She shut her eyes, her hands pressing her breasts.

"Yes."

"You seem to have made a pretty squalid mess of your life, Margot," he said, without looking at her.

She sat motionless, her hands clenched.

"Well, all right," he went on. "Everyone is entitled to lead the life they choose." He suddenly crossed over to a chair and sat down. "You know it is hard to believe you've done this, Margot. It is not going to be easy to get you out of it either."

She leaned forward, her hands now so tightly clenched the knuckles showed white.

"You won't let them send me to prison, will you?"

"No, I won't let them do that."

He stood still, staring out of the window while he thought.

Except for the sound of her quick, frightened breathing there was complete silence in the room.

I watched them, not moving, aware of the gun he held in his hand.

After a minute or so, he said, "Now listen to me, Margot; you must leave St Raphael immediately." He took from his wallet a flat packet of money and tossed the packet over to her so it dropped into her lap. "You'll need money. Go to your aunt's place. Stay there and try to behave yourself. I will make the necessary arrangements here. Take Brandon's car. It's outside, so use it. I want you to drive as quickly as you can to your aunt: do you understand?"

"Now wait ..." I began, but stopped as Creedy lifted the .25 and covered me.

"Keep your mouth shut!" he said. "I need very little persuasion to shoot you. It would make my task a lot easier if you were dead. Don't give me the excuse." Still keeping me covered, he again looked at Margot. "Do you understand?"

She nodded.

"Yes."

"Then get off."

"You will make it all right for me?"

"Of course. Get off now. Take Brandon's car. I'll see he is compensated." As she got quickly to her feet, he went on, "I hope the new life you are going to find will bring you more happiness than your old life has done."

She wasn't listening. She was looking at me, her hand holding the roll of money tightly, her eyes glittering with triumph. Then she ran out of the lounge, down the verandah steps and seconds later I heard the Buick start up.

"You might fool her, but you don't fool me," I said to Creedy. "You're not human! No jury would ever put her into the gas chamber. You can't do this to her!"

"No daughter of mine is going to rot in a jail," he said curtly and, getting to his feet, he slid the gun into his pocket and walked over to the window to watch the tail-lights of the Buick disappearing up the rough road towards the promenade.

I turned and ran out of the bungalow.

Creedy had driven himself down in a big, black Cadillac. It stood under the palm trees, its lights still on. I ran across to it, slid under the driving wheel, started the engine, swung the car around and drove at a racing speed after the Buick.

III

Margot had a long start on me. I could see the twin red lights of the Buick as it left the rough road and turned on to the promenade. I was some five hundred yards behind her.

I slammed the Cadillac over the road; the car shuddering as its wheels banged into the potholes at high speed. As I got on to the promenade, I caught a glimpse of the twin red lights as Margot whipped the Buick into the turning that led to Franklyn Boulevard. I wondered if she were going back to her apartment to get her clothes before leaving town and that raised my hopes.

I was scared to drive too fast. Rankin had said there were thirty prowl cars on the road. To be stopped now for speeding would ruin my chance of catching up with her.

Again I caught sight of the Buick as it fled up Franklyn Boulevard and I swore under my breath as it swept past the Franklyn Arms. So she wasn't stopping off at her apartment. I wondered if she had spotted the Cadillac, and I increased speed slightly, closing the gap between the two cars.

She was driving fast, but not dangerously fast. I spotted a patrolman standing at the corner of an intersection. I saw him stiffen as the Buick went past and he stared after it, not sure whether it was going fast enough for him to whistle after it. I took my foot off the gas pedal and touched the brake, slowing as I drove past the cop. Then I accelerated again.

I saw now she was heading for the mountain road. Then suddenly a big prowl car swept out of a side turning and slid between me and the Buick. If I hadn't slammed on my brakes I would have smashed into its rear bumper.

The Cadillac slowed, and I lost sight of the Buick as Margot turned on to the twisting mountain road. The prowl car ahead of me surged forward, took the first bend of the road with a screeching of tyres and stormed after the Buick.

What I feared might happen had happened. Rankin had been speaking the truth. The order to nail me, to manufacture an accident, had gone out. The two flat-capped cops, driving in the prowl car, had recognized my Buick and they were carrying out their orders. It was too dark for them to see who was driving. They would naturally assume that it was me, leaving town. I was sure now the order to manufacture a smash had come from

Creedy. He had known that Katchen's prowl cars had been alerted to hit the Buick at sight. He had put Margot in the Buick and directed her on to the mountain road. He knew as soon as she realized a police car was after her she would try to get away. He knew she wouldn't stand a chance of out-driving a police driver. This was his way out: no publicity, no trial and a worthless, degenerate daughter out of the way.

There was nothing I could do to stop this now, but I kept on, sending the Cadillac roaring up the twisting road, my spotlight on to warn traffic coming in the opposite direction that I was on my way.

I heard the long wailing blast of a police siren ahead of me. The bends in the road prevented me seeing the two cars, but every now and then I caught the flash of their headlights as they whipped into the turns.

Then suddenly I saw them ahead on the higher level of the snake-back road and I slammed on my brakes. I wouldn't have believed it possible for Margot to have driven so fast, for she was now a good mile ahead of me. I jumped out of the car and stood on the grass verge, looking up. The road wound up the hill and long stretches of it were in sight.

The prowl car was only twenty yards or so behind the Buick: its headlights blazing on the Buick's bumpers, its siren screaming.

No one could hold that speed on such a road for long. Ahead I saw the first of the hairpin bends. Margot must have seen it too. The prowl car driver knew the bend was ahead for he had already cut speed and had dropped a hundred yards or so behind the Buick. Margot came to the bend at something like sixty miles an hour. I heard the screaming of tortured tyres as she crammed on the brakes.

The long white fingers of light from the headlamps swung out into the black void like antennae of some huge insect sensing danger.

I felt my heart suddenly lurch as the Buick left the road and shot off into space. For a brief, unbelievable moment it seemed to be driving through the air. In the silence I heard Margot's terrified scream: a sound that chilled my blood, then the Buick turned over, and a moment later it struck an enormous boulder, bounced away from it, slithered in a fog of dust, uprooting small trees and loosening rocks, sending them banging down the hillside. Then with a loud, dull crash, it came to rest not two hundred yards from where I was standing.

I ran as I had never run before. My one thought was to get her out before the wreck caught fire. The car lay on its side, wedged against a huge boulder. As I started the short climb up to it, I could smell the gasoline fumes. I reached the car. It was too dark to see into the broken interior. With a shaking hand, I took out my flashlight and sent the beam probing into the car.

Margot lay curled up against the driver's door: a little trickle of blood ran from her mouth and down her chin. Her blonde silky hair hid most of her face. I saw her fingers move: then slowly close into fists, then open again.

I reached inside and gently pushed aside the soft gold hair. Her eyes were closed, but at the touch of my fingers, she opened them and we looked at each other.

She tried to say something: her lips moved.

"I won't leave you," I said. "They'll get you out without hurting you ..."

Futile words, but I couldn't think of anything else to say.

She moved her head slightly; then her face stiffened. She tried once more to say something, then she made a pathetic little grimace and died.

As I stepped back, the headlights of a car came sweeping up the road. A Lincoln pulled up and Frank Hepple tumbled out and came running over to me.

"I spotted you following her and I came after you," he said. "Is she dead?"

"Yes."

He went over to the shattered Buick, took a flashlight from his pocket and peered into the car. I sat down on a rock, took out a cigarette and lit it. I felt pretty bad. Maybe she had killed Sheppey, but that was over and paid for now.

Hepple came back. He went to his car, took a camera and flashlight from the back seat, returned to the Buick and took a couple of shots of her. Then he came back.

"Come on," he said. "I'll drive you back. I guess you're ready to talk now."

I looked up the mountain road. The patrol car had turned and was coming down the snake-back road fast. I got into Hepple's car.

Creedy wasn't going to escape the publicity he feared, I told myself. The *Courier* had the gun that had killed Thrisby. The police couldn't hush that up. Hepple would be able to prove it was Creedy's money that had financed Cordez and Hahn. When the story of the drug organization came out with Creedy's name linked to it, it would finish him in St Raphael City.

I drew down a lungful of smoke and leaned back.

"Yes," I said. "Now I'm ready to talk."

James Hadley Chase

An Ace Up My Sleeve

When three very different people come together, all out for the same thing and prepared to go to any lengths to get it, the stakes are likely to be high. But, for a wealthy middle-aged woman, an international lawyer and a young American, games of bluff and counter-bluff quickly develop into a dangerous and deadly battle. As the action hots up, Chase weaves a fast-moving story of blackmail, intrigue and extortion with a hair-raising climax.

The Fast Buck

International jewel thief, Paul Hater, knows a secret that everyone wants to know – and will go to any lengths to uncover. How long can he remain silent?

When Hater is arrested in possession of a stolen necklace, the police use every possible means to persuade him to reveal the location of the rest of the collection. He remains silent and so begins his twenty-year prison sentence. Having exhausted all their leads, the International Detective Agency, acting on behalf of the insurers, must patiently await Hater's release before they can hope to find out more. But just as his day of release approaches, Hater is kidnapped by a ruthless international gang determined to force the secret from him and prepared to go to any lengths to do so...

JAMES HADLEY CHASE

HAVE A CHANGE OF SCENE

Larry Carr is a diamond expert in need of a break. So when his psychiatrist suggests he has a change of scene, he jumps at the opportunity to move to Luceville, a struggling industrial town, and become a social worker. This, he thinks, will give him all the rest he needs...until he runs into Rhea Morgan, a ruthless, vicious thief who also happens to be extremely attractive. He falls headlong into the criminal world and embarks upon a thrilling, rapid and dastardly adventure in true Hadley Chase style.

JUST A MATTER OF TIME

An old lady's will seems to be causing quite a stir. Suddenly everyone wants to get in on the action, everyone that is, including a master forger, a hospital nurse, a young delinquent, a bank executive and, to make matters worse, a professional killer. With such ingredients, a showdown seems inevitable and James Hadley Chase adds enough suspense to keep you guessing right up to the very last page.

JAMES HADLEY CHASE

MY LAUGH COMES LAST

Farrell Brannigan, President of the National Californian Bank, is an extremely successful man. So when he builds another bank in an up-and-coming town on the Pacific coast, he is given worldwide publicity, and this new bank is hailed as 'the safest bank in the world'. But Brannigan's success came at a price and he made many enemies on his way up the ladder. It seems that one of them is now set on revenge and determined to destroy both the bank and Brannigan himself.

YOU'RE DEAD WITHOUT MONEY

Joey Luck and his daughter Cindy were small-time criminals going nowhere fast...until they joined forces with Vin Pinna, a hardened criminal on the run from Miami. They began to set their sights higher and turned their hands to kidnapping. But their hostage, ex-movie star Don Elliot, seemed to have different ideas. He wanted in so they formed a 'quartet in crime' and this time the stakes were higher still – eight Russian stamps worth a million dollars.

'realistic and suspenseful'
Observer

OTHER TITLES BY JAMES HADLEY CHASE AVAILABLE DIRECT FROM HOUSE OF STRATUS

Quantity		£	$(US)	$(CAN)	€
	AN ACE UP MY SLEEVE	6.99	12.95	19.95	13.50
	AN EAR TO THE GROUND	6.99	12.95	19.95	13.50
	THE FAST BUCK	6.99	12.95	19.95	13.50
	GOLDFISH HAVE NO HIDING PLACE	6.99	12.95	19.95	13.50
	HAND ME A FIG-LEAF	6.99	12.95	19.95	13.50
	HAVE A CHANGE OF SCENE	6.99	12.95	19.95	13.50
	HAVE THIS ONE ON ME	6.99	12.95	19.95	13.50
	HIT AND RUN	6.99	12.95	19.95	13.50
	HIT THEM WHERE IT HURTS	6.99	12.95	19.95	13.50
	JUST A MATTER OF TIME	6.99	12.95	19.95	13.50
	KNOCK, KNOCK! WHO'S THERE?	6.99	12.95	19.95	13.50
	LIKE A HOLE IN THE HEAD	6.99	12.95	19.95	13.50
	MAKE THE CORPSE WALK	6.99	12.95	19.95	13.50
	MORE DEADLY THAN THE MALE	6.99	12.95	19.95	13.50
	MY LAUGH COMES LAST	6.99	12.95	19.95	13.50
	NOT MY THING	6.99	12.95	19.95	13.50
	SO WHAT HAPPENS TO ME?	6.99	12.95	19.95	13.50
	TELL IT TO THE BIRDS	6.99	12.95	19.95	13.50
	THE WHIFF OF MONEY	6.99	12.95	19.95	13.50
	YOU HAVE YOURSELF A DEAL	6.99	12.95	19.95	13.50
	YOU'RE DEAD WITHOUT MONEY	6.99	12.95	19.95	13.50

ALL HOUSE OF STRATUS BOOKS ARE AVAILABLE FROM GOOD BOOKSHOPS OR DIRECT FROM THE PUBLISHER:

Internet:	www.houseofstratus.com including synopses and features.
Email:	sales@houseofstratus.com
	info@houseofstratus.com
	(please quote author, title and credit card details.)
Tel:	Order Line
	0800 169 1780 (UK)
	800 724 1100 (USA)
	International
	+44 (0) 1845 527700 (UK)
	+01 845 463 1100 (USA)
Fax:	+44 (0) 1845 527711 (UK)
	+01 845 463 0018 (USA)
	(please quote author, title and credit card details.)
Send to:	House of Stratus Sales Department House of Stratus Inc.
	Thirsk Industrial Park 2 Neptune Road
	York Road, Thirsk Poughkeepsie
	North Yorkshire, YO7 3BX NY 12601
	UK USA

PAYMENT

Please tick currency you wish to use:

☐ £ (Sterling)　　☐ $ (US)　　☐ $ (CAN)　　☐ € (Euros)

Allow for shipping costs charged per order plus an amount per book as set out in the tables below:

CURRENCY/DESTINATION

	£(Sterling)	$(US)	$(CAN)	€(Euros)
Cost per order				
UK	1.50	2.25	3.50	2.50
Europe	3.00	4.50	6.75	5.00
North America	3.00	3.50	5.25	5.00
Rest of World	3.00	4.50	6.75	5.00
Additional cost per book				
UK	0.50	0.75	1.15	0.85
Europe	1.00	1.50	2.25	1.70
North America	1.00	1.00	1.50	1.70
Rest of World	1.50	2.25	3.50	3.00

PLEASE SEND CHEQUE OR INTERNATIONAL MONEY ORDER
payable to: HOUSE OF STRATUS LTD or HOUSE OF STRATUS INC. or card payment as indicated

STERLING EXAMPLE

Cost of book(s):..................... Example: 3 x books at £6.99 each: £20.97
Cost of order: .... Example: £1.50 (Delivery to UK address)
Additional cost per book:.............. Example: 3 x £0.50: £1.50
Order total including shipping:.......... Example: £23.97

VISA, MASTERCARD, SWITCH, AMEX:

☐☐☐☐☐☐☐☐☐☐☐☐☐☐☐☐☐☐☐☐

Issue number (Switch only):

☐☐☐

Start Date:　　　　　　　**Expiry Date:**

☐☐/☐☐　　　　　　　☐☐/☐☐

Signature: _____

NAME: _____

ADDRESS: _____

COUNTRY: _____

ZIP/POSTCODE: _____

Please allow 28 days for delivery. Despatch normally within 48 hours.

Prices subject to change without notice.
Please tick box if you do not wish to receive any additional information. ☐

House of Stratus publishes many other titles in this genre; please check our website (**www.houseofstratus.com**) for more details.